the fog garden

Other Books by Marion Halligan

The Golden Dress (1998)

Collected Short Stories (1997)

Those Women Who Go to Hotels (with Lucy Frost, 1997)

Out of the Picture (1996)

Cockles of the Heart (1996)

Wishbone (1994)

The Worry Box (1993)

Lovers' Knots (1992)

Eat My Words (1990)

Spider Cup (1990)

The Hanged Man in the Garden (1989)

The Living Hothouse (1988)

Self Possession (1987)

the fog garden

marion halligan

a novel

A SUE HINES BOOK
ALLEN & UNWIN

First published in 2001

Allen & Unwin
83 Alexander Street, Crows Nest, NSW 2065, Australia
Phone: (61 2) 8425 0100   Fax: (61 2) 9906 2218
Email: frontdesk@allen-unwin.com.au
Web: http://www.allenandunwin.com

National Library of Australia Cataloguing-in-Publication data:

Halligan, Marion.
The fog garden.

ISBN 1 86508 471 9

1. Title.

A823.3

Text design by Mary Callahan
Typeset by Pauline Haas
Printed by Griffin Press, South Australia

10 9 8 7 6 5 4 3 2 1

For Lucy and James

Acknowledgements

Thanks to my friends and family for their love and kindness and comfort. And to my agent Margaret Connolly, for being a friend as well as an agent. My thanks also to the Literature Fund of the Australia Council, the Commonwealth Government's arts funding and advisory body, whose support over the years has given me time to write, and particularly for the Senior Fellowship which made this book possible.

Extracts from Dante's *Divine Comedy* are from the translation by Dorothy L. Sayers (Penguin, 1974); 'The Unquiet Grave' is published in the *Norton Anthology of Poetry* (W.W. Norton, 1983); 'Pale Hands I Loved Beside the Shalimar' is from a collection of Four Indian Love Lyrics by Laurence Hope; the poem discussed on pp.260–1 is 'The Countess of Pembroke's Dream' by A. D. Hope, in *Selected Poems* (Angus and Robertson, 1992); references to my other books appear on the following pages: *Lovers' Knots* pp.74, 97, 237, *Spider Cup* pp.160, 200, 291, *Wishbone* pp. 98, 160, *The Golden Dress* pp.128–9, 208 and 'Here Be Unicorns' (*Collected Stories*) p.128.

lapping 1

introduction 9

the lineaments of gratified desire 11

at concerts 36

vermilion: a short story 38

the sins of the leopard 56

old happy times 60

the boat 73

the moral ground 82

the thirsty cat 95

not like a loser 97

a good death 110

referential friends 120

a measure of kindness 122

the unquiet grave 131

life is dangerous 138

flights of pigeons 165

love potion 175

her silken layer 192

the weirdo's kitchen 211

a year and a day 213

remarrying 232

listening to herself living 234

her own mistress 251

the sons of heaven 278

lapping

LOWER SNUG, TASMANIA

11.12.98

For Graham, who died, 18.11.98

I DO NOT CRACK. I do not crack. Though it could be thought that I might. For instance at the moment when the man nestles his hand in the hollow of his wife's neck, and leaves it there, comfortable, habitual. Or when she gives him his formal greeting kiss when he comes home at the end of the day, a kiss almost never highly enough prized. Sometimes even regarded with scorn.

No. I do not crack. These are gestures too small to measure the immensity of loss. Even as emblems. It would be sentimental to collapse under them. My edifice of grief is much weightier. My grief is a great cathedral and the hand

1

nestling in the neck is a small bird perched on the corbel of one of its arches.

The water flows in, and slides back. It is cobbled with lozenges of light like those impasto strokes with which Impressionist painters rendered transparency. When you stand in it the lozenges make patterns on the sandy floor of the bay, like mullioned windows in reverse; the leads holding the clear panes together are yellow sunlight, moving, shifting, but not breaking up on the sandy bed. And with that shapely regular irregularity of leads.

These are the hardest things to write down, the patterns of light on the sandy lake bed, I cannot quite get exactly how they are. Of course it is the pattern of the sunlight broken up by the ripples of the water, I know that, but that is not what it looks like.

Last night, dark, but still there was a faint shadow of light defining the bay, we watched the yellow beam of a torch trudging back and forth across it. Someone out floundering, looking for the fish lying on the bay's bed, to spear them. The person invisible. Our lights go out, it's a failure of the electricity, but his torch beam trudges on, back and forth.

In the hot afternoon, the cries of the children swimming off the jetty. Very close, very present, full of the pleasure of cold water on a hot day.

A friend of mine said to me once: men adore me, but they do not stay with me. I've pondered this often. I do not know that I can say that you adored me, though maybe at moments you did. Certainly at moments, and probably more of them than were offered by those men who didn't stay. But you did stay with me.

Even when once you tried to leave, tried very hard, and couldn't manage it, what was important was your unableness to go, not the thinking you might. On the third last day of your life you said, I am only happy when I can look at you.

I remember when you used to drive the terrible old turquoise-coloured Holden, that you bought while I was still overseas, I would never have agreed to that colour, and whenever I used to turn the corner into our street and see it parked, my heart would lift. You are home, you will be there to greet me, it is the first thing that will happen. Perhaps with a kiss, more likely words.

In the night gulls cry. One makes a sound like a tied-up whipped-down dog, yipping and grim, relentless. Another like a tin can being beaten by a stick. Another has that wail of a baby which squeezes parents' hearts, that sound that isn't hunger, or discomfort, or pain, which has no cause but fear, and who can be surprised that a baby should cry with fear. Don't we all, if some of us noiselessly.

A fourth gull sounds like the ring of a mobile telephone. People twitch at the sound: is it mine? No, not even someone else's, it's a bird.

The cries die out in the night's silence. And then I can hear it, the water lapping. The ripples sigh towards the shore like glimmering exhaled breaths, to spend themselves in waves small as sighs. But more rhythmic and more determined than human sighs will ever manage. The water laps, it soothes, and sleep may come.

On the hottest day we go to the beach and picnic beside the water. There are a lot of young women with small children.

3

The water is cold as gin and tonic against our middle-aged legs, but the half-naked little kids are deliriously happy. Two tiny girls have built a dam, a deep hole with a solid much-fortified wall, in a clever place where the waves will fill it with water but not wash it away. The only father makes sand castles, pressing the sand in a bucket, turning out perfect towers. Until he gets too ambitious, and piles one on top of another, and they all collapse. This is when his child shows interest.

Four dolphins swim past, two pairs, gliding in and out of the water, slowly, luxuriously, keeping close in couples, but how quickly they cross the bay and out of sight.

In town, the weather still hot, we sit at a cafe beside a fountain, a big pool of water with bronze clumps of mush-rooms or clouds or whatever. It celebrates southern exploration, it seems. A child gets in and paddles, and tips over lengthwise, now he's wet he may as well stay there, and suddenly the basin is full of children, all neatly dressed, swimming and crawling, under the metal clouds. Two little girls in party dresses with long skirts that dry billowed like spinnakers have seal heads and sodden draggle-tailed garments, their voices are hoarse, they whisper with horrified delight, it's so enormously improper to be swimming in such party clothes. Two small boys white as chicken breasts have no clothes on at all. I have not felt so gladdened in a long time, the children are not just happy, they are full of awe, that they are getting away with this. Swimming in their clothes.

A lot of deaths have happened here. Angry deaths, cruel, resisted, deaths that came too soon. I was going to say that were never welcome, but that would not be true, even wicked

4

unnecessary deaths can sometimes be better than life. In the next bay was a convict station, and now it is a place claimed by aborigines. A lot of deaths. Of course that is true about everywhere, but this place has the reputation for it. There are dreams of innocence, and sagas of betrayal, and cruel ruins testifying to the wickedness of humanity made legal. The lucid water is smooth as a mirror, today the flagged and pebbled floor of the bay is covered with it as by a pane of glass; this water has no need to remember. Its lapping washes away memory.

It is fanciful to talk about sighs and exhalations where the bay is concerned. And sick. The breather would be sick. The rhythm is too rapid, and the sound too liquid, it would be panic and drowning to breathe thus. But for the sea it is comfortable, and comfortingly inexorable; it will keep on. The ripple waves run in, with liquid frilling and popping sounds, they turn and plash on the rocks of the shore, and so it happens, over and over. A storm won't stop them, nor will the huge burning weight of the summer's heat. The lapping is always there, and it soothes like a stroking hand, even though there is no meaning in it. Except perhaps that you would have liked it too.

Today is four weeks. The longest time in thirty-five years in which I have not spoken to you. If we were apart we spoke on the telephone, every day, several, many times. Even at long distances we talked with extravagant frequency. I remember the soft intertwining of our voices, weaving our lives together. Our breaths knowing each other's pattern, catching, slipping, quickening; sometimes I think *our breaths mingling* but not of course literally, but as our hearts beat at the opposite ends of these lines which are not even lines any more but pulses through space, these our voices slipping through the vast icy spaces of the universe, sliding off satellites, still I believe wandering through the cosmos inextricably woven together, I think those breaths were the most erotic of our acts. I think John Donne would have liked the ethereal unspoken sexiness of our idle phone calls. Once in that last year we watched the television together, me in our kitchen, you in hospital, and chuckled and sniffed and criticised, it was fun.

Even that time apart you still rang up; I was amused by the pretexts you found. The children, remembering to pay the phone bill (you told me to use your credit card), was I watering the garden. I hardly spoke; I sat and breathed very stilly, and let you talk. You were courting again. It was exciting, your voice cutting through the pain of your absence. And I was angry, too; I knew this wasn't right, for me or you, your not being here with me, so why were you doing it. And shortly you stopped. And we were not parted again.

When, on the last day of your life, I rang you and you said you didn't have enough breath to talk, I knew that was the end. I knew it was time for you to die.

People ask me, Are you all right? Oh, I say, yes, I'm, *all right*. This means, No, of course I am not all right but what the hell is the point of saying so? What good will it do? And my friends understand this, that we are talking a sort of code, that I am not all right but then I am, as much as can be expected, that I am not cracking despite the hand like a bird nestling in the shoulder; who said that life is like a bird flying in one end of a great banqueting hall and out the other? The warriors are feasting, the feasting goes on, but the bird, it is a sparrow, flies

6

in one door and quickly out another, back into the winter, the storm, the cold, and that small space is our human life and all the rest is the winter and unknown. Bede, it was, the Venerable Bede, and he meant all human life, I think, everybody's, not just one person's.

But my bird perches there, in the cathedral of my grief, high up on one of the corbels of an arch. You knew all the vocabulary of cathedrals. Corbels and bosses, groins and squinches, you would point them out as we stood heads bent back looking at them, and now I can't even remember the names, let alone the meanings, you it was who kept them for me.

Summer holidays have begun; some children on the jetty whose pale red roof can be seen as Chinese or Venetian but not with much conviction, throw a dog into the water and cheer while he swims to shore. A small boat bobs, before and aft. In the garden a cicada winds itself up. The water is no longer lucid as a mirror; the tide is running in small ripples that fragment the light into facets but never break. Water washes away stone, like the great natural arch we saw yesterday, created by violent waves throwing themselves against the cliff face, scouring it out with sand and chips of rock, flinging compressed air against it so that it finally falls away and leaves an opening like a great door, a portal in the cliff. I read that in the guide book; it is surprising about the sea being full of compressed air when it is violent. And dripping wears rock away too, a constant gentle dripping, though centuries are needed. Maybe millennia.

I don't know about my cathedral; it will need a lot of lapping to wear it away.

Footnote

14.6.99

When I came up with—I was going to say chose, but I didn't, it chose me—that cathedral as an image of my grief it was because of the enormous mass and weight of it, and its complication, its manifoldness and indeed manifestness, and I wanted to oppose this heavy edifice to the water lapping, and notice the piece is called Lapping, not The Cathedral of Grief, though that is partly so that the cathedral will be a surprise when it comes, and also because the water lapping will eventually wear it away, though not for a long time. The cathedral is an imaginative construct, the water a natural one, and I was supposing that the latter would endure for longer.

But what I did not realise then was that my cathedral would be a place where I could sit and be happy, for moments, that it would be a place of comfort and solace and peace. And that it was a miraculous work of art, whose beauty is to be marvelled at, and whose contemplation will lift and hold the heart in a dark joy. And that dwelling in it will make happiness and sorrow and pain, love and sex, music and words and pictures and all the terrifying world to be felt so intensely that I will ache with the desire of them. And that the ache of that desire will be exquisite and addictive.

My cathedral is a truly Gothic edifice, in that it is going to be a long time in the building. I am still constructing it. Not all the parts match, but they never do, that is part of a cathedral's richness. And I am glad that the lapping water will not in my lifetime succeed in eroding it.

introduction

I WOULD LIKE YOU TO MEET
Clare. She is a young woman in her fifties. A bit over a year
before the end of this novel her husband died.

Clare isn't me. She's like me. Some of her experiences,
adventures, terrors, have been mine. Some haven't. We have
the same profession. Both of us have had to come to terms
with being widowed, and sometimes we have made similar
choices. Not always. Her voice is quite like mine. She enjoys
a similar bowerbird cleverness, a kind of sly sharpness in
the collection of matter. That understands the shred of
blue plastic may be more valuable than the chunk of lapis
lazuli.

But she isn't me. She is a character in fiction. And like all
such characters she makes her way through the real world
which her author invents for her. She tells the truth as she sees
it, but may not always be right.

9

A reader could think that, since Clare is my character, I can make all sorts of things happen to her that I can't make happen to myself. This is slightly true, but not entirely. Clare like any other character has become her own person, and there is an invincible integrity in that. She knows where honesty lies in her own life. And it is not quite as it does in mine. In my world I can choose to behave honestly or not, but I cannot fudge what life does to me. I can't become prettier or richer or a more successful writer or have more lovers simply by willing it. In theory I could do these things for Clare; write her a lovely lover, why not. Send her off happily ever after. But only if it is not betraying the truths of her life and character as I have imagined them.

The first piece in the book is about me. The rest of the novel is about Clare.

Marion Halligan

lapping

CLARE WAS WRITING A STORY
about an elderly woman, an old woman, really, in her
seventies, whose slightly younger neighbour visited her four
times a day and made love to her. She thought of saying
fucked her, but it wasn't really one of her words. Bonked was
a bit jokey, and having sex . . . well, that might be better.

She got the idea for this story from Kirsten, who liked to
stand leaning just inside the doorway of Geoffrey's room,
telling dirty stories. Clare didn't like the word *dirty*, the
grubbiness of it. Kirsten's stories were sexy, they uncovered
and manipulated the funny points of sex, made you laugh,
made you squirm. Like the one about the two friends,
women, drinking tea; one looks out the window and sees the
other's husband coming up the path with a gorgeous bunch
of flowers. Aren't you lucky, she says. The other groans. You
know what this means. This means I'll be on my back with

my legs in the air all night. Why, says the friend, haven't you got a vase?

This joke makes Clare squirm. She can feel those prickly flower stems poking into her own vagina, how dry and scratchy they would be. But she laughs, the gruesomeness only makes you laugh more.

You can hear the pause when you tell women this joke, says Kirsten, there's this sharp intake of breath, and then they laugh. She sits on the bed and pats Geoffrey's knee on the punch-line, very delicately, the idea of a pat, more than an actual touch.

There are buzzers outside, insistent nagging bells, and eventually Kirsten drags herself away. It's after that she comes back and tells them about the old lady. A mild problem of incontinence that she wants dealt with so she can get back to her neighbour popping in and pleasuring her four times a day. When Clare walks down the corridor she shiftily stares at all the old women she can see, wondering which she might be. Of course there's no telling. And Kirsten is discreet in her way, she will describe the condition but not the person.

Kirsten makes it her business to collect sexy jokes. She's a ski instructor as well as a nurse, working alternate seasons. She loves telling her stories, does it well, the right speed, and pauses, the deadpan tone highlighting the punch-lines. They keep Geoffrey well entertained as he lies dozily waiting for the chemotherapy drugs to feed into his arm. Kirsten isn't actually supervising this, that's another nurse who continually comes in and stands and watches that the flow is right, brings hot packs, cold packs, to relieve the stinging of the drip as it goes in. You have to pay constant attention to chemo doses.

And since it is highly toxic and burns, you dress in layers of proofed clothing, two pairs of gloves, goggles.

I see, you're the floor show, says Geoffrey to Kirsten. He collects some jokes in return from their son, who has a good memory for them. One of the enormous whole lifetime of things that Clare and Geoffrey have in common is an inability to remember jokes. Whereas for Kirsten it is a third profession. She's off to Aspen for the ski season in a little while. It will be duller in the ward without her; plenty of affection and kindness, but not this saucy fun.

When she drags herself off to do some work, which she seems to do so much less of than talking, but maybe that's what patients like Geoffrey are seen to need, he dozes a little, the chemo slowly dripping its death-defying poison into his veins. Clare reads, a Ruth Rendell novel, you need something gripping in these circumstances, the kind of book that demands to have been read rather than to be being read. Nothing contemplative or you will get switched on to contemplating the wrong thing. Sometimes Geoffrey opens his eyes and she smiles at him. He strokes the back of her hand with his soft fingers. She loves his arms, the neat flatness of his wrists, the way his watch wraps round, his hands that are so delicate in their touching. She fell in love with him in one moment, when they were going dancing and he stopped the car outside the hotel and instead of getting out turned to her and took her face in these hands and covered it with tiny kisses, hundreds of them, his lips faintly brushing her face, so that her heart tumbled and fell and she was in love. He'd kissed her before, urgently, sexily, and filled her with desire, and desire there was in these kisses, but a desire of infinite patience, of time to discover and to know love. Kissing was all he could do now, his lips as soft and sweet as ever, so sweet, but not kissing for long, he didn't have enough breath, and his body was too frail and close to pain for anything but the lightest momentary touch.

Four times a day, eh, he said. Remember when we made love five times a night.

She did. She does. This is how they live their life these days. Now that it is halted in this place of his illness. Clare believes that once you have done a thing you are doing it forever. They are still those young people, in their twenties, beautiful (she didn't think so at the time but photographs show it) and full of health, making love, dozing, waking up and doing it again, so that the next day her fanny felt like a crushed pulpy flower exulting in its own tenderness. Her fanny remembers.

Five times a night. He repeated the words a few days later when they were having drinks with friends. Clare was amazed. Geoffrey was normally the most private and shy man, he never said anything about his own gifts or prowess, never boasted. It was as though now he knew he was dying he wanted it on some small record.

And not just one or two nights either, he said. A great many, often. In those days.

Once you have done a thing you are doing it forever. And one day not too far away it will be his death, and she will be living it on her own for the rest of her life.

Geoffrey dozes again, and Clare lets her arm rest against his leg, no pressure, and thinks of the old lady and all that surely rather greedy sex when she more than twenty years younger has none. She doesn't think this out of resentment or envy, but as a curious fact. Geoffrey has not been well enough for a while now. That dizzy erotic pulpy haze is a long time ago, so are the games and familiar bliss of married habit. Their love is in their eyes, in gentle touches of the hand, in words spoken in soft lilted voices that caress the skin of the mind as surely as the body. And in worry and short snaps of anger. There are moments when each thinks the other would be a better person just by taking a little notice. Quickly over, these, they both realise it isn't likely to happen, now.

But sex, as such, no. Clare has put it behind her. Is happy to be celibate, though that's hardly the word for so consuming a relationship as hers with Geoffrey. Feels no itches, no urges, no aches in the loins or longings in the fanny. Is contemptuous of those who do. Men her age who suddenly discover they're gay. That's not a problem, they should just control their feelings and not wreck the lives of all those around them. Is scornful of middle-aged people who run away from old marriages with young lovers. Quotes Hamlet telling his mother Gertrude, who since he's thirty must be over forty at least, that at her age the heyday in the blood is cold. Clare makes her garden and thinks of her new novel which has a scene with a fat girl sitting on top of her lover and energetically bonking him. Erotic writing, her own not other people's, is the only thing which is much of a turn-on these days. And this will be comical as well, when she manages to sit at a piece of paper and write.

When Clare becomes aware that she has this story forming out of Kirsten's gossip she's pleased, stories fit better into disordered lives. She hasn't written much lately. Too busy. Not so much washing, ironing, cooking meals. It's that Geoffrey wants her to stay with him, keep him company. The four-times-a-day mysterious woman in her story isn't the main character, that's someone else, called Vivian, a widow, leading now a tranquil solitary life. Growing flowers in terracotta pots. There's a nail punch, from Clare's own youth, this woman's wooden floors need a bit of work, there are nails sticking out. She has to do it herself, not having a husband. Since she's got this widow character Clare won't be able to show the story to Geoffrey. She knows that the woman has to be a widow because of the story, nothing to do with Clare herself, but Geoffrey can't be expected to see that. The widow meets Rennie, the amorous one, who is worried about her satin bedspread, under all this pleasuring. Not much done with the sex, it's there, as a fact, not particularly erotic, readers will have to take it into account and set it into their own view of life. Clare writes sex so that other people slot their experience into her words, she's not a lot into fluids and members and panting and heat and sticky exchanges, prefers to let her readers use their imaginations. One person's ecstasy may be another's comedy.

When the chemotherapy is finished and everything is unplugged, the bed lowered so Geoffrey can slide from it into the chair, she drives them home along the winding road by the lake. They've been watching it through the seasons. Now it's late spring, the willows frilled pale green, the poplars darkening, the grass just beginning to yellow after the rains. The sky is high and faintly clouded, you could imagine it waiting for someone to paint in some cherubs, except that the scale is wrong in this wide hill-scalloped landscape. There will

16

be a Manchurian pear in the story. The husband will have described its colour in autumn as vermilion, and his wife will remember that, it will be important. The dead husband isn't Geoffrey, vermilion isn't particularly a Geoffrey word.

She takes him home, and settles him in bed, then goes out shopping. Miriam and David are coming for a drink tonight. They come most weeks, David ringing up and making the engagement, he having more time, being retired, while Miriam is still working. She'll be a bit weary so Clare will get some nice things to eat. The woman in the fish shop says the oysters are from their farm at Bateman's Bay and will be freshly opened, so she buys several dozen and some prawns.

Geoffrey feels good on the day he has chemo. The day after he is exhausted, and the day after that very tired, but the first day is okay. They sit around the long table in the kitchen, drinking white wine out of tall oval glasses and talking. So much to say, so many conversations to have, with friends of so ancient a date. When their children were small, and David, dark and lean and fierce, was beginning his career in the law, the first time they met was at a function, a dinner dance, the men their wives' partners, their wives who were colleagues, Clare part-time because she wanted to be a writer, but didn't like to say so, so many people wanted to be a writer and nobody thought you'd be successful.

I didn't think David would be at all like that, said Clare the next day. A stupid remark, immediately realised.

Oh? What did you think he'd be like?

Clare couldn't think of an answer that wasn't rude. Maybe that he would be more serious, more grave, less lean, capering, mischievous, more handsome? She remembers still the embarrassment with which she cast round for an answer. But not quite what the answer was. Fatter? Browner? Older? As time passed David grew stouter and greyer, and his ambition which was maybe what she perceived in his fierceness all those years ago carried him cork-screwing upwards through his profession. He was impatient, rude sometimes, bossy. But now he had slowed down and was sweet-natured, you could feel his affection.

They all knew that David fancied Clare. In the old days he'd put his hand on her leg under the dining table, pinch her nipples in the kitchen. When she thought of him she thought of a small wriggling movement she made to get out of his hands, a sort of undulation that removed her from his touch and yet was a kind of game, too. They always kissed at meeting, and he'd put his hand on her ribs where her breasts curved. It was only ever a moment. It was her breasts he liked, because they were big. Geoffrey and David had conversations about how they liked tarty women. Clare thought both would have liked their wives to be more tarty than they were, now. But it seemed a bit late. Looking back at photographs when they'd had small waists and long legs (perhaps not so long, but good, shapely, with fine-cut ankles) under the tiny skirts that this day's vulgar young call pussy pelmets, skirts which had shocked their mothers because they'd had babies as well, small children, and where was the comfort for a small toddling child in a bare leg, or worse, a fish-net tight? . . . Looking back at the photographs . . . well, what could you say, it was another country and the wenches have grown plump and comfortable and the well-cut short and paler versions of their tumbling titian curls and dark Cleopatra fall are now, they suppose though they have never let themselves find out, a stiff and sombre grey, and love has grown plump and comfortable too.

> *Oh love is handsome and love is kind*
> *And love's a jewel while 'tis new*

And when 'tis old, the song is wrong, it doesn't grow cold, it grows cosy, it grows plump and comfortable and still kind. Kinder, perhaps.

Or perhaps the wenches aren't grown fat, but dead. Dead as a photograph of a dead Diana, dead as the young Audrey Hepburn, the luscious Marilyn. Not forgotten, but never to be flesh again. A number of seven-year renewing cycles have passed since then. And maybe Clare remembers better what Miriam was like all those years ago than she can recall herself.

Geoffrey turned the wine in his glass, it was a Tyrrell's, semillon, called riesling when it was made, old and pale, grown strong and rich in a quite austere way. He had always loved wine, and could still drink it, not a lot, but he tasted it thoroughly, and ate some of the oysters whose cool puckery flavour made the wine zing in the mouth. David and Geoffrey had a conversation about Latin gerundives, but Clare didn't really listen.

Another time David and Miriam brought a jar of salmon caviar, quite a lot, and they had it on black bread with ricotta. The fat little juicy globes burst their brilliant vermilion in their mouths, and that evening they drank champagne, a pleasant quite good Australian bubbly, and recalled the night when Miriam and David had got naturalised and they had a party with a great quantity of French champagne, and David kept coming past with a bottle in each hand saying, Drink that up this one is different, so she'd finish what was in her glass and he'd pour another. She must have got very drunk; she felt wonderful but suddenly on the way home she had to ask Geoffrey to stop the car and she leaned out and vomited by the side of the road, somewhere in the middle of the wolf-haunted pine forest.

She remembered what she'd been wearing, green snake-skin sandals with a high wedge heel and strap, such as might have been worn by a woman of a different generation to seduce an overpaid oversexed overhere Yank, and a strange short shifty dress of some gleaming grey fabric (bought very cheap) that dropped over her breasts into a slight swishing A-line.

No you weren't, said David, you were wearing a red dress, tight and short, with straps.

No I wasn't, I never had such a dress, I couldn't have been.

Yes you did. You must have. I remember it so well.

So perhaps she had. David was so sure. There was a red sundress once, tight and short and straight, leaving you nowhere to be except upright and breathing in; would she have worn that to the party? And it must have been another party when she was sitting on the floor and David put his arm friendlily around her and suddenly with a quick little flick of his fingers her bra was undone. That was definitely the grey dress. How did you do that, she hissed. She had to cross her arms over her chest and go to the bathroom to do it up.

But not for some years had his nimble fingers inscribed their little murmurs of lust on her body, in this impudent and reproved game of sex played with desire but no expectations, not for some years had she hissed and wriggled out of his tricky embraces. She supposed he didn't think it appropriate, under the circumstances.

How is Quentin, Clare asked Miriam.

Don't get her started, said David, it'll be the photos next, and before you can blink she'll have you watching the full-screen movie.

You know perfectly well we don't own a video camera, said Miriam with her placidity that like a bowl of cream caught and drowned David's buzzes of irritation.

Words, pictures, doesn't make much difference.

Quentin was a gorgeous boy, two years old, with corn-coloured fuzzy hair and violet eyes. It's funny, said Geoffrey (for Miriam did have photographs), that a child can look so like his grandfather and yet be so handsome. For the beautiful child was the image of David, as well as quite like his granny as well.

Clare and Geoffrey don't have grandchildren. Not yet. But Geoffrey never will have, now.

Geoffrey was saved from pain by morphine. It wasn't a high dose, but constant. You have to have enough for it to rise above the pain, said the doctor, to rise higher than it and then fall back down and completely quell it. Clare thought that this must be a metaphor, and could you trust a figure of speech in so urgent a context? Except that it seemed to work. Such a dose would cause addiction problems to you or me, said the doctor, but since he is using it all up to deal with the pain it isn't addictive. If the pain went away tomorrow he could stop tomorrow, instantly, no problem.

Maybe nobody would be addicted to any opiums if the pain stopped, she thought, but that seemed too romantic a thing to say.

The morphine also made him constipated. Later that night, when she was wheeling the chair out of the lavatory where he'd spent more than an hour waiting for enemas to work, and they hadn't, Geoffrey said sadly, The body fails. It's no good.

She leaned over the back of his chair and kissed his ear, little butterfly kisses that brought her near his skin, his flesh, his smell that was as sweet as ever. The body isn't you, she said, it may be behaving badly but inside it you are still you, still you. She breathed the words in his ear and rested her head for a moment against his, only for a moment, even the touch of love is quickly intolerable to the very ill.

They kissed goodnight, little soft kisses between trembling lips. The oxygen hissed. Odourless, tasteless, coolish, a faint wind. She bent over him, held back all but her lips kissing his, not for too long.

Kirsten sends a postcard from Aspen. She has met a man and fallen in love. Fancy that. Geoffrey imagines her entertaining him with her jokes. At the bottom of the message in tiny letters, so small he can't read it even with his glasses, and Clare has to peer up close with her short-sighted eyes, Kirsten has written, *no merkins necessary*.

That is because Geoffrey was the first patient she'd met who knew what a merkin was. A pubic wig, he'd said, and Kirsten was impressed. But she didn't know why such a thing might be necessary, and he could tell her. That venereal disease could make for bald pubes, and so false hair was necessary. Leading to terrible jokes, about merkins lost in

22

public parks, and presented to cardinals as the pope's beard. Even constructing them into false vaginas. Kirsten was charmed with so much information.

Thought you must have had one, she murmured, even Kirsten couldn't say this in her usual cheerful loud voice. So gorgeous. All those red curls.

The hair on his head was that colour once, said Clare. Before it faded to this pale buttery yellow; I envy it, it's like being a blonde.

Clare couldn't quite believe they were having this conversation. Geoffrey smiled and blushed.

False vaginas, said Kirsten, how do you mean?

In the absence of a real one. You'd use a merkin and a bag of cotton wool, or some such. Same principle as those blow-up dolls, which I believe you can spend a fortune on in certain sex shops. The merkin, of course, a kind of synecdoche, the part for the whole.

Clare gets this joke, which is a bit erudite for Kirsten. She wonders what she will do when Geoffrey is no longer here to tell her things, how she will cope without his vast store of odd facts. His wit. His black irony. And who will translate bits of Latin for her?

. . .

When Geoffrey died it seemed as though Clare had given him permission. Not directly, but saying to her daughter, I wish he could go to sleep and not wake up. It was the first time she had formulated the thought in the present, always it had been, not yet, not yet. And her wish was what Geoffrey did. She kissed him goodbye at seven o'clock, at nine-thirty he was sleeping peacefully, by ten, still in that same deep sleep, he had died.

At just after seven she had made her wish, because she thought he had struggled enough, that it was just too hard for him to keep on breathing. And she was afraid that his death would be a terrible long agonised drowning in the tumours that were invading his lungs, that was what she was wishing against. She was grateful for that gentle slipping away. The night before he had asked to keep his bedroom curtains open so he could see the meteorite shower but it turned out to be too cloudy. The evening of his death he'd drunk two glasses of Fleuri, his favourite wine by that time, for its mildness and delicacy. She'd tasted it faintly winy on the sweetness of his breath when she'd kissed him.

She went back to the hospital in a taxi. His skin felt cool, like himself, not as it did later, in the mortuary chapel, cold and ice-hard. She stayed for several hours, talking to him, touching, kissing his cheeks, holding his hands. She found the nail scissors in his sponge bag and cut off some strands of the red-gold hair to keep.

.　　.　　.

She discovered that the long rehearsal for grief of his dying was no preparation for the real thing. Practice hadn't helped. Geoffrey's affairs were neat, not complicated, no debts, but she was astonished at how pioneering she needed to be to settle them. It was as though nobody had ever died before, and the whole process had to be rediscovered, perhaps invented. Eventually it was done, and she thought, this is the beginning of my new life. She'd tried out the word *widow* in her mouth a few times; the taste was strange, not bitter or sour exactly, more mysterious. Of course not sweet; perhaps salty? And it was very very large. Needing a lot of chewing on and sucking at before she could know its flavour.

She did register the fact that she was on her own now for the first time in thirty-five years. On her own. She could say *free*. Not her own choice, but the word was there. So was *adventure*.

She got invited out to dinner a lot and never took her car because she liked to drink wine. When after one of these dinners an old friend put his arms around her, one warm April night giving her a hug goodbye, after dinner, and she put her arms around him, hugging him back, a lot of her friends gave her hugs these days, and she knew she needed them, her loose shirt slid away and his hands touched the skin of her back. The others were in the garden smelling the heavy night scent of the mandevilla, she could hear their voices talking about how heady it was, almost too heavy, and she stood longer in the hug than was simply friendly, perhaps, she wasn't sure; she was too busy feeling the way that his touch had got into her blood and was flowing all around her body.

Of course you realise Clare that men your age prefer younger women. So says her friend Thea. Young women, in fact. Statistically speaking, it is very unlikely you will find another partner. There's more chance of you getting electrocuted in the bath.

25

She doesn't want another partner. She's had one, a lovely one, for thirty-five years. You don't expect or need to repeat that in a lifetime.

But her body would like someone to make love to it.

Well, I'll just have to take up with younger men, won't I, she says defiantly to Thea. Young men.

.   .   .

The thing about writers is that they put everything that happens to them into words. Sooner or later. Sometimes they write them down, sometimes they make stories out of them, sometimes they are too hard to deal with now and have to be put away till later. Sometimes the happenings are a long puzzle that no solutions seem to fit. And sometimes they need to be invented.

She could think of a lot of words for this sense of a man's touch flowing through her body. They all sounded straight out of a Mills and Boon novel. Surging. Pulsing. Over-whelming. Electrifying. She laughed sarcastically at herself. Evidently Mills and Boon are getting it right. Electrifying. Forsooth.

Electrifying gave her a picture of Frankenstein's monster. Mary Shelley's monster. Wired up and plugged into a storm, so the lightning could zap him into life. It was always seen as so violent and jagged an act, but perhaps it wasn't. Perhaps it was gentle and powerful and full of pleasure. *Frankenstein, a Genevan student of natural philosophy, learns the secret of imparting life to inanimate matter* . . . she is beginning to see that her matter has been inanimate for a long while.

26

Now she finds herself thinking of sex all the time. She is still full of grief, but these thoughts of sex have become an extension of her grief, this sharp unfocused desire that suffuses her blood and makes her juices run; she had forgotten what puddles are possible. Once she hunkers down to get a book from the bottom shelf and drips on the floor; she laughs, it's funny, but she is delighted too. Dry vaginas are another of Thea's stark warnings.

And so the writer sits at her desk early one cold autumn morning (minus four, already!) wrapped in a rug of small Afghan squares, pink and blue, white and pale lemon; Geoffrey used to wear it and it smells of him. The golden elm outside the window is still entirely green, but the Manchurian pears that inhabit this suburb have reached their full dazzle of vermilion. The Manchurian pears are always the first. Later, if the sun shines, she will drive past several she knows, for already their leaves are beginning to fall, their quiver and dazzle of brilliant colour is slowly dropping away into piles of browning litter on the grass, blowing and crushed on the asphalt road. It's important to look at them before it's too late.

And so the writer sits, and writes about Manchurian pear trees, but in fact she is choosing where her narrative will take her next. Or perhaps she is letting the narrative choose . . .

Bodies on a bed, who have breathlessly but slowly stripped one another of clothes, whose hands have rubbed silk knickers against smooth skin, have stroked breasts offering themselves cupped in black lace (the kind they called jelly-on-a-plate bras when they were teenagers) and now naked are endeavouring to consume one another. Straining, pulling together, apart. He kisses her breasts, his tongue flicks around her nipple and she takes off into a flight of orgasms like a flock of birds. He is kissing and licking. Her stomach and armpits and ribs. His mouth is between her legs, his tongue . . .

She has always believed in writing sex scenes that aren't explicit, so readers can use their own imaginations, offering a delicate kind of literary foreplay that they can take to their own erotic conclusions. Oh, but his tongue . . . her back arches, and she takes off in another flight of orgasms.

When he comes between her breasts she smooths it into her skin with languid fingers. Geoffrey always said it's good for the skin, she tells him. Well, he says, we better keep it up, and they giggle, and lie together, sticky and slightly squelchy, making patterns with their fingers on one another's skin, he runs his nails furrowing into her flesh but she has been careful not to mark him, there is no explanation for the reddish tracks of passion down a husban's back. And safe in this happy enfolding of a man's arms for a little while she talks to him of Geoffrey. She tells him how sex with him feeds into her grief for Geoffrey, nourishing it, soothing it, she has always known that sex and death are a powerful combination but hadn't thought that death could feed into sex like this.

Le petit mort and *le grand*, he says.

It is a kind of dying, this abandonment. This is adultery, which she has never practised but has imagined often enough. A lot of the characters in her books commit adultery. She has always enjoyed imagining it for them. And guilt? My grief needs this, she says to herself. It is comfort, that is all. There isn't any betrayal.

They teach themselves to talk at the same time as kissing.

She says to him: What if you fall in love with me?

His role is the seducer's. Is it necessary to sound warnings? She is the mistress, not the good woman of thirty-five years standing.

I won't, he says. I love you, I have loved you a long time, you are my dear friend. But I won't fall in love with you. We aren't twenty any more.

She knows this is true, about falling in love with her, and is glad of it, though some wicked little slitty bit of her would like it not to be, would like a mad bad dangerous grand passion to storm into their lives and not care what damage happened around it, but she is mainly glad that they are too old and full of consequences to let it happen.

If we could do this whenever we liked, she says, we probably wouldn't. Hardly ever. If we were married, or partners in the eyes of the world, we'd probably go to a concert, or something.

It is because it is illicit. It is adultery, not marriage.

And shouldn't try to become marriage. Should stay adultery and illicit and stop soon.

Not yet.

And so they lie together, on more than one occasion, not too often, and she takes off in flocks of orgasms, and he tells her she is the sexiest person he has ever met, and she is pleased, she who believed the heyday in her blood was cold. Ah, she was mistaken. But needed to be, to survive. Then.

They talk about marriage. You get married when you are twenty, he says, and it's a matter of compromise. But you have to be careful that you compromise with integrity, that you don't fake it.

Faking compromise. It's a nice idea. Subtle. He is a subtle man.

Marriage is a construction, she says, over the years, you both make it. It's complicated, and you have to see what a structure you've built. Look after it, value it.

But sometimes it is just that structure that gets in the way of people simply being.

The thing about couples, he says, is that they become complacent. That's dangerous.

She plays Alfred Deller, his dark deep counter-tenor singing, *Ah love is handsome, and love is kind . . .*

You mean fat and happy and comfortable, she says. Growing plump on pleasing one another.

She is getting thinner now she has lost Geoffrey. She thinks how pleased he would be with this slimmer self.

But maybe in growing plump on pleasing you aren't any more the person you were, he says.

The wife isn't the wench she was, you mean.

He sighs.

Ah, she says, we are none of us the people we were. Not you, not me. Not your wife. Certainly not Geoffrey. We have all changed. We change one another. And isn't it mostly a good thing? Or anyway a necessary one. I'm not twenty-two with waist-length hair and ignorant, or anyway innocent and with everything to find out. Thank god.

They turn from the pleasures of conversation to the

pleasures of sex. She lies back and lets his mouth cover her body with its nips and tingles of lust until she is driven wild by it. I like the way you don't stop even when you've come, she says, and they clutch one another in laughter. And then they go back to talking about marriage, which is proving to be a topic of great fascination to them both.

Anyway, he says, we wouldn't be any good at living together. We're both too fond of setting our own agendas.

She wonders about this. People thought she set the agenda in her and Geoffrey's life, but did she? Maybe in certain things, houses, holidays. But she did what he wanted, she was a faithful wife through all their years together, he had his way. She set out to please him.

Power in marriage isn't always obvious, she says. It's like outsiders never knowing what makes a marriage tick. Often the quiet one is in control, the noisy one zips and zaps about but the quiet one is the strong one.

I was fairly noisy, he says, but they were pretty much my agendas that we followed.

She knows what Geoffrey would say. He would say, all this talk of power. Disdainful. Marriage is about partners, sometimes one is strong, sometimes the other. Power isn't what marriage is about, not good marriage. She thinks of her present feverish behaviour. Geoffrey saved her from that. Calmly, and dismissively sometimes, comfortingly, he saved her from barbs, from unkindnesses, attacks. He was the still point of her life to which she always returned. She needs to find another one. Invent another one.

She has another question. What about love, she asks. You know, how it is said that there is one person who loves more

31

than the other; one who loves, one who is loved.

He doesn't know. Is it a question you can ask, he wonders.

It is the kind of question that gets asked in not very good novels, she says.

Maybe my wife would think she had loved me more than I loved her. But I don't know that it would be true.

She has at moments thought the same; that she loved Geoffrey more than he loved her. Maybe all wives think so.

How can you measure love like that, he asks.

Sounds like a song, she says.

Maybe it's like a cistern, she says. It fills and empties. It's all flux. The Greeks thought so. Life is made of flux. Very juicy.

His fingers . . . she can't write it down.

Eventually she comes back to this. Maybe your wife doesn't know how much you love her, she says.

No, that's probably true. I'm not good at telling her.

You know that?

Yes, but it doesn't mean I can do anything about it.

They talk on like this endlessly. In bed. On the phone. Over coffee, and glasses of wine. In company, and out. There is so much to be said. So much to be understood.

What I like about you, she says, is that you haven't come to the end of yourself. You aren't finished. You can still learn. Change.

Maybe I shall learn to be a good husband.

Why not? It could be a kind of courtship of his wife, all over again. It will be more difficult than the first time, because of all the constructed past behind them. But she thinks he might succeed, that he will put his energy and his love into this second wooing and make it happen. She is not jealous, she admires it, wishes it well. It is nothing to do with what they are up to, here on this bed. That is marriage. This is adultery, illicit, doomed but not yet. This hours of pleasuring another body is the sort of thing you don't often do when you are married. At the beginning of course, and afterwards on high days and holy days, but married lives have mostly got too many interesting things in them to want to spend a whole afternoon smearing one another with bodily fluids. Witness these conversations, they are about marriage, their marriages to other people, not this adultery. Adultery which she has never practised, but has written about, often enough.

It functions on an absence of history, a lack of commitment. These hours now. *Baisers volés*, sings Charles Trenet. It is not just the kisses that are stolen, it is little snatches of another life, that will have to be given back. And in her case, the nourishing of grief. It is Geoffrey's death that she is exploring, through her abandonment to pleasure.

Geoffrey is what she thinks about, all the time. It seems to her that he gave her permission to go back to her sensual self, encouraged her to do so. Saying at the dinner party: we used to make love five times a night. Telling the story of their first meeting to their children. How he sat next to her at lunch in the university hall of residence. How she was wearing very small shorts (it was the summer, out of term) and her hair in a long plait. Why did she interest him? Because she was so sexy, of course. Of course. Oh, he liked her mind, her conversation. But what made him come and sit beside her that very first time at the long hall dining table was her sexiness.

She lies in bed. She can arouse herself very well. Like adultery, something that she's not made a habit of. She takes to sleeping naked, which she hasn't done for years. When you sleep in a house with small children and sick people you have to be ready to jump out of bed and get to them before you wake up properly, you don't want to take time covering your nakedness. She puts linen sheets on the bed, has a shower, rubs into her skin a fine white lotion scented with Arpège and called *lait délicieux*, delicious milk. When she stretches in bed, luxuriating in the cool silky smooth sheets, turning over on her stomach in simple-minded delight, she gives herself an orgasm; the linen against her nipples has set her off. She's impressed with herself. She smiles and feels her face smooth itself into an expression of delight, knowing, innocent, inward. The lineaments of gratified desire. Blake's words slide through her head:

> *In a wife I do desire*
> *What in whores is often found*
> *The lineaments of gratified desire*

She loves the weightiness of *lineaments* and *gratified*, the small cool words, *wife*, and *whore*. And *desire* twice.

To be prized in wife and whore. And in oneself. This is another story to tell herself. The free and independent woman who pleasures herself. No need for adultery. For a man. Or a woman. Though that is also a thought. She knows a lot more interesting unattached women than she does men.

So she lies in her bed, stroking her breasts. This is the present moment, it is good. Like looking up from her desk at one of Canberra's huge sky sunsets, or the grassy yellow of the Monaro Plains perceived in Rosalie Gascoigne's fragments of old soft-drink crates, it is a solitary occupation. Everyone dies alone, she's read that often, and the nurses in the chemo ward had told her how often they had observed it to be true; a mortally ill person will be surrounded by family and friends, who wish him not to be alone at this last moment, but the person waits until they are all gone to die. As Geoffrey did. We die alone, and in our most secret beings we live alone. Desire presses bodies together, plaits together minds, but what keeps sex going is the knowledge that each time you haven't finally made it work, you haven't merged with the other, you still have to part, and there is melancholy in that, but the rekindling of desire as well.

If she were more agile perhaps she could put her lips to her breast and kiss it.

. . .

What has happened to us is always happening. Geoffrey dies. The girl with the long plait and the small shorts puts her tray on the table, the red-haired man sits beside her. The night is dark, the rain falls, the road is long and clumsily winding, but in the car the girl and the man have so much to say, are so in love with their conversation, that they don't care how long or dangerous the drive is. She has already fallen in love with him, now she thinks she could marry him. See them there, a man and a woman, in a little car driving through the night, forever.

And maybe . . . maybe what hasn't happened yet, the possibilities, all those outcomes, maybe they exist too, eventually and all at once.

at concerts

WHEN CLARE READ THE FIRST
few pages of her widowing story at a literary festival on
the Gold Coast some people cried. She had never read
anything so newly written, so unlived with. Part of a story
that wasn't finished, even. In her home town she would not
have read anything so raw, but somehow distance made her
reckless.

She could hear the breath-stilled quiet of the audience.
Her own voice was flat, unable to bear any emotion, so the
words had to work on their own. Afterwards some women
came up and talked to her. One said she was a widow and
Clare had got exactly how it felt. The next day at breakfast
when she was talking to a publisher, it was a formal event, a
conversation about writing and editing and publishing, a
woman made a comment, as part of the discussions and
questions afterwards. She was a pretty woman, rather plump,

with soft blonde curly hair that was probably grey underneath, and her voice was gentle. She said this:

> I do so miss having a man in my life. When I go to a concert and a couple come and sit next to me I always hope it will be the man who sits beside me, just so I can feel what it is like to have a man beside me again, not touching, just the feel of a man sitting beside me. But they never do, it is always the wife who sits next to me, and the man on her other side.

Clare didn't write that down straightaway, so couldn't swear to having got her words verbatim, but that was the tone and the rhythm and the sadness of her words. Wanting so much to sit by a man. And the sigh of the audience when she finished; they knew what she meant.

vermilion: a short story

THE FLOOR IS THE COLOUR OF honey. It's knotty old pine gone yellow under varnish, but it looks viscous and golden, and the flawed wood has a patterned richness that once was the life of the tree. The contour lines of its knots and swirls and granular shadings are evidence of growing and branching and flourishing, now preserved and mellowing under these honeyed glazings of varnish. Smooth it is under bare feet, warm and even comfortable to the skin, not of course sticky like honey; like resin, perhaps, like amber, preserving all the knots and grains and irritations of that past but still witnessed busy life.

Except for several nails that have worked loose, and up, to catch at bare skin. Somewhere there's a nail punch, used when these floors were new, before the varnish. Vivian remembers it, remembers the work with it, going along the rows, tapping with a hammer, not forcefully but accurately, sliding up and down with bare feet to check the job well done, and remembers where it came from, this deft tool, the solid iron nail punch over all the years a tiny weight on her conscience.

Make sure you bring it back, said Sid, Maggie's father. She and Maggie had been best friends through school and after, and it wasn't yet apparent that they wouldn't be through their married lives as well. No falling out, nothing dramatic, just two husbands who weren't drawn to one another, and living in different cities the women not quite making the effort needed. But back then, freshly married, they were still near enough the young women they had been, even visiting one another at their parents' houses, talking about their own new houses in those other cities, when Vivian had described all the floors to varnish, and how the nails stuck up, and Sid had said, Here, this is what you need, best to do it properly in the first place, and had loaned the nail punch. Not something he used often, but something he liked to have, and was keen not to lose. Of course, Vivian said. Of course she would bring it back. But somehow she never had. And had never forgotten she hadn't.

There was another thing she remembered about Sid, from when she was seventeen, some years before. Hot summer, and she was visiting Maggie. She can still remember the dress she was wearing, the way that certain dresses stay in your mind all your life, their colour and shape and how you felt wearing them, the nearest you will ever get to the person you were then, while others are entirely forgotten, unless in surprise you find a bit in the rag bag, or if there are careful needle-women around, in some piece of patchwork. This dress was made of seersucker, and the crinkles of the weave formed

39

stripes in colours of toffee brown, with white and cream; it had a fitting bodice, a waist with a belt, a full flaring skirt. The sleeves were small and the neck wide and quite low, lower in the back than the front. It was a satisfying dress, a dress with verve. Her mother had made it, and got it right for tightness of waist and lowness of neck, which didn't always happen.

Sid came up behind her. She and Maggie were walking down the narrow hall of her house, his house, Maggie already round the corner in the dining room. You've got a mole, he said.

She knew she had a mole. It was quite big, the size of a pea, but flat. It was on her back, her shoulder-blade, it sat just above the graceful curve of the neck of her dress. She thought of it as a beauty spot. If she'd been a woman at another moment in history she might have put it there herself, a round brown patch glued on to draw attention to the backward dip of her dress. As it was, nature was doing it for her, and she was pleased.

Sid put out his hand and tweaked the mole. Took it between thumb and forefinger, pinched it, turned it. Cruelly. Shockingly. Vivian's eyes filled with tears, she went stiff and jumped out of his grasp, twisted round, saw his grinning face, and ran into the dining room after Maggie. Her face burned, and so did her back; the mole felt damaged, as though he had almost pulled it off, and for days after she could feel the rough stinging pinch of his fingers. It had taken only a moment to happen, in that darkly carpeted silent hall, but it was a moment like a cleaver chopping through her girlhood. Maybe not severing it, but damaging. Sid changed from a man known as fathers are, taken-for-granted good, strict, unfunnily joking, kind, changed into her equal and her antagonist, a mean person who had enjoyed hurting her. Whose smile was dangerous, because it belonged to a diminished person. She never felt quite the same about her mole after that, he'd spoilt its serene and saucy beauty, and after her second child was born she had it removed, in case it should turn into a melanoma.

Later still, she could think, lecherous old man. Though he was much younger than she is now. And looking through the narrow wooden box where are kept the screwdrivers and hammers and a couple of old rusty files that she's never known used, for the nail punch that has sunk to the bottom untouched for years though it is something you like to have, her fingers pinching its round cold solid smoothness, she thinks, maybe I never gave it back to him, because of the mole.

Of course, you'll have carpet one day, Maggie said, and she replied, Oh no, I hate carpet. Tony didn't care for it either. That was one of the lucky things about being married, that they did it for reasons of sex (it was long enough ago for it to be difficult to have any, and certainly it seemed impossible to live together, without this ceremony, as well as pleasure in one another's company), and then discovered that they both didn't like carpet, and did like lots of fresh air, the windows open for breezes blowing through whenever it was at all warm. What about draughts, Maggie said, wooden floors are so draughty. No, said Vivian, all that wax, it keeps the draughts out. Wine got spilt on it, and newly nappyless children sometimes peed on it, watching with a certain pleasure the globular puddle that formed, sometimes pushing at it with their fingers to see it stretch and blob across the wood. It was easier to be brisk and cheerful and do your best not to give a child hang-ups about toilet training when the puddle was quick to mop up and did no damage. When the parents got older and had more money they bought rugs, old oriental ones, but still there was plenty of deepening yellow wood. You could hope caught-short grandchildren peed on that and not the rugs, but rugs were tough, weren't they supposed to be cured with camel dung?

It was odd that the nails were beginning to pop up again. Vivian hunkered down. Tapping the hammer against the punch. Having to do it on her own. Saying to herself, so, so, how is it any different from going to the pictures or shopping or being in bed on your own? Don't think of it. But of course it was its being the first time that caused the thought, the first time on her own, and the last time being so long ago, and so immense and exciting, their new house and new life . . . and she was getting sentimental about nails. No, melancholy, you could say melancholy, because there is a pleasure in remembering, it happens again if you remember. You're a girl again, a young woman, your legs are limber and everything is easy and there's so much time. And the young man you are intending to spend your life with is dipping a wide brush in varnish and making jokes about painting himself into corners.

The hammer bangs down. The nail punch jumps. There's a dint in the soft honey-coloured wood. Bugger.

Hooroo, calls a voice through the screen door. I didn't know you were a home handyman.

It's Rennie. Rennie is a new friend. She lives in one of the townhouses on the way to the shops. One day Vivian was passing her house and music was pouring out. It was *Lucia di Lammermoor*, the septet. The seven voices looped and soared and plaited the familiar marvellous pattern, she had to stop and listen. She sat on a low brick wall and raised her head and stared at the pale green leaves of a silver birch trembling in the music-filled air. Love and death. Love and death.

Why don't you come in and listen? A woman had come out into the courtyard and was gazing at her.

It's nearly over, said Vivian.

We can play it again.

Okay, she said. Thinking it was time to do something different, even a small thing like this.

That was how she met Rennie.

Have a glass of white wine, said Rennie. I told a lie. We can't play it again, it's the radio.

She stood with her hands clasped, smiling a naughty anxious smile. Vivian wondered about her age; the same as her own, perhaps. She had grey hair cut short, in little curls over her pink scalp. Her shape was cylindrical, under a pink and blue striped silk dress with a loose tie where the waist ought to be. Her legs were long and slender and shapely, and she wore flat little red leather shoes.

What pretty shoes, said Vivian, admiring their softness, and the red grosgrain ribbon binding them.

Yes, aren't they, said Rennie, I get them from the ballet shop. Very comfortable. Poor feet, they need a bit of comfort in their old age.

Rennie's feet looked as though they might have had a lot of comfort. They were broad but not bulgy, no bunions showing through the fine soft smoothness of the red leather.

Just a minute, she said, and came back with a bottle of wine already open and two glasses.

Vivian looked at her watch. It's ten to five, Rennie said. Definitely time.

So began the friendship. Both widows. Living in this suburb where people their age were moving out and young couples moving in and so frantically busy with jobs and children they had no neighbourly leisure. Vivian the more reticent, waiting to be asked, Rennie likely to wander in, as now, hoorooing through the wire door.

I'm not handy, said Vivian, I just can't stand nails sticking into my feet. She explained that she walked round the house barefoot, most of the time. Liking the smooth warm glaze of the wood against her skin.

It looks like honey, said Rennie. Not sticky, of course.

Vivian made coffee and they sat in the garden. They talked about that for a while, the black speckles on the rhododendrons, the nuisance but prettiness of the forget-me-nots, the honeysuckle with its sweet childhood smell and rampaging habit.

Remember pulling the centre out and sucking it.

The honey taste.

There's a lot of work in a garden, said Rennie. It needs a man.

Oh, said Vivian. You can say that. A gardener would do. Or me working harder.

They sipped their coffee.

Vivian, do you have any problems with . . . with . . . dryness?

Well, I water a lot . . .

Not, not gardens. Dryness, you know . . . down there.

Oh. Well, not as far as I know. I mean, it doesn't bother me.

44

I mean, when you're having sex.

But I don't have sex. Not any more.

Rennie frowned a bit, but her mouth turned up.

You do? said Vivian.

Mm. Perry, next door. He pops in, well, several times a day.

Several . . . ?

Two or three. Four sometimes.

Gawd. He's . . .

Yes.

So. Where. What. Vivian began questions and abandoned them. Perry, she said.

Yes, he's a nice man. A good bit younger than me, he's only sixty-six. Of course, I don't let on how old I am.

Sixty-six.

Mm. He's retired now. His wife died and he moved into the townhouses. His daughters thought he'd be safer. But he still grows roses. Red ones, they smell lovely.

And he comes to visit you.

Yes, said Rennie. Her face and scalp were glowing rosy pink. But, you see. Well, it's not so much the dryness. There's these creams and things. But, you know . . . you know when you laugh a lot you get caught short a bit, well, that tends to happen, I don't like that. I mean, the bed cover's satin, it shows.

Have you, spoken to your doctor . . .

Dr Alex? Oh I couldn't. He's such a handsome young man. How could I ask him something like that? What would he think of me? Rennie gave Vivian a reproachful–flirtatious look.

I'm sure he wouldn't care . . .

I would.

Well, what about another doctor? I go to a woman, Nicole, she's terrific . . .

Oh, but I couldn't give up Dr Alex. I've been going to him for years.

Nicole's good with women's things. Menopause, and that. I'm sure she'd know about incontinence.

Incontinence. It's not as bad as that.

Three or four times. A day. It's probably stress.

Oh, it's not stressful.

It might be, in a localised way.

Maybe I'll get a chenille throw, said Rennie. One of those really fluffy ones. Rose-coloured.

Rennie's sitting room was extremely rosy. She had a sofa covered in blue linen with big pink cabbage roses, and armchairs in a deep terracotta with bunches of them. The curtains were heavy cotton striped in the same colours. There were real roses in blue and white Chinese bowls, and paintings in gilded frames. Vivian recognised it as the English country house look, and was surprised that she liked it; the entire thing was so whole-hearted you couldn't help it.

Rose chenille, Vivian said.

A deep colour. Nothing pallid, said Rennie.

What about, the sheets, said Vivian.

Oh, we don't get into bed, it's not that kind of relationship.

Is that because of etiquette, or passion, Vivian asked.

Rennie ate another ginger biscuit. No wonder she was a cylindrical shape. Today her dress was green, a pale sage colour that was pretty without being sickly, tied with a bow around her fat waist. It was the kind of dress Vivian's mother would have worn; she didn't know you could still get them. Vivian was wearing black straight trousers and a big white tee-shirt; her waist wasn't very thin either, no way would she tie a bow round it.

Rennie dipped her biscuit in the coffee. She didn't answer the question, in her tranquil polite way. She often didn't, Vivian had noticed, and at first it had seemed to her rude, but then she decided it was because Rennie didn't know the answer; she thought about it, but nothing came to mind, and then she forgot.

So Perry came and pleasured Rennie on her satin quilt, soon to be protected from Rennie's unreliable bladder by a rose chenille throw. Etiquette or passion? Lust, I reckon, said Vivian to herself, and snorted a bit.

What? said Rennie. Vivian didn't answer, she could play that game too though she wasn't good at it yet.

I mean that velvety kind of chenille, said Rennie. Not that terrible half-bald candlewick stuff. Tidiness, she said, I couldn't stand having to make the bed four times a day.

When she'd gone Vivian punched in the rest of the protruding nails, then remembered she'd left the coffee cups in the garden. She turned on the hose and stood gently spraying the plants in pots, that always dried out too fast. Then she got herself a glass of wine and sat in the twilight. Dusk after rain, she said, smelling the wetness and enjoying the words, though it wasn't rain but hosing. There were mosquitoes so she lit a candle.

Linda next door looked over the fence, so Vivian asked her in for a drink. Oh I can't, I'm flat out, she said, I shouldn't, oh well just for a minute, a glass of wine is what I need.

Linda was a thin young woman with a son of eight. He's

watching telly, she said, leaning back in her chair and taking rapid pecks at the wine. She was a single mother; every fourth weekend Matthew flew to Melbourne to see his father. Linda worked in Parliament House, she was secretary to a junior minister, personal assistant was what she called herself, a terrific job except that when the house was sitting she often had to stay late, eight, nine, even ten o'clock.

My father's coming to live with me, she said, pulling a face. I hope it's a good idea. Seemed silly, him living on his own and me paying a fortune to have Matthew minded after school.

The words *It'll be good to have a man around the house* came to Vivian's mind but she didn't say them. Rennie words. Though Rennie's man was not about the house, he was on the bed and off again, home. And Vivian knew that it wasn't a man but the particular one that counted. After all those years with Tony she couldn't imagine fancying anyone else. Yet when she met Linda's father, who was called Tom, she couldn't help thinking of him like that; blame Rennie, Rennie's Perry, three times a day, four sometimes, on the bed not in it. Tom was a small nuggety man, with brown skin and heavily corded arms; he wore a hat low down on his head and spectacles that went dark in the sun. She was surprised that his voice had quite a thick accent; his English was good, he had learned it well, but too late in his life to sound like a native. He strode about the garden in old R. M. Williams boots, pruned all the trees and swept up the leaves left over from last autumn. Vivian spent more time in her garden. Tom tipped his hat to her, but wasn't conversational. Vivian remembered an expression of her mother's, how she would say someone was a worker. Usually a woman. She's a worker, she'd say, no adjective, it was stronger like that. Tom was a worker. Not to be confused with a fast worker, that was to do with sex. Like Perry. Or perhaps sometimes trickery, cheating. A worker was somebody who was visibly so, it didn't apply to people who thought and read and wrote, who worked in that way. It was physical. Vivian hearing it wished it could be said of her, though she didn't particularly prize that kind of on your feet all day activity. I bet he never reads a book, she said to herself. She wondered if Perry ever read a book.

She became conscious of Tom being there, next door. It made her feel peculiar; youthful, a girl again, not a comfortable feeling, who wants to be a girl again. Not since that time had she looked at a man with speculation. Not since before she was married. She'd looked at men over the years, discreetly but closely, paid attention to their sexiness, flirted with some of them, but always from the safety of being married to Tony. In play, not need. And now Tony was dead, she'd believed herself looking from the safety of having been married. Out of curiosity, not real interest. But now, blame Rennie, she didn't seem safe any more. Of course, nobody else had to know. But she did, and it unsettled her.

Tom climbed the ladder and pruned. He seemed a keen pruner. Vivian fiddled in her garden, it was looking unusually neat. She planted white petunias in pots, with blue salvia and pink impatiens, very pretty they looked. She imagined herself offering Tom a cup of tea, but never did. Or would he like coffee. Europeans often did. After school he and the boy Matthew put their heads together over jobs in the garden, or disappeared into the house. Often there was hammering to be heard.

By the side fence that separated their gardens was a Manchurian pear tree. Vivian could see it from her kitchen window. In autumn its leaves turned a dazzling vermilion colour, so full of light she would stand and gaze at it and feel her heart glowing and trembling like the tree. This autumn Tom took to it with a chainsaw. Lopping the branches down to the trunk. What are you doing, she shrieked, rushing out of the house, forgetting the difficulties of conversation. Cups of tea might be too intricate but the beautiful Manchurian pear was simple.

He turned the saw off. Looked at her. It's a pity, I know. But I can't leave it here and build the carport. It's exactly in the way.

But you can't chop this tree down, she shouted. You can't destroy something as beautiful as this.

The leaves on the chopped-off branches were still living and full of light. Vermilion. It wasn't often you had a word like that in your life. Tony had come up with it, when the branches first showed above the fence. Its leaves are vermilion, she said in a hopeless voice.

Tom gazed at them, too. Do you believe that trees go to heaven, he asked.

What?

That trees go to heaven. That they have an afterlife, as well as us.

That tree was making heaven for us here. You've ruined that. Who will forgive you for that?

She turned and strode inside her house. Leaned against the sink, shaking, not looking where the chainsaw whined and slashed. For hours that day and the next it laboured at destroying the tree. The carport was built, with lengthy headache-screaming noise of drills and hammers. It was a kind of roofed pergola. Tom planted banksia roses which would soon grow and cover it with a mass of yellow blossom in spring. But she mourned the vermilion tree, the mysterious trembling light that had made her heart glow. Even bare in the dead of winter the memory of its colour had been alive. And its summer green was a pleasure too. But now it was gone this memory had lost its power. Often she found her eyes filling with tears. She hadn't wept like this for Tony. Her face had ached but the tear channels had been tense and dry as salt pans and all the weight of her sorrow had stayed trapped in her head. Maybe if he'd been here the tree would have been safe too. Tears ran down her cheeks in grief for Tony's lovely lost vermilion. She kept her eyes turned away from the bleak wood and metal of the carport.

Linda put her car under the carport and Tom used the garage as a workshop. He and Matthew spent a lot of time there, but at least the hammering was muted.

It was winter. Vivian and Rennie drank their tea and coffee and white wine in warm inward rooms. How's Perry, Vivian would ask, and across Rennie's face would flit that sly visceral blind look that is the intelligence of sex. She'd get rid of it with a quick little giggle. Oh Perry's fine. As ever. Rennie had bought her rose-coloured chenille throw. Two in fact. One to use, one to wash. They had big swaggy tassels in the corners. Rennie was pleased with them.

In the spring, when her roses were just beginning to bud, Rennie died. Quite suddenly, instantly in fact, on her bed, one afternoon. Perry found her, said the woman in the newsagent, with the round important eyes and careful air of one who has gossip but is nervous of offering it. In fact, she said, I heard he was with her, you know, and they . . .

They were great friends, said Vivian.

It's a good death, said the newsagent, quick, like that.

Mm, said Vivian. Well, a good death is what we all hope for.

That's what people had said about Tony, a good death, and so maybe it was, but hard for the rest of them, with no warning, no preparation, no time to get used to it.

She met Perry at the funeral, a white-haired small man, nimble and grief stricken. You were a good friend of hers, too, weren't you, he said. We who are left must comfort one another. As she left he asked for her phone number. Perhaps we could have a cup of tea, he said, wrinkling his small brown eyes.

That would be nice, she said, but felt panic in her throat.

One morning Tom knocked at her door. He had with him a rather large object, made of some reddish-brown highly varnished intricately grained wood. It looked like a butler's tray, an oblong shallow box on crossed over legs, and it was full of sand.

I thought you might like to have this, he said. He picked it up and she stood aside to let him in. He scraped his feet on the mat, then stepped carefully inside. His boots creaked and clicked on the wooden floor. I hope you have a place for it, he said.

Oh, she said, meaning, what is it? what's it for? what's going on? Oh.

He pulled two little wooden rakes out of his pocket. It's a sand garden, he said. The Japanese have them. They are charming . . . like a charm.

He used the smooth side of one of the rakes, stroking it across the sand until it was perfectly smooth, taking his time, putting his head on one side, protruding his tongue.

Now, he said, you make patterns. He turned the rake to its pronged side and drew a wavering line through the sand, forming ridges that curved and crossed one another. The sand flowed and sifted in the wake of the rake's passage.

Some people have stones, round smooth ones, and make rings around those, but I like just the sand. I like to be pure, said Tom. Here, you have a go. No, make it smooth, start again.

It seemed to take a long time and at first she was anxious about being slow and clumsy, but Tom stood solidly calm and so contemplative of what she was doing that she took her time, and smoothed the sand, then furrowed it. Her strokes were stiff, and awkwardly angled, but she supposed they'd become more fluid with practice.

You see, the rakes are different sizes, so you can change the patterns, make them coarser or finer. Tom frowned as he said this. I believe that Japanese people often start the day with them. They begin with raking it all smooth, and then they let the rakes in their hands form the patterns. They say it calms the spirit. Maybe it does.

Maybe it does, she said to herself. Though she could also imagine herself forgetting about it, and walking past wherever she found to put it without registering, the patterns neglected, fading, collecting dust. But perhaps not. Perhaps she'd get into the habit of its curious austere beauty. Accept its daily ritual.

Her hand slipped and the rake flicked over, scattering sand that pattered down on the floor. Under her feet it crackled like spilt sugar.

You have to cultivate a delicate touch, he said. You won't find it difficult.

It's an unusual present, she said.

I suppose it is. He smiled. His glasses out of the sunlight were paling, she could see his eyes hopeful, with a faint anxious squint.

An amazing present. I wonder what made you think of it. She said this, not asking a question, not sure she wanted to know. I hear you hammering often.

I like to keep busy. The evening is reading, but the daylight is for keeping busy.

I like to read in the daytime sometimes. It feels wicked.

Do you like to feel wicked?

Well, it's only a very little bit. I can't feel very wicked about reading a book in the daytime. Not these days.

I see you work hard in the garden.

Oh, I like to potter a bit. It's a useful hobby, she said, her cheeks warm. Ah . . . how about, a cup of coffee?

I should be getting back.

Or tea? I could make tea.

He frowned again. She walked towards the kitchen. The sand crunched. I'm sure you can spare a moment for a cup of . . . whatever.

He followed, his boots clicking and creaking.

Perhaps a glass of water.

If you like. I think I'll have some coffee. A good worker deserves a break, she said.

He looked out the window. When the rose grows you'll hardly see the carport. The banksia rose has a profusion of flowers.

Yes, well, it's not a Manchurian pear, though. Not vermilion. She was afraid her eyes were going to fill with tears.

Things rarely are what they were. We all learn that.

She filled the jug and set it to boil. She filled a glass with water for him. Did you decide, would you like some coffee as well? Or tea?

Oh, he said, okay, coffee. He patted his breast pocket. And we'll have a bit of this. He took out a flat glass flask full of colourless viscous liquid.

Slivovitz. His voice was proud.

Plum brandy, she said.

People say brandy. I prefer alcohol, he said. But yes, made out of plums. A friend of mine has a still.

I didn't know you could do that.

Oh, it's not legal. We'll have a bit in our coffee.

Isn't it a bit early?

How, early? How is an early or a late time better for a little alcohol in the coffee? It is good, the time does not matter.

Like reading in the morning.

But not even a little bit wicked. You will see, it is not the taste, it is the feel, the warm, the glowing.

She could taste the slivovitz in the hot sweet milky coffee, it bit through the familiar drink. It was a hard taste, a bit dangerous, it made her gasp. But she saw what he meant about the warm feeling. Down her throat, into her stomach, and flowing out from that dark pit, warming places she'd forgotten.

the sins of the leopard

That day we got no further with our reading . . .

But we could listen. Not like those long-ago lovers, those two who could get no further with their reading, with their startled glances and trembling lips. They put the book aside, stopped reading of the loves of others, and fell to making their own story. One kissed away the other's smile, as did the lovers in their book, and on they went from there. So we 700 years later could lie in bed and hear it read to us, and no need to stop the kissing of our trembling lips.

This is adultery with technology, and a great help it is. No more claiming to be a Luddite. Not with devices so useful. Take the phone for instance. Switch it through to the mobile. Nobody knows whether you are at home or out of town. It rings and you answer, firm-voiced, no trembling of the lips now. Spouse, or the plumber, the good friend coming to visit; one lies poker still while the other speaks the mundane details of daily life. Afterwards they murmur, breathless again, of how the person at the other end would marvel could they see what was actually going on. Marvel, or be filled with fury at the betrayal. Technology does not cancel out betrayal, just makes it easier.

A pander was that book, and he that wrote it, says the voice out of the machine. Referring indeed to the narrative of Lancelot and Guinevere, which is what the lovers were reading.

Oh, she says, I know this bit.

It's supposed to be the most famous of all.

I didn't know that. Well, it's probably because it's the saddest.

At least Dante had his lovers only as far down as the first circle, he says. Could have been worse.

And they are forever united, she says. *Hand in hand, drifting on the dark wind.*

The thing about lust, he says, is that it is a shared sin. So it's not wholly selfish.

Dante is told by Virgil his guide that the first circle is for people without hope. Things aren't too bad. Not like the lowest frozen level, where Judas has his head forever locked in Lucifer's jaws. Lucifer the bright one, the son of the morning, now filthy and matted and shaggy-hairy, encased eternally in ice. Endlessly chewing on the head of Judas, whose legs hang out and jerk in the air. Judas of course the wickedest man ever, as is Lucifer the wickedest angel, both betrayers of their lords. But going on forever without hope is clearly not pleasant for people whose only sin is to have died without Christian repentance.

She wonders if it is tempting fate to listen to *The Divine Comedy* on a compact disc after making love, this greedy ecstatic plotted-for illicit love-making, to be kissing and stroking and listening, not always with attention, and this is a new experience for her, who has always read every word so carefully, to be listening to these moving cadences as one listens to music, drifting in and out of its sense, the soft seductive voice speaking only privately for them, and so she wonders, are they wishing the same fate upon themselves, inviting it, summoning it; will they end up forever punished. Like Francesca and Paolo, who read together in their book about those other adulterous lovers, and looked on one another with the same illicit passion, Francesca the wife and Paolo the husband's brother. The husband ugly and lame, and Francesca given to him in marriage because of his bravery (and his wealth), the lover handsome, *this lad with the lovely body*, she sadly describes him to Dante. The story goes that the beautiful Paolo was sent to woo her, that she was allowed to suppose he was the one to be married to, and that is why she accepted. But extenuating circumstances don't help, it is still wrong to put your reason in thrall to lust. So here they are, shadows driven on the wind, *hopeless of any rest*.

The thing about adultery is that it has been going on a long time. It isn't new. Though it is always news. Always dark, and full of delight, and dread. And death. Paolo and Francesca killed by the angry husband, stabbed as they lie in bed together, *in flagrante delicto* and all its heat, so there is no moment for repentance, not a second; condemned forever to hell. The punishment for sin is sin itself, experienced without illusion. Maybe this is the punishment for all adulterous love, to be left with the sin, and none of the delight that went with it. Maybe they will be punished in this way.

Punished? Of course not, he says. You can't accept even the simple principle of it. Think of that first level, the no-hope lot. Everybody who isn't baptised is there. From Adam up to the time of Christ.

Not Adam, I don't think. Isn't he in the rose of heaven.

Is he? Well, all the rest of the Old Testament. Moses. Virgil. Babies. Virtuous Moslems. Not to mention Buddhists. How can you believe in a god who is so mean about punishing people? Good people. It can't be true.

He says this while kissing her. They have taught themselves to kiss while talking. This may allow for profound utterances, possibly lengthy ones, but certainly it means that argument is difficult. Something has to be lost in a kissing conversation, and it is the chilly powers of reasoning. But she doesn't want to argue, of course she doesn't believe in hell at all, not this souls in everlasting carnal torment version.

But then, she doesn't believe in adultery either.

old happy times

SCREWED TO THE WALL IN THE laundry is a rotisserie and grill. When it's closed it's a flattish stainless-steel oblong, then when you pull the front panel down the electric grilling mechanism rises up, and the opened door forms a base. You can hang a grill pan on levers at the back, or fasten a spit so it turns slowly and produces crisply browned roasted meat: chickens, beef fillets, legs of lamb. Altogether it is a cunning device.

On the front is a notice, on a largish yellow post-it note. It says, in bold block letters:

CAREFUL!
LIFT BY
THE EDGES
HANDLE LOOSE

This message is written in pencil and stuck by its narrow gummy edge just where you put your hand to grasp the broken handle. It has been there for at least three years, perhaps four.

The machine isn't used every day, but frequently enough, and the label has stayed stuck all that time, isn't even greasy or dog-eared or curled, and the pencil writing has not smudged or faded.

It is Geoffrey's writing, and every time she opens the thing by the edges, not the handle, which is indeed loose, being attached on only one side, she marvels with a kind of bitter marvel. This frail little scrap of paper, and it endures, while Geoffrey is dead. Every time she reads his admonition, looking at the handwriting she loves, she has this thought. It endures, and Geoffrey is dead. Was ill for more than a year before that. The label was written in the days of his good health, the pencil strokes are vigorous, they believed there was a lot of life left to him, still.

Once, a long time ago, they had an argument, she was angry and accused him of caring more for objects than for people. He was careful, he liked to look after things, to polish shoes and keep cars clean and preserve the gleaming surfaces on furniture. But people, she said, you do not care so much for people. We can always get a new table, or a car, or a pair of shoes, but if I am hurt or injured a new me is not so easy to come by. I may not easily be mended, either.

At the time she was meaning they had just bought a marvellous Hiroe Swen pot, large and darkly glazed, with a great bird scraped into the clay underneath. She had considered it a kind of token, a promise of faith, a return to their ways of doing things, but then thought it wasn't honest in that way at all. She wanted to drop it on the terrazzo doorstep so that its fragments were the first thing he saw when he came home in the afternoon. But she could not bring herself to do so, it was too beautiful as a work of art, it did not deserve to be destroyed in a conjugal quarrel. And she thought even more bitterly, I can be hurt, but I cannot hurt this inanimate thing.

What she did instead in the middle of a fury as visceral as the grief she now feels was smash a drinking glass in the upstairs bathroom and scratch her wrists with it. She drew blood, but knew even in her fury that she could never cut deep enough to make it a real act. He was furious with her too, did not believe she would do it, thought it was a threat, mainly he thought it was a threat though he was afraid too. And held her in his arms, and bound up the scratch, and cleaned up the glass that had strewn its sharp shards all over the floor.

He was wounded when she accused him of caring more for things than people, and she knew that it was a clever angry remark, intended to hurt. And it wasn't true. Not at the bad time. Never did he stop caring for her. Never stop loving her. Even in the year of his dying he took care of her, listened to her, paid attention. She knew it at the time, and how much more now when he isn't here.

I was good at being married, she writes to Oliver. Her old lover, her lovely heart-breaking illicit love, from when she was twenty-one, a girl with long straight hair and a tentative expression. He hasn't seen her since those days, but now they email every day. He writes back: I can see that, from your letters. She thinks of this; thirty-five years, learning to be good at being married, it came naturally but needed training into, as well. And now it is a skill she may never need again. She is entirely engaged in developing a quite other skill, in becoming good at not being married. She appears to be a success at that too, she pays her bills, entertains friends, maintains the house and garden, lights fires, orders wine. Even does her job, in a minor way; she keeps being asked to do small well-paid writing tasks, and if the novel is not getting written, well, it takes an orderly and calm mind as well as house to write novels, and that she may one day achieve, too.

Besides, she is writing stories, which she describes as unpublishable. A friend says, Oh, I expect somebody might take them, some time, you shouldn't worry too much, and she says, No, I mean unpublishable by me, not by anybody else.

She discusses the nature of fiction with Oliver. It is about illuminating the world we live in, she says. That's why we read, she says. To make sense of this difficult world. No, he writes back, it is about language. Language is what literature is about. But then he agrees you need both; life without language is tedious, language without life is sterile. What's more, it's about consolation, she says. Like all art, it fills us with desire, which it doesn't quite assuage, but itself is some comfort.

Oliver started writing to her after more than thirty years of absence, of silence, because he had searched out copies of her books and read them. I knew you would never be a routine I-love-a-sunburnt-country writer, he said, in that first letter, a delayed love letter he called it, but I did not know what I was missing. Clare wondered if he had not got hold of the books sooner because he was afraid she'd be no good. Protecting the old love turned into a novelist from failure, and disappointing him.

She thought of all the characters she'd turned him into over the years. They may have done what you did, she wrote, but I did not see you as quite such a baddie. I hoped not, he said, I was fairly sure not.

Later, in the middle of the year of the epistolary novel emails, he sent her an amazing bunch of flowers, signed with the name of one of the characters she'd loaned some of their story. Making him charming, not the seducer and betrayer she sometimes rather maliciously turned him into. A sad story, this, of meeting in later years and parting. Not at all prescient, as it turns out.

But she did not keep up that first renewed correspondence, not then. She did not tell Geoffrey about it, and let it lapse. When Geoffrey died and she had to learn how to live without him she wrote again to Oliver, wanting to tell him about this immense thing that had happened to her, and then she was telling him about all her life since she'd seen him, constructing its narratives for him and for herself too, creating for him the person that those more than thirty years have turned her into. And in return he pays attention to them, and to her.

She sends him the stories, too, and he tells her how much he likes them.

Clare takes pleasure in her survival skills, she is happy sometimes, has fun sometimes, even has small flashing moments, not usually those of fun or pleasure, when she is not conscious of grief. She makes the curious discovery that grief feeds off happiness, and pleasure nourishes it. Grief grows fat and richly fleshed, and sits in her chest like a big suety pudding.

She treasures the yellow sticky label on the door of the grill. It's a message. Neat and syntactical. She can believe he is still taking care of her. CAREFUL! He often said careful. It was one of his words.

Careful. Careful didn't help. Careful couldn't save Geoffrey. All of her care didn't work.

There are other bits of paper around the house in his handwriting. Shopping lists, addresses, the names and numbers of compact discs he planned to buy. She tucks them back into books and boxes and kitchen drawers so they will turn up their small random memories of comfort at unexpected moments.

One of the things that Geoffrey said to her in his dying year was that she was the love of his life. Of course, she knew that, but the words are a precious gift that she can take out and gaze on. She can slip over her head the necklace of pearls he gave her for their thirtieth wedding anniversary, wear her rings, pin on the tiny antique coral brooch she bought in Tasmania because he had rung up some jewellers and discovered that corals are the token of thirty-five years married. And she can hold in her hands the words: You are the love of my life.

In the bottom of a drawer full of junk she finds the card he gave her one Christmas, to go with a tiny silver cherub holding a pearl: *Happy Christmas to a pearl among women, love from Cupid.* You could have expected years more of such small fond jokes. In that beloved writing, black ink, cursive, firm, eminently readable.

One day of his illness he said, I don't suppose I shall ever go to Paris again. I wonder, she said. Probably not. I may not, either. But you've done it, she said. Think how well you've done it. Over and over. Think how well you know it.

That's true, he said.

She sighed. And anyway life is full of things we'll never do again. Or do at all. We'll never have a baby again. And think what a nice thing that was, it's sad it won't happen. We'll never learn to ski. Or tango really well. But think of all the things we've done, and loved doing. I think we've done everything we wanted, don't you?

He smiled, and she could see her words pleased him.

And as I say, I doubt I'll get to Paris again myself.

(Even when she said it she suspected she wasn't telling the truth. Now: in her filing cabinet now is an airline ticket. Melbourne Singapore London Paris Singapore Melbourne. She is still greedy, still wants.)

Not everything she said to him was comforting. Once she was miserable and muttered to him, The person who dies is all right, they are alive and then they aren't. But the other person has to stay alive and full of grief and who is going to comfort them?

Even though she was upset she was trying to keep her words vague: *person, them*; not *you, me*. But then she said, You're all right, I am here looking after you. But what will happen to me when I get sick? There'll be nobody to care for me. I'll be all alone. I'll have to go to the hospice. I'll have to be among strangers.

This made him cry, and she did too. She was heartbroken by what she had said, and put her arms gently around him, and they both sobbed, until she took a deep breath and turned a sob into a breathy little giggle and said, Oh well, with a bit of luck I'll fall under a bus and it'll all be over nice and quickly. He smiled too, and the moment went away, but she was aghast at her words, still is, she cannot forgive herself for them, they were cruel and selfish, her feeling desolate was not enough to excuse them. After all, she is alive, and full of energy.

But the words are true. He will not be there to love her when she's dying.

Once she said, I'm trusting you to plan me a decent funeral. Some good music.

What about the Entry of the Queen of Sheba, he said, and sang it.

Oh yes.

This was not the time to talk about that. He would not be planning her funeral. She said, None of us knows the moment of our coming hither or our going hence.

> *Men must endure*
> *Their going hence, even as their coming hither.*
> *Ripeness is all.*

She remembers studying *King Lear*, and how you recognise that this is a precious moment in the play, not its message, or its note of hope, or anything so neat, simply that, a precious moment, to be paid attention to. They are both enduring Geoffrey's going hence. But whether ripeness is a word to be applied is another matter.

She said to him, You know how you nearly died when you were a baby, when you had whooping cough. Well, you could say that all the years since then have been a bonus. Sixty-three is a lot better than being a baby. Sixty-three already.

His face opened in that particular soft luminous smile which showed her words pleased him.

Mm, he said.

To herself she said, But seventy-three would have been better. Eighty-three.

It's a bitter winter, cold and wet, she lights her fire and sits by it with a book. She has been reading Dante, since listening to a recording of the Cantos of Hell, in quite other circumstances. She thought that Geoffrey would have a copy somewhere, and so he does, a Penguin edition, translated by Dorothy Sayers, a curious piece of work which endeavours to keep the *terza rima* of the original and so is not altogether successful as English. But it has good notes which explain the literal and allegorical meanings of the text. The beasts, for instance, which Dante meets at the beginning, when he's been lost in the Dark Wood and trying to get out of it by climbing the Mountain. There's

a Leopard, nimble and light and fleet
Clothed in a fine furred pelt all dapple-dyed

which comes gambolling out and hinders him, so he has to keep retreating. Then there's a Lion, *swift and savage*, making straight for him, *with ravenous hunger raving*. Third is the Wolf, *gaunt with famished craving*, and Dante is driven back, in terror and despair, and that's when Virgil comes to lead him.

The beasts, says Sayers, are the images of sin. To be identified with Lust, Pride, Avarice. Or with the sins of Youth, Manhood, and Age. 'The gay *Leopard* is the image of the self-indulgent sins, *Incontinence*; the fierce *Lion*, of the violent sins—*Bestiality*; the *She-Wolf* of the malicious sins, which involve *Fraud.*'

Her lover saying that lust is not the worst sin because it is shared, it isn't selfish. The Leopard is gay, he gambols, his coat is beautiful. And his sin is a sin of the young. Of incontinence.

On the contrary, she says to herself, very self-contained, it is. And nothing to do with being young.

She considers Sayers' remark, that the place, hell, is not remedial, since once you've got there it's for all eternity, but that the idea of hell is remedial, if you use the fear of it to keep you out of it. She doesn't know why she finds these ideas so potent since neither she nor Geoffrey believed in hell, except in the sense of the mind being its own place, and making a hell of heaven, a heaven of hell. Geoffrey believed death is death, the end, final, absolute. She doesn't, though she doesn't know how it isn't. But she doesn't believe that all that remains of him is in a plastic casket inside a cardboard box on a high bookshelf. His ashes that they will decide what to do with one day.

Polly who practises Catholicism but is unsure about eternal life says it's okay not to know, and okay to think that one day we will. Or not, says Clare. Or not, Polly agrees.

She remembers Alec Hope telling her he was learning Italian so he could read Dante in the original. Now reading this sacred text of Western civilisation she has her own dialogue with its author. Arguing often. As with the lines:

> *The bitterest of woes*
> *Is to remember in our wretchedness*
> *Old happy times.*

This is Sayers. She finds another simpler translation:

> There is no greater sorrow than to recall a time of
> happiness in misery.

She thinks of the year of Geoffrey's dying, and how they remembered their past, forming it into little stories for one another's delight. Like small beautiful objects passed back and forth between them, to admire the craft, the skill, the intricate detail, the devotion. Old happy times. She believes that the past is alive, that it should be more alive than the future, that things that have happened should be talked about with as much pleasure as those you are planning to make happen. (How much more so when there is no future.) That the past should be dwelt in as energetically as the present, remembering how much was invested in making it come to pass.

Ah yes, she thinks, but they were happy then, Geoffrey was alive, even if he was dying, they were together, they were remembering old happy times in a present happy time, and they knew it. It is a gift to know you are happy.

And Dante has a word to say. Context. You can't quote me out of context. I am talking about the lovers in hell, remember, the adulterous pair, doomed to remember not just their past happiness but their old wickedness.

But they are together, she says to him, that must help. Hell doesn't seem so bad like that. Hand in hand they are.

Ah, but consider, it is for eternity. What is it that Joyce says about the raven? Well, not Joyce, but his character, the priest . . . if every grain of sand from every beach in the world was piled up and a raven came once every million years and took one grain away, by the time he'd got rid of the whole pile of them just one second of eternity would have passed.

Imagine how that would have terrified all the little hell-believing kids. Imagine how Paolo and Francesca feel, vexed by the blasts, hopeless of any rest, endlessly whirling and wailing.

But when she looks at the text of Canto V again she finds Francesca saying:

> *Love*
> *Took me with such great joy of him, that see!*
> *It holds me yet and never shall leave me more.*

Love holds me yet . . . And so it does. In her own time scale she gets pleasure from remembering. She looks at photographs, at his name written in the front of books, at his gifts to her, at the things they bought together, furniture, pictures, carpets, pots; at the words he gave her. Most of all she believes she can be a time traveller in her mind. She's in hospital, in the second year of her marriage, having a miscarriage, she is lying in bed, he is holding her hand, the curtains are closed. The nurse pokes her head in, curt: Time to go. Your wife needs to rest. He leans forward and kisses her, the kiss goes on and on, his mouth is on hers, time flows over them, ages later the nurse bustling back, the nurse's shocked voice, but somehow respectful, she has felt the power of that kiss, miscarriages are her business but the small curtained space is full of the passion that makes babies in the first place. He goes, and she lies dazed in the secret dreaming happiness of that kiss, her lips tremble now with the tender gentle power of it, thirty-however many years later she sits dazed and trembling in its aftermath, it is fresher

71

in her mouth than the coolness of his just-dead skin in that last hospital room.

The grief of the memory of all this loss fills her with a kind of happiness, a bitter pleasure that she desires and cultivates. That nourishes.

She is roasting a chicken, quite plain, the skin rubbed with cut lemon, then the pieces put inside it, the spit poked through as carefully centred as possible so that it will turn smoothly, the bird trussed with string and tied in place.

She goes to the grill, to open it and switch it on to get good and hot before she sets the bird turning. Its own fat will run over it and brown it before dripping into the pan beneath, it will be tender and succulent and dark golden brown, though some people will not eat the skin, far too rich and fatty, far too dangerous.

She grasps the door.

CAREFUL!
LIFT BY
THE EDGES

Careful she is, sliding her fingers in behind the rim, pulling it down. The yellow post-it note flutters. Careful. Don't spill any grease on it. It's to be treasured, this little yellow note. A message from beyond the grave, she says to herself. Laughs. That's your kind of joke, Geoffrey.

the boat

LIFE IS DYNAMIC, SAYS CLARE TO
her lover on the telephone. He usually telephones in the
morning, and they talk about things like original sin and the
immaculate conception and enlightenment and Sartre, about
Huit Clos and the movie of it he saw as a student as well as
existentialism, he said once that he'd been using the words
existential angst for thirty-five years and had only just
understood what they meant. Anguish in the face of an
uncaring universe, he said. An indifferent universe. She said
she thought that was what everybody feared. Not being seen
with the eyes of love. Anger is better than indifference; a
tearing terrible fight with someone you love preferable to his
not paying attention to you.

Clare has only just formed this life-is-dynamic idea into
words, and she likes it, it is new and exciting for her and she
has not yet obliged herself to think that it would be certain

73

that somebody had said it all before. The thing is, she says, life has to change, and it doesn't at all mind changing in the direction of getting better, but if it can't do that, it will change in the direction of getting worse. And that's the thing with marriages, if they don't get better they get worse. People want them to stay the same, but they don't, they can't, a simple smug easy content may seem nice, but it can't happen. At first it's usually all right, because being a couple is all so new, and exciting, terrifying even, and finding out about sex—well, in my day anyway, she says—and getting a house, and children, and them growing up, and jobs, and you growing up, except that I'm not sure you do, really. But then everything seems to be done, you're established, there's nothing new, and that's when it changes in bad ways. Of course, she finishes up (these telephone conversations allow for very long exchanges, they don't interrupt one another much, just breathe quietly), I'm sure there's nothing new in this, it's just that I haven't particularly thought it before. I don't think. But I expect someone has.

Probably some Greek, he says. The doctrine of becoming, was it? That the world is made of becoming.

Is that Heraclitus, she asks. The same as flux, maybe. Didn't he say that? That no one steps twice into the same river.

Clare put that not stepping twice into the same river in a book once. She thinks it is a powerful image. She likes the idea of calling a book after it, one day. *The Same River.* Has done so, but only in a book.

Wasn't he the one that said *most men are bad*, he asks.

Probably. After all, I am wicked, she says, savouring the idea, but not happily.

74

And that the world is a vast battlefield. He reckoned that you can't get rid of war or there'll be nothing left, because war is the father of all things.

Who's their mother, she wonders.

I don't think he says. Heraclitus the Obscure, he was called. Or the Dark.

Oh yes. Dark.

They are both dredging up memories of Philosophy 1, or some such, and not getting far. It is existentialism he is reading now, not the ancient Greeks.

This conversation is because his wife has found out about them and there has been a huge blow-up, nights of tears and storming, anger, misery, terror. It is a change all right. And curiously, for the better, this angry intertwining beating anger brings the husband and wife together, almost the whole way across the politeness that has parted them.

I thought it would, said Clare. I knew it would. It's a gift I've given you.

The discovery has stopped the marriage sinking further into badness. Not that it was very bad, it was contented enough, not unhappy. Very civil. It just wasn't as happy as two people together loving one another can be. We are getting older, his wife might have said. This is maturity. Serenity is not to be sneezed at.

The lover says that a state of not being unhappy is in fact unhappiness. He has been unhappy, he's been in a bleak black depression. Now he is happy, Clare has made him so. Or he has been, until he saw the pain he is causing, now.

He had thought he could tell his wife about it in a rational manner, and that she wouldn't mind too much. Would agree that parting was the only sensible thing to do. That she might even be glad to see the back of him.

I see that you did not know about anguish, says Clare.

No, he says.

Whereas Clare is an expert in anguish. Ever since her daughter was born, and the doctor said, If you believe in having babies christened, I would christen this one. And they did, not because they were religious but because so small a life demanded some ceremony. But the baby didn't die. But needed two heart operations, and they were risky; after the second Clare heard the intensive care nurse tell her sister on the telephone from Brisbane that her condition was critical but stable. What a cold weight was in those words. Then Geoffrey's heart attacks. And the time . . . still too painful, just say: when he thought he might want to stop being married to her. As her lover might have to his wife, but hasn't, and in Geoffrey's case not so quickly resolved. And then Geoffrey's death. After a long illness. Another cold and weighty phrase. Clare is well schooled, long-learned, in anguish. And all its clichés.

I could not believe that one person could be so shattered, her lover says. He uses plain words, like *awful*, and *terrible*, and his voice invests them with a power that mostly they have lost. His voice, and his stricken face. He does not think he can inflict that much pain on anyone, he says.

This anguish went on for several days and mostly nights. And he doesn't leave her, he won't, but he must stay friends with Clare. Yes, says his wife, and she wants to, as well. Friends is the word here, friends, and no more.

★

Tomorrow is Clare's wedding anniversary. The first since Geoffrey's death. She sits at the computer and tears run down her cheeks. Lucky it is not paper and ink, there would be big blots and puddles on the page. Maybe the computer will spark and sizzle and die, and the email she is sending to Oliver in England will fizzle with it. I am living in interesting times, she tells him, in the manner of the Chinese curse. Do you think it is better to be full of passion and excitement and terrible pain, and know you are alive, she asks him, than content and complacent and no pain but no passion either? Clare is going for passion and pain, which is just as well, since she's got them. Pain, anyway. Her tears fall, for her dead husband, her widowhood, her lost lover, all her lost lovers. What if email had been invented in Oliver's day, would their affair have been different? It doesn't help with this one. Email is only as good as the emailer. Don't swear any terrible oaths, she said to him, her newly lost lover, just say that this is what you intend to happen. Her mind wants a friend, her body wants a lover, and she, who is neither mind nor body but an indissoluble mixture of both, wants both friend and lover. Her tears fall, she doesn't sleep, lies with itching eyes. She knows she cannot have what she wants, but his wife doesn't, she believes she can have it all. So Clare thinks, and who knows if she is right. She imagines herself saying to this friend, there are prices, you know, you can have things but there are prices. Maybe some people never find this out, but she doesn't know anyone who has lived scot-free.

She reminds herself that she has given her lover's wife, her friend, an important gift. The friend might not recognise it now. Clare has shown her how terrifying life might be. Clare has known for a long time, she's often told her friend, who has nodded sagely, kindly, sympathetically, but telling is never enough. It has to be shown. The burnt finger makes the child know the stove is hot, as no words can ever tell. The old clichés reveal their truth, again.

She has shown her friend that her husband loves her and will not leave her.

Her lover, now just friend, takes her out to lunch; he's remembered it's her wedding anniversary. How does he know this? It's a marvel. They go to the restaurant in the sculpture garden. I'll show you my favourite sculpture, she says.

Is it the couple making love, he says.

No, which one's that?

The Henry Moore.

I've never noticed they're making love. They're not.

They are. You look.

Mine's much more innocent. Childhood. Holidays at the lake. It's down here. She turns to the side of the pool.

After lunch, he says, let's get a table first.

The fog sculpture is working. She sits sideways in her chair so the sun shines on her thinly stockinged legs—she used to wrap them in warm winter trousers for cold winter days but now it is sheer stockings with lace tops and erotic misery keeping you warm—and watches its white vapour eddy and billow and rise in rags of mist among the reeds and through the casuarinas. Each needle is coated with hundreds of droplets of water and the low sun turns them into tiny points of light so that all the trees and the reeds are spangled with glittering spheres.

I think the fog garden is the most beautiful thing I have ever seen, she says, and he agrees.

The mist eddies on to the deck of the restaurant and settles its droplets on her hair, not spangling it because her head isn't in the sunlight, it seems to be laying a greyish veil over it.

Remember that song? He says the words in a lilting voice, almost music, under his breath:

> *I loved her in the summertime*
> *And in the winter too*
> *And the only only thing that I ever did wrong*
> *Was to shield her from the foggy foggy dew*

I thought that was a rugby song, she said, drunken student yobbos waving stubbies.

They did sing it, all those long drawn-out ooh sounds was what they liked. But it's a folk song first. And here's the foggy foggy dew.

They pay half each for lunch, as friends do. They walk around the Henry Moore. You can see lovers in it, penises, vaginas, thrusting and rearing and lying open, but the two parts don't touch, they thrust and loop and follow one another's shapes but never meet.

If they're lovers it's tragic, she says.

Why? I see them as lovers.

But they're not touching. They're straining together, but not touching.

It's an image of copulation; don't you see it?

Desire, maybe, but it's not happening.

She can see that it is possible to imagine that maybe they will come together one day. The metal's tension will snap and all that mighty weight will grind together and fall upon itself.

What a cataclysm, she says, and he laughs and puts his finger on her cheek.

A great bang, he says.

She averts her eyes from the mechanism of the fog sculpture as from sordid detail, the racks of tiny nozzles through which the water is forced into the fine mist whose white billows roil and creep across the pond. She knows what they look like from all the times they weren't working, were always being sent back to Japan for repairs. It's really too fragile, people said. Too finicky. But somebody's clearly worked something out, for now the fog sculpture always functions, every day from twelve to two.

We probably wouldn't be any good, living together, she says. Don't you remember, you said we wouldn't, at the beginning, there'd be no question of it, we were both too fond of our own agendas. That's why it was safe.

He shakes his head. We would, we'd be good, he says. I never did mean that, even when I said it. We'd be good.

Yes, she says. Sadly. She's never slept with him, never got up with him, but she too doesn't believe that they wouldn't be good at it.

You said you weren't going to fall in love with me, she says.

Ah, yes, I did, and I was telling the truth. I wasn't going to fall in love with you because I already had, oh, a long time ago.

He puts his arm round her, squeezes her in a hug. They aren't lovers, they're friends, this is the sort of thing friends can do; only lovers, adulterous lovers, must be secret in public, and entwined they walk through the winding bush-scented paths of the garden to a small private space with a bench overlooking the lake. She forgets to show him her sculpture, the one she likes best, after the fog, the boat made of rusty bronze half on the bank, half sinking among the reeds, reduced to a sketch of its timbers, reminding her of those boats by the holiday lakes of her childhood, rotting away in the shallow water, spongy, frail, broken, and it is a thing of wonder that this weight, this mass of bronze, so solid, should capture so perfectly that decay.

the moral ground

SHE WAS TALKING TO HER LOVER on the telephone about the sin of onanism. She wondered if she should think of him as her ex-lover, though she still loved him and he loved her. But they weren't supposed to be making love any more, now he had decided he was going to stay married to his wife. She'd thought that was always his intention, but he hadn't, for a while he thought his wife would tell him to piss off and he could get together with his lover. But his wife was keen for him to stay. And this wife values honesty above all things. The truth is important to her, more than morality. The only way we can keep on being lovers, he said, is to deceive her, and I cannot do that. I cannot look in her eyes and lie.

He did say, Perhaps we can hold one another, and touch, and kiss, he said, so long as we don't actually do it, and he invested the funny little sharpish pronoun with all its old adolescent eroticism. But she said no, he might be a lapsed Catholic but he knew that you can't avoid sin by weaselling about with words. And you can't avoid dishonesty either. She in fact did not entirely believe that they needed to stop doing it; what she was promising was to have no designs on her lover as husband, to have no intentions of taking him away from his wife, and she didn't think a bit of sex made any difference to that. Especially not given the conversation that they were keeping on having. She had always named what they were doing as adultery, which needs a marriage in order to exist, adultery its own little box, precious and shut away, she wouldn't Pandora it open and let it loose to ravage another woman's life. An ambiguous little box, that could be so delightful to one, so bitter to another. Ambiguity is her favourite mode. But it was her lover's honesty that was at stake, and if he believed it had to go like that, well, it did.

Her other reason for knocking back the heavy petting was not so theoretical. Thanks to the threat their love affair had been to his marriage it seemed to have got back to sex, his wife had recovered her libido and a nice time was being had by both. Only she, the mistress, this other, had to be celibate. She thought it might be easier to be totally so than a bit. How far can you go, was a question they asked when they were young. David Lodge used it as the title of a novel, back in the sixties. About married contraception, as she recalled. Catholic friends had read her copy; Elvira had asked to borrow it because Bruce had seen a review and thought it sounded interesting. But it had also been about virginity, degrees of it, virtual virginity, people could say these days. Did fingers count, that sort of thing. But the Bible had always been clear, lusting after in the heart was as bad as fucking. So if you lusted you might as well do it, her lover had said. But not now was he saying that.

Ah yes, she'd said, but what about being tempted and resisting? That's very virtuous. That's the gift of Eve to the world, the chance to know evil and to choose good.

But it wasn't virtue that was moving her. In these circumstances she thought that pretty thorough celibacy might be easier than allowing desire to have its way, so far, but stopping when it got keen. There isn't much delight in promising pleasure and then denying it. And she hates the thought of quick furtive couplings. Our sex has been splendid, she said, it's been glorious. I don't want anything less.

But talking on the phone was all right. Which was where they were having this conversation about onanism. When they were really lovers they talked sex on the phone. Long breathy silences, little seething sighs, dreamy fragments, giggles. What are you doing . . . what are you . . . aah . . . what is . . . how do . . . what do your fingers smell like . . . ah . . . yes . . . Remember when people used to say fishy . . . No not fishy, he says, that must have been old weeks-unwashed whores, things could get a bit fishy then, I reckon . . . but not you . . . you smell exquisite . . . and he talks her into having an orgasm in her large leather chair with her feet up on the bookcase and her fingers inside the silk knickers she's taken to wearing. Why don't you jump in the car and come over, he says, I would welcome you . . .

He is not talking on his cordless phone, or his mobile, neither is she, he does not trust phones that are not wired, he says, but when she asks him why he says, I'll tell you sometime, not on the phone. He was once a bureaucrat, does he know something or is he just bizarrely careful? Paranoid, even.

But now they are talking about an article in a magazine he gave her, called 'The Rehabilitation of Onan'. It's actually to begin with about myths of masturbation. She thinks these myths are one of the most tragic and cruel tricks ever played on children. The article says it all started in 1710 when a quack called Bekker wrote a tract about it, *Onania*, saying that the consequences of masturbation were retarded growth, priapism, gonorrhoea, fainting fits, epilepsy, consumption, loss of erection (priapism and loss of erection? Both at once?), premature ejaculation and infertility. Women were only likely to suffer hysteria, imbecility and barrenness.

It's terrible, she says, people have got enough brains not to believe such rubbish, in the sense that they don't stop doing it, but they still believe a bit, so they're worried about it, they do it but it makes them miserable, when it ought to be a pleasure.

The article mentions Tissot, a Swiss doctor, who reckoned that the body is in a state of continuous decay, drastically exacerbated by any kind of activity, and that sexual activity is by far the worst kind. The loss of one ounce of sperm is equal to the loss of forty ounces of blood, Tissot said. So semen must not be wasted.

People still have that sort of idea, he says. Look at all that business about footballers and cricketers. Should they have sex the night before the big match? Or should they save themselves?

I think sex re-energises you, not the opposite, she says. This is one of her regrets; she misses the pleasure, the abandon, of making love to him, and as well she loved the sense of being full of energy that it gave her. Young, and light of foot. This makes her think of one of her favourite lines, which always fills her eyes with tears: *So light a foot will ne'er wear out the everlasting flint* . . . Juliet, who will die soon, running to be married.

Hereditary insanity is another one of the side effects of masturbation. No problem for Clare, she is well past menopause, no more danger of passing this on to her children. But will she be safe? The logic being, lunatics often masturbate, so masturbation will turn you into a lunatic.

Of course it won't. She can see logic's clunking failure in that proposition. And she knows how rational she is. Sadly, bleakly rational, she has no choice, given the way her mind works. But her body is still rebellious. And her heart aches. It's full of grief, for all her lost lovers, but most for her lost husband. She wonders if she will ever get not to think of him for a whole day. A whole hour. She misses the way sex made grief splendid.

Tissot recommended clean living, healthy exercise, light meals, cold baths, as the best antidote to masturbation.

The ideal of the English public school, the former lover says.

The writer of the article has dug up some weird facts. A German called Vogel suggesting infibulation of the foreskin. (And we think it is only women who have suffered genital mutilation, she says. What about being circumcised, he says, who isn't.) Some English fathers fitting their sons with small penis cages, a kind of boyish chastity belt. Sometimes lining the cages with spikes. And there was an apparatus which would ring a bell in the kitchen if the youth had an erection in the night.

I wonder what would happen then, she says.

Maybe the under-parlourmaid was sent up to do something about it.

You wish, she says.

I bet the lad did. It's a nice thought, tweeny sent up to relieve the young master.

More like papa with a cane.

Now, the article goes on, the Catholic church has calmed down, masturbation is not such a sin, really. A Vatican spokesman says: *We are not saying fine, go ahead and enjoy yourselves. It is still objectively wrong, but subjectively it might not always be sinful.*

He gives a delighted shout of laughter. Objectively wrong but not always subjectively sinful. What on earth does it mean?

Isn't it a casuistry? Typical Vatican.

The next day he rings her again. I've found a nice footnote to our masturbation conversation. He always has a reason for ringing.

So have I.

What?

Oliver to whom she writes everything that happens to her including interesting conversations though she is a bit elliptical about what is going on—someone is in love with me, she said, and he replied, I am not surprised—Oliver has told her that in gaols in Western Australia prisoners were made to wear great rough leather gloves, thumbless mittens, to stop them playing with themselves.

Isn't that gruesome, she says.

She hears the hiss of his breath. A pained laugh. Maybe they got to like it.

Makes me think of scrubbing your nipples with a nail brush when you're pregnant.

Good god. Why?

Supposed to toughen them up for breast feeding.

Did it?

Dunno. But it was certainly horrible. I think it was one of those things that were fashionable for a while. Awful con tricks, but just about everybody falls prey to that sort of sadistic fashion at some time—like all the cholesterol dieting stuff. A bit earlier, a bit later, you'd have missed it. Just hope you don't die of it in the middle.

Mm. What doesn't destroy us makes us strong. Now, listen to this. This is Voltaire on the subject. *It is amusing that a virtue is made of the vice of chastity* . . .

Vice of chastity! I like that.

. . . *and it's a pretty odd sort of chastity at that, which leads men straight into the sin of Onan and girls to the waning of their colour.*

I must remember to get some blusher.

I haven't noticed you losing your rosy colour. Of course, he says, in his didactic mode (she always falls in love with men who like to practise their pedagogy on her, she likes listening to them, though she doesn't always take the trouble to remember what they say, so they can tell her again), of course, he says, and Voltaire doesn't seem too aware of it, in the Bible the sin of Onan isn't actually about masturbation.

He spilt his seed upon the ground, she says. Isn't his sin the frustration of conception, isn't that how the Catholic church interprets it?

Yes, they do, he says, but . . .

Terrible useless method, she says. I got pregnant once, doing that. And horrible for both the people concerned, I love it when . . . I love being come inside, and it's so hard to pull out in time, and dangerous.

He could come in your mouth.

Why do men always want to come in your mouth?

Why not?

Ha. Anyway, I was good at getting pregnant. Very fertile. A bit scary. But I was also a bit prone to miscarriages. Had one that time. Do you know, she says, I've been pregnant five times? Five times, and two children. Imagine if I had five children.

Would you like that?

Yes. Easy to say now, I suppose. But I think a lot of children would be nice.

Now she and this lover are triply infertile: her tubes tied, his vasectomy, her age.

Interesting, isn't it, she says, you had a vasectomy, I had my tubes tied. Neither of us asked it of our spouses. We submitted to the knives.

Shows what good and generous people we are.

Or not the ones with the power.

You're a bit preoccupied with power, aren't you. I don't think I was ever powerless.

Weren't you? People thought I wasn't, but I don't know. Not wanting to do things, talk about things . . . there's great strength in that. He hated the thought of a vasectomy, couldn't bear it, so I got done instead.

How old were you?

Thirty-eight. Old enough, I suppose.

I was twenty-nine.

It certainly was good not to have to worry about pills and foams and all that junk. Remembering to make sure you had them. Though of course it did fill you with desire. I mean, thinking you shouldn't, because you didn't have the necessary, and how you longed to. She sighs, recalling a night travelling in France, when she was using something called Delfen foam (silly spritely name) and she'd run out, how overwhelmed they were, how sweet the longing, how sharp and poignant the fear. Not another baby, not now, not at their age.

Anyway, she says, you were telling me about Onan.

Oh yes. Well. It's really about Old Testament marriage laws. Onan had an older brother, who was a bad lot, so God killed him. As was God's wont in those days. According to these laws Onan was supposed to take his brother's wife and father children on her, for his brother's sake, sort of surrogate descendants for his brother. And Onan didn't want to do that, so he spilled his seed on the ground, in order not to impregnate her. God wasn't too impressed with that either, and killed him as well. But it wasn't anything to do with masturbation, not unless you think that fucking a woman without intending to make her pregnant is a kind of masturbation.

Hm, she says. She likes the way he can remember these things.

And it's not even really about contraception, it's about that certain law that Onan broke.

Of course, she says, the wily old Catholic church can always cite scripture for its purpose, even if it's slightly twisted scripture.

She gets out her Bible concordance, which was a present from her first lover, so she tells people. (What sort of contraception did they practise, she asks herself, it's all so long ago and vague. Withdrawal again, probably, and it must have been just luck that she didn't get pregnant then. Making love on a cliff above the sea, and never enough time.) Well, the concordance wasn't really a present, he lent it to her and she never gave it back, he could have been annoyed, but she's always seen it as a gift from him, and precious, as itself, enjoying its usefulness. And when she writes to Oliver and confesses, he says, I know you have it, I have always been glad that you do.

There are an awful lot of references to seed in Cruden's Concordance of 1761, all meaning offspring, progeny, descendants, heirs; and prosperity depends on them, so cursing them is a terrible thing. Considering God is so close, and given to slaying, it is this world not the next that needs to be populated. That is what the law is about: population. Not wasting a fertile woman. God is chopping so many of his people off, those left need to keep procreating in this. Onan knows that the seed will not be his, the child will be considered his brother's child, so when he goes in unto his brother's wife he spills it—it again—upon the ground.

There is a gloss in the Genesis reference, to the New Testament, where Mark tells the story of the Sadducees questioning Jesus about this kind of law. There were seven brothers, say the Sadducees, the first one married a wife, and died childless, so the next brother took her, and so on. Right down to the seventh. All died. Then the woman died.

An unlucky family, her lover remarks. Seven brothers and all dead. And no children?

Maybe it was the wife that was infertile.

Anyway, this is a story about a trap. Jesus is asked, *Therefore, in the Resurrection, whose wife will she be, of the seven?*

This question-trap is because the Sadducees don't believe in the Resurrection.

Jesus' answer is: *Ye do err, not knowing the scriptures nor the power of God. For in the Resurrection they neither marry, nor are given in marriage, but are as the angels of God in heaven.*

Aah, says her lover, her not-lover, does that mean there is no sex in heaven? When sex is the nearest most of us come to bliss on earth. What will heaven offer us that is better?

Foie gras to the sound of trumpets. Oh, she says, you know you don't believe any of this. You know you only believe in bliss on earth and this is all there is.

I do. But what about you?

I've told you. I don't know. I think we don't know. That that's an appropriate way to be. But I don't believe Geoffrey is just nowhere.

There is his seed . . .

How is that better for him than dying childless? When he was alive it might have comforted him, but if there really is nothing else how is it helping him now?

That's why we have to live our lives to the full now. Have all the pleasurable experiences we can.

Then come and fuck me, she wants to say.

She says, You know, the cat brought a mouse in the other day. A present. Carrying it in gently in her mouth, through the cat door. Let it go and it ran off, goodness knows where. Useful cat, brings in mice, instead of getting rid of them. Anyway, I thought of that mouse, and me sitting at the word processor, and making coffee in the plunger, and talking on the telephone, and that mouse could have seen me doing all those things and not had the slightest inkling of what any of them meant, could not even begin to see that I was doing them, let alone what they signified. So, maybe, we understand our world no better than that mouse does. We run around in it, survive—the mouse squeaked a terrible squeak of terror, but it was alive and perfectly functioning—but we don't understand it.

Well, we can certainly believe what gives us comfort.

I'm not saying that for comfort. I'm saying it because it's a good image of how the world might work.

We'll never know.

If you're right, we won't, she says. But I like to think that death might be some kind of understanding.

You may not like it. You might end up in one of Dante's circles. In limbo, or worse, down with the adulterous lovers endlessly wailing.

Hell's an image.

But Dante's is a very good one.

Remember Manning Clark . . . quoting Dostoevsky . . . saying he wanted to be there when everyone suddenly understands what it has all been for.

Some of us think we know.

Hubris, she says.

They have been talking for more than an hour. It is time to stop. Take melancholy leave. He will be late for the dentist. She is sorting letters to give to the National Library under the tax incentives for the arts scheme. Letters and papers, mostly from the eighties, strange to see her life in these second-hand

pieces of paper. Cool documents, mostly, rejections, accept-
ances, requests, invitations. Some a bit more passionate. But
mainly the shapes and outward manifestations; her real life is
elsewhere.

She should write him a love letter. He is as nervous of
words on paper as he is of cordless telephone calls.

the
thirsty cat

CLARE WAKES UP IN THE NIGHT
and hears the cat lapping a saucer of milk by her bed. Lap, lap, lap, very regularly its rough little tongue rasps against the china saucer. It's a thirsty little cat, and the saucer must have quite a lot of milk in it, for the sound continues for a long time.

At first she was puzzled by this, for she had left no saucer of milk. Her daughter goes to bed with two glasses of water, one covered, for herself, the other for the cat, who likes to forage her drinks. But Clare never takes water to bed. If she is thirsty she gets up and goes to her bathroom for a drink. So she lay and listened, wondering where the milk could have come from. Until she realised it was not a cat drinking but her bedside clock, ticking.

But even though she now knows that this is what the sound is, still when she lies in bed awake it is the sound of a cat lapping that she hears. And thinks of her life as a saucer of milk, and knows that one day that so comfortably regular greedy little tongue will run out of milk, or perhaps will get tired of lapping, and stop.

not like
a loser

WHEN CLARE'S LOVER TOLD HER about existentialism and how its central idea was that the universe was indifferent to humanity, at the very least, if not actively hostile, she objected to this as a world view. But events made her think of changing her mind.

She'd had her share of anguish, she wasn't denying that. But until recently anguish had been resolved. More or less happily. She knew that her novels had moderately bleak endings; quite happy, but not entirely so. Happy is the word that keeps occurring, because happy is what endings are supposed to be. One she finished by allowing some characters a happy beginning. Everyone deserves at least one, she said. But endings aren't usually happy. The real end of the novel is death, as it is the real end of life. Who was it said all life is a preparation for death? The novel that ended with a happy beginning was a hundred-year novel, so a lot of people died, sometimes in ways that are described as tragically, but the overall feeling was of death as something natural, normal, part of the way that life goes on. But that is death, the end of life, whereas her novels end in contingency, in compromise. In characters becoming sadder as well as wiser, and you have to hope that the wiseness makes up for the sadness. They tend to learn that the price is higher than they might have thought, and that you can't escape paying it. In one novel she had intended to kill off all her main characters, either that or turn them into vegetables, which is a kind of living death, but they dug in their toes and wouldn't let her do it. She often explained in writing workshops how it was they dug their toes in; they simply made the whole novel stop. She couldn't get it moving until she offered some other fates, then they all quite gladly went along with her. To ends that were much less glamorous, exciting, final, than death and idiocy, needing to make the most of small kindnesses, and affection, and the momentary beauty of lemons in a blue bowl.

And yet despite all this she managed to believe that the universe was benign. She realises with a shiver of embarrassment that she had somehow supposed that if she behaved well the world would treat her well. Though maybe she shouldn't feel so embarrassed, the world had treated her well, and she couldn't think of anything she'd done that was actually morally wrong, well, not anything major, although if she thought of things that she'd failed to do she could find cause for reproach there. So there did seem to be a kind of correlation: behave well and you will be treated well.

But then she found herself paying the price of her husband's early death. Of course you could say that it was

Geoffrey who'd paid that, but if he was right that was just a moment of annihilation, waited for indeed but still in life and knowing love, while she is paying the price of his death over and over. When she thought of the cost of this she began to wonder about benign.

About this business of the universe being hostile, she said to the man who had been her lover.

Not hostile, I didn't say hostile, just indifferent. Not caring one way or another.

I used to think it was benign.

So it is. To human life generally. That is how we survive on this planet. But not to any one individual. The species survives, but the individual is of no account. It's not paying attention to any one person. And even if we say it is benign because it allows humanity to flourish in it, you have to remember that we have evolved to do so; we have made ourselves to fit it. Indifferent is the word for the universe.

Along with Rhett Butler; frankly my dear it doesn't give a damn. It's hard to accept.

You are used to people loving you. You want the universe to love you too.

Not to love me. To be kind to me. To be kind to the people I love.

Only people can do that.

Her daughter has to have an operation. It will be dangerous. Clare knows now the impotence of wishing and wanting; they won't change what will be. She keeps hearing a Lady Bracknell voice in her head. *To lose one parent may be regarded as a misfortune; to lose both looks like carelessness.* The same must be said of losing both a husband and a daughter.

Carelessness. The word does a clumsy hysterical dance in her brain. All the care in the world, and it will make no difference; it will look like carelessness.

Her daughter is in hospital, all ready, settled into a pastel pink and turquoise room, her clothes packed away, her mind prepared, that is, its acceptance held at a fragile point of balance by great will power, when suddenly the anaesthetist, a cardiac anaesthetist, notices she is taking aspirin to thin her blood, prevent clotting. She could bleed to death. Notices? Surely it is one of the first things that everyone involved should have paid attention to. The first question to ask.

She has to go home and wait until her blood is rid of it. The terror of it will have to be faced all over again. Of doctors saying, You know that this is risky, don't you. It's dangerous. We can't be certain nothing will go wrong. Yes of course she knows the risks, she does not need to have them rehearsed for her.

As the surgeon said to Geoffrey when he was taking out some wisdom teeth, under a general anaesthetic. There is the possibility of paralysis on one side of your face. Of destroying nerves so you won't be able to taste things any more. Of something going wrong with your tongue. And then, of course, there's death.

And so her daughter has to go home, and contain her fear for . . . well, as long as it takes.

That isn't the universe being hostile, that's doctors making a monumental stuff-up, her lover says.

Her friend Polly comes in after work to drink wine with her. Clare has lit the fire. The central heating is perfectly efficient, but the fire is a pleasure. And one of those things

Clare is proud of herself for managing. In Geoffrey's last year they didn't often have fires, because it was too much effort for him to come and sit in front of them. Now she brings in wood and collects fallen twigs from the oak trees for kindling. She makes a neat fire. When her son comes to visit he takes over this job. When she is critical of his fire-making (fires are a patriarchal activity, he says; if this were Bosnia he'd be the head of the family, she'd have to do what he tells her) he calls her a fire fascist. These wintry evenings (at a time that would still be the afternoon in the summer) she sits beside her fire and reads Dante. Slowly, paying attention, making notes. She is much taken by the lines:

> Then he turned round
> And seemed like one of those who over the flat
> And open course in the fields beside Verona
> Run for the green cloth; and he seemed at that
>
> Not like a loser, but the winning runner.

She wonders why she likes them so much. There is a particular melancholic cadence to them, and a kind of mysterious triumph as well. And that last line of the canto, it falls very beautifully, its shape just right. It's the rhythm, perhaps, here it works especially well, as Sayers' attempts at translating into *terza rima* don't always. And maybe there's the idea of seeming not a loser, but the winning runner. Though of course however beautiful the lines he is a loser, he's in hell; he's Brunetto Latini, once Dante's neighbour, a man who taught him a lot. He's here because he was a sodomite. Dante asks him to sit down and talk to him, but he can't: *Should one of our lot rest one second, a hundred years must he lie low*, which means that he has to let the flames consume him, he isn't allowed to beat them off. His face is scorched, his skin is shrivelled, his face scarred.

As well as being a sodomite, a man of perverse vice, he was worldly and did not care for the soul. That's not helping him here. He asks Dante to keep his Thesaurus, his Treasure Book, handy, because he is still alive in that.

Brunetto these days is the name of a restaurant in the next suburb. With an apostrophe s.

Polly taps on the glass, Clare has left the curtains open over the french windows so the fire will welcome her as she comes up the path. She looks up and sees Polly's laughing face, her hair turned into a halo by the misty streetlight, that round head of curls that used to be fair and is now silvery.

Your hair's a silver-gilt halo, says Clare.

Well, I am a saint, of course, says Polly.

With a tarnished halo, says Clare.

What a picture, Polly says, the fire, the yellow chair, the book. She sits in the other yellow chair; in her red dress she looks like a parrot tulip.

Dante, what's more, says Clare, and Polly hoots. It's a construct, she says.

My life is a construct, says Clare. She gets a bottle of sauvignon blanc, some olives, and a bowl of hoummos with little toasts. She loves these visits of Polly's; the delight of them sits happily within her grief. Polly shares her enthusiasm for curious facts, sometimes of a theological nature. Ever since they were blue-stockingy girls living in a university hall of residence with rather risible Oxbridgean pretensions.

Why are you reading Dante, asks Polly.

Ah, if Clare were to tell her.

Do you know, she says, that the usurers and the sodomites are paired in hell?

No. There must be a good reason?

Because the sodomites make sterile that which should be fertile, and the usurers make fertile that which by nature should be sterile. Namely, of course, money.

Blimey, says Polly. Come to think of it, usury's interesting stuff. It's one sin that doesn't exist any more. Nobody can possibly be blamed for being a usurer any more. Well, not unless they're loan sharks, but that's a different category.

Yes, that's greed and extortion and menaces and stuff. But ordinary grasping bank-type usury is eminently respectable. We should all be merchant bankers.

Ha, says Polly, taking a mouthful. Good wine.

It would be better if I were a merchant banker.

Funny to think of sins going in and out of fashion.

Some never do.

(Polly doesn't know about the lover. Clare thinks she doesn't. And now he isn't any more she need never find out.)

She tells her of her thoughts about the benign or hostile universe. When Geoffrey was dying she talked to Polly about life after death. They both agreed that they didn't know but didn't believe in simple absolute snuffing out.

I think it's something to do with being good girls, good women, says Clare. We can't believe that it's not of value. That there aren't any rewards.

We can't help believing that somewhere out there are the scales, says Polly.

Clare is much taken with this image. Over the years they've sent one another photographs from Romanesque tympani and column capitals of St Michael weighing souls, on balances like those they learned to use in school science, and devils pitchforking the heavy ones (how heavy is heavy?) into the gaping maws of hell. Quite literally sometimes, huge open mouths with jagged teeth.

And we continue to live as though the scales are within our experience, says Polly.

It's an Egyptian idea too, says Clare. Wasn't it Anubis who weighed the souls of the dead? Against feathers, wasn't it?

When she tells her lover, her former lover, about the scales he says, Yes, of course, there have to be scales. It's what you weigh in them that matters. And what you weigh it against.

You mean moral behaviour, choosing what is moral for you.

Yes. Is it truth, or goodness. But how do we know what they are? You know, I liked it when you could believe in God. You knew where you were. You had faith . . .

Couldn't you choose to believe in God again?

He doesn't let me. Faith is a supernatural gift from God which enables us to believe without doubting what God has revealed.

Is that the catechism?

Of course. And God does not give me his supernatural gift of faith. I can't do anything about that.

God is dead, so we must invent ourselves.

Sartre again.

He and Polly have both been Catholics. Polly still is. But even that isn't simple any more.

Clare says to Polly, Why are all the women we know so full of pain?

They have been to a reading, of some short stories, and there was such pain in them the audience was flabbergasted. Immensely excited, because they were so good, the pain had been turned into such a work of art that the listeners felt its wounds, the words were so exact, very simple and so much stronger than their lightness would have suggested. Load-bearing words, somebody called them. And they make you feel exactly what load it is they are bearing. Clare looked out at the room from the booth where she was sitting. In that slice of it she could see five widows, three women whose husbands had left them for other women, usually younger, two whose husbands had simply left them, two whose husbands had come to the conclusion that they were gay. Another whose lover had gone back to his frightful wife. She could see two actual couples, men and women together, but she didn't know them. And a number of lesbian partnerships, and who knows what sorrow had to be lived through before this safety was reached.

Clare tells her former lover's wife that she is one of the few women she knows who are not full of pain. She's had a shock, she's been furiously angry, but she has recovered her happiness.

They were sitting by a fire in a clubby sort of bar at the Hyatt drinking glasses of white wine. An expensive act. But necessary.

I would have coped, she said. I'd have chucked him out and not given him a second thought. I'd have thrown myself into my career, worked hard, moved up, I'd have taken control of my life and become a successful woman and enjoyed life.

We are all that, said Clare. We all do that. Look at me, I zip through the days, I have fun, I have a great time with my friends, my work goes well, I've got plenty of it, I love my house and my children and my way of life. All of this happens, it happens to all of the women I am thinking of, we are all successful and busy and fulfilled. And deep inside, full of pain. I mean, she goes on, not bowed down, lugubrious, lachrymose, groaning . . . She is about to say, like one of Dante's damned souls drifting and running, eternally tormented, but decides this isn't a good image. Like, like Niobe, all tears, she finishes.

Well, I suppose you might think of Gertrude. Remember? *Or ere those shoes were old* that she wore to her husband's funeral, there she is jumping into bed with the next one, betraying the old one.

Clare remembers what a quick ear her friend always had for a quotation.

O, most wicked speed, to post
With such dexterity to incestuous sheets.

she finishes. I've been a lot of things, but not incestuous. The thing about quoting the classics, she says, is that you can always find something to fit. More or less. You may have to chop off its feet or stretch it on a rack, but there's precedent for that too.

Beds, and lying in them. Hah.

I always wondered why if you fell into the hands of Procrustes you couldn't just curl up, says Clare.

That would make you into one of those people who can't lie straight in bed.

Isn't lying always crooked?

They are at their old games. Though now the edge of the fun is sharper. It wounds like a paper cut, drawing little blood, not very visible, but stinging for a long time.

What's happened to our generation, she asks Polly, pouring more of the modest sauvignon blanc into her glass. I don't think our mothers were unhappy at our age. Were they?

Probably, in different ways. They just got on with it. They couldn't change anything, so they made the best of it.

I think my parents were happy. They loved each other. Were a comfort.

Some people are lucky. Still are.

Another time is made for the operation. Her daughter closes down her life again, wrapping herself away from any outside contact. The winter is cold. Her chest was clear, let's keep it that way.

Clare drives her into the hospital, drops her at the door, parks the car. The room is another of the pink and blue and pale turquoise pretty. Safe and dull. Far too hot. A view of cold suburbs against the hill doesn't cool it down. Neither Clare nor her daughter likes hospitals.

Early in the year her daughter spent five days in a Melbourne hospital, having tests. Overdue, these, but life stopped when Geoffrey was ill. She was put in a kind of holding ward, no television or phones, no comfort, there were simply beds for people passing through on their way to surgery. It was the only ward they could find space for her. If you think the set-up stinks, said a nurse, write to the minister.

Every night there was a different person in the two-bed ward, being prepared for an operation the next day. Usually a man. Even the usual segregations didn't apply. Early on there was a Greek man, who spoke no English; he was very hairy, and a Jehovah's Witness. All through the day registrars and residents came in and shouted at him: You don't want any blood? No blood? What if something goes wrong? You might need blood. Are you sure you don't want any blood?

The man looked rather wild-eyed. No blood, he said. When he first came in his adult daughters explained in clear English to the admitting doctor that he was a Jehovah's Witness and that it was against his religion to have a blood transfusion. That doctor wrote it down. So why do they have to keep coming and shouting at the bewildered man, Are you sure you don't want any blood? You don't want any blood? What if something goes wrong?

Clare hadn't come across a Greek Jehovah's Witness before.

He's having bypass surgery. That means his chest has to be shaved. It is thick with long black stiffly curling hairs. So is his back. That has to be shaved too. And his arms. And his legs. They are not sure whether they will take the veins for the bypass out of his arms or his legs. His groin must be cleared too. It takes a long time, scraping away, to do all this shaving.

Afterwards, the hair drifts in large clumps over the floor. For days. The room is cleaned every day, a languid woman comes in with a mop, then a duster. So how is it that it happens that the hair runs around for days? Even so desultory as the mopping seems. The hair clumps together with the other dust in the room. The slut's wool. Clare sitting reading by the bed, overwhelmed by that paradoxical mixture of boredom and fear that hospitals and wars engender, sees out of the corner of her eyes a large black hairy creature running out from under the bed. A rat! No. A clump of hair. The Greek man goes, presumably to a successful operation and a new life, another man and then another takes his place, but still the hairy rats run round the linoleum floor.

In this pink and blue room, with its carpet and television set and private if surgical bathroom, Clare unpacks her daughter's things into drawers and wardrobe. Her daughter bends over and peers under the bed.

What are you looking for?

Just checking. To see if there's any hair running around.

Ah, yes. She is her father's daughter. Humour as black and hairy as the rats it conjures up. Clare laughs and laughs, and maybe it is the laughing that fills her eyes with tears.

Not like a loser, but the winning runner. Why do those words keep saying themselves in her head?

a good
death

CLARE WONDERS IF SHE SHOULD
stop writing about Geoffrey for a bit. Write a story for its own
sake. She feels like some simple action. Adventure. Murder.
An opening line pops into her head one morning when she
isn't getting up, is dreaming herself into words. *Carl decided to
kill his wife because he couldn't bear to hurt her.* She writes it
down, and later in the day, filling in time in a cafe, she scribbles
away at it. Using the backs of some heavy cream paper flyers
left on the counter, advertising a cathedral concert of
Monteverdi's Vespers.

a good death: a short story

Carl decided to kill his wife because he couldn't bear to hurt
her. He loved her dearly and couldn't bear to cause her the
pain he knew would result from his actions. He did love her,

very much, and had for a long time, in different ways, from when she was a beautiful sixteen-year-old. But he did not want to live with her any longer, and he knew that would cause her more anguish than he could stand.

But if she died quickly, unknowingly, painlessly, then he could grieve and after a decent interval go and live with the woman he was in love with. It was only necessary to find a good manner of death, something comfortable for her, and also not one that he could be blamed for. He didn't want to get caught and have to spend years in gaol. It wasn't that he was all that unhappy with his wife, he just wasn't deliriously happy as he was with his lover, so he'd be better off with things as they were than being in prison for the rest of his life. If he told his wife he wanted to go and live with his lover . . . well, he couldn't quite imagine what would happen. Her heart would be broken, she would be full of rage, she would believe he had destroyed her life. She might even think of suicide.

He didn't plan to tell his lover about his plans to kill his wife. She wouldn't approve, might think it was a callous thing to do, when what he was being was tender-hearted. Not wanting to hurt. The other thing was, he knew it would be safer if no one else knew. He trusted his lover, of course, with his life he would have, certainly with his happiness. But he also knew that the best way to get somebody to keep a secret is not to tell it to them.

He didn't come up with the idea of murdering his wife straight away. He started off in a 'what if' kind of way. What if she had a heart attack and dropped dead. What if she was hit by a car and died instantly. The instantness was important, he didn't want her to suffer. What if she slipped in the bath and hit her head on the tap at a specially vulnerable place on her skull so that she wasn't just knocked out or concussed. But it wasn't a very hopeful process, this what if. It could be a long time, or never, before it happened. It could happen to his lover, or himself, first. He started to wonder how you might nudge what if along through maybe and past happenstance to fact.

The newspapers were full of reports of a court case, the trial of a policeman who'd killed his wife by injecting her with heroin. He hadn't done it himself, he'd paid some men to do it for him, they'd tied her up and done it and stood in her kitchen drinking beers out of the fridge while they waited for it to work. It took a long time, the men got drunk on the beers while the woman in the next room watched her death coming and lived through its agony. Carl thought that would be the worst thing, knowing your death coming and having no power to stop it. The policeman's girlfriend was on trial too, as an accomplice.

To Carl this seemed the apotheosis of how not to kill your wife. It was messy, crude, cruel, and the bloke had got caught. It seemed particularly ironical that the man was a policeman; you'd think such a person would have some sharper sense of what would work and what wouldn't.

And certainly such a method wouldn't do for him because his wife had never used heroin, knew nothing about it, and neither did he. He wondered why the policeman hadn't done it himself, why he'd had to hire people to do it; that was probably where the messiness came in. And the unreliability. He certainly wouldn't get somebody else, apart from the expensiveness of it, the waste of money that could be better spent elsewhere, that was where you would lose control, that was where danger would especially lie. The policeman seemed to have been estranged from his wife, he wondered why it couldn't just be left at that, him off with the girlfriend, the wife deserted. There was some problem with custody of a small child. This wasn't a problem for Carl, his children were grown up; provided he decently mourned his wife and that wouldn't be difficult, he would really be sorry, they would be happy to see him settled again, he was quite certain of that. His lover was younger; his children could even be relieved that she would be the one to look after him when he got old, the job wouldn't fall to them.

Carl started reading a lot of books of true crime stories. Fiction wasn't any good to him, a fiction writer could start at the end and work back, keeping utter control of events in a way that wasn't possible to a person living them. The thing to be learned from the true crime stories was that it was usually minor and entirely unforeseen things that gave the game away. In the case of really clever murders, that is. Anybody as stupid and clumsy as the policeman trying to buy his wife's death was bound to get caught, and deserved to. But really clever people who had taken every possibility into account got caught by the unexpected, a door sticking, a light bulb failing, the cat bringing in a mouse. The person who never went to the casino being there that night, the cleaning woman coming late because she had to take her dog to the vet, the neighbour choosing that day to have his trees lopped out of the way of the electricity wires.

The real problem was the alibi. He was beginning to appreciate how difficult it is to have a perfect alibi, unless you have an accomplice, and that is even more dangerous. That was what trapped the policeman, thinking that paying someone else would allow him to construct an invincible alibi for the time of the crime. Since his wife was already someone who did drugs, an overdose was a clever idea, it just hadn't worked. Or it had worked, but not secretly. And the hired help were no good. You could see how anybody prepared to commit a crime for money wasn't likely to be a very trustworthy person, and not a very nice person. Quite different from somebody preparing to commit a crime out of love, and a desire not to hurt.

Carl thought if he just kept thinking, and reading around the subject, a good idea would come. In the meantime he was more and more in love with his lover. He pretended to have enrolled in a course at TAFE two nights a week in order to have time to spend together. He'd quite fancied doing French in case they ever got to Paris one day but then thought he might get caught out not having learned any, so he chose photography instead, since anybody can take photos, he already knew how to do that. To make it look real he bought an expensive new camera and spent quite a lot of time pointing it at things, and even took some pictures, using black and white film and photographing objects of no interest to anyone and calling them compositions. He made a point of doing homework. He posed his wife, she was called Dianne, against backdrops of bunched-up curtains with light coming sharply from strange angles. She didn't look very good in these portraits, which was partly his lack of skill, but when he looked closely at her in the flesh she wasn't looking too hot there, either. Her skin had lost its rosy colour, even in her fifties Dianne had pretty skin, but then age has to strike sometime. And maybe he was comparing her with his love, who was that good bit younger. She was wearing a lot of make-up, which had never been a habit of hers, and it didn't suit her.

That's rather a dark lipstick you're wearing, darling.

Oh, I like a bit of colour, she said, with quite a coquettish smile.

He was wondering about electrocution. They'd once had an electric espresso coffee machine which had stopped working and when he'd taken it in the repairman said it was a wonder nobody had been killed because it was wrongly wired up so that any time it was turned on it was alive, touching the metal could have been lethal. How can that be, Carl had asked, I've been using it for years. It's been wrongly wired for years, said the repairman. You've been very very lucky.

He could wrongly wire up some appliance and when his wife used it she would get a shock and it would kill her. Instantly. But he might be implicated. What if he made it go bung and took it to be mended and then he redid it, wrongly. But that would implicate the tradesman, who would point the finger at him. And what appliance? They didn't have anything like that simple old ethnic coffee maker any more. Mostly these days appliances are sealed units, you can't interfere. Too dangerous, otherwise.

A car accident. Him driving, but not hurt much. But he didn't know how to control that. He might be killed, or badly injured, she might be badly injured but not killed. And you only had to look at wrecked cars; some were mangled beyond recognition and the occupants had walked away, others barely dinged and people killed. Falling over a cliff when they were out for a walk? But she would see him do it, know for that however many seconds of her fall to death that he had done it, and he did not want her to think that of him, even for a few seconds. And anyway she might survive. Or pull him over with her.

Poison then. But he didn't know anything about poisons. Maybe if they had rats, and he put baits down. But how would he get them into her, and just how did they work? He didn't want any long-drawn agony. Thrashing, and foaming, and drumming heels. That would be hideous.

Dianne wasn't interested in sex any more. He'd been doing his duty, and of course he enjoyed it, she was his wife and he loved her, even if she didn't make him deliriously happy the way his lover did, oh the agonies of parting from her afterwards. But now she turned away with a regretful little kiss on his cheek. She didn't actually say, Not tonight dear, but that was what she meant.

She was losing a bit of weight too. It looked good. She'd got rather dumpy. Shapeless, a bit bulgy. Of course she was a grandmother. Now she was much neater, more her old shapely self, and was wearing smarter clothes, more fitting.

Thinner. More make-up. Smarter clothes. Coming home late from work and no explanation. Off sex—with him. Ha ha. The penny dropped. How could he have been so slow, so stupid. She had a lover. That was the explanation.

He suddenly felt a sickening acid wash of jealousy fill his gut. His wife and a lover. He'd murder the beast. He squeezed his fists together round the brute's imaginary neck. The tension of his squeezing made the veins in his own neck stand out in cords. But then he began to think rationally again. His gut was still full of acid, but his mind was functioning. Seeing, as it had been trained to do, a window of opportunity.

An amicable parting, then. That would be a lot more expensive, of course. With her death he'd keep her half of the house, and some of her superannuation, and there was a decent insurance policy. They'd made their wills, and left everything to one another, each trusting the other to leave it to the children in the end. But he could adjust his thinking to a lot less money; he'd made some nice plans depending on it, the Paris thing, and so on, but it was his lover he wanted, her body, her presence, he didn't need a lot of money as well. And he hadn't come up with a decent murder scenario; it could be the best solution.

But his wife, and a lover . . . He still felt sick, the betrayal of it, he wouldn't have thought she could ever do such a thing. She deserved to die, being unfaithful like that.

When Dianne came home from work late he confronted her. I've been wanting to talk to you, he said.

She smiled a wan smile. I've been wanting to talk to you, too. But she stopped, waited, so he had to go on.

You're looking very smart these days.

Again she smiled, an odd smile, he thought it was maybe a secret sly sexy smile, which disturbed him, but that didn't seem quite right. It was sly, and knowing, but with more fear than sex in it.

It's my old clothes. Haven't you noticed, now I've lost a bit of weight, I can fit into my old smart clothes.

Oh, he said. He hadn't noticed, he'd thought they were new.

You've got a lover, he said.

She looked at him, and gasped.

It's all right, he said. I won't stand in your way. You must follow your heart.

Her gasp turned into a laugh, into long and not very pretty laughter, into hiccups, and a sob.

A lover, she said. A doctor. A lot of doctors. I've been having tests. After work. I didn't want to tell you, in case it was all right, and then you needn't have worried. But it isn't. All right.

She leaned against him, and he put his arms around her, hugging her tight. Her voice was muffled against the shoulder of his tweed sportscoat.

It's cancer, she said. It started in the cervix. But I didn't, didn't get it found out in time. Now it's mest . . . mets . . .

Metastasising, he said.

Yes. Spreading in all sorts of places.

We can get chemotherapy. Radiography.

They might give me a bit more time. But they won't cure me. And it won't be very much more time.

Why didn't you tell me? I'd have come with you. You shouldn't have had to go through this all on your own. There were tears in his eyes as he stared over her head.

Well, I thought it seemed the best way. And you didn't seem, seem very interested.

He hugged her closer. Oh darling, he said.

She stretched her head back out of the hug. Carl, she said, I want you to promise me . . .

Yes?

I've got some pills, some morphine, the pain's quite bad already. And some syrup, I can take little sips of that on top. Oh, but Carl, I'm afraid of the pain. Promise me, Carl, if it gets too bad, you'll help.

Help?

Help me, put an end . . . Oh, to die. I don't want to go on living if the pain's unbearable.

Oh my darling. He squeezed her harder, and she winced. I couldn't bear to see you suffer.

. . .

This is Carl's ending. But it's not how it was.

Go back to where Dianne says she has cancer. This sad loving scenario spools through his mind as she begins to speak. But she says something different.

It's cancer, she says. In the cervix. But not too bad. They think they'll get it in time. Surgery, then chemo to make sure it all goes. It won't be fun, but with a bit of luck it won't be fatal.

She looks at him with a small smile, brimming with tears. He puts his arms round her so he won't have to look into that brave frightened face.

Oh darling. We'll beat it. You know us, never conquered. I'm not going to let a silly thing like cancer take you away from me.

She hugs him back. Oh sweetheart, she says. My own sweetheart.

referential friends

WHEN SHE SPOKE AT GEOFFREY'S funeral Clare said, He was my Latin dictionary, my English grammar, my entrée to the French language, my Thesaurus, my mentor, my critic. She had got into a wonderfully lazy comfortable habit over the years of asking him instead of looking things up herself, knowing he would be perfectly precise and right. Or else he'd say he didn't know, but that didn't often happen. Sometimes, since, Oliver has filled those roles; she has emailed him and asked for help, especially when she was in Adelaide for a month and missing her reference books. What sort of kidney did Leopold Bloom eat? She was sure it was pork, but a Joyce scholar had said it was ox. Of course it was pork. Oliver fixed her up with the Greek word for garden, the reason for using a certain tense, the real meaning of celibate. She argued about that; if people use it to denote not having sex, that's what it means now, even if originally it meant not being married. Especially since there isn't another word.

Often Geoffrey could be a dictionary of quotations, but it had always been Miriam who was best at that. If Clare's mind was a rag bag, Miriam's was a card index, neatly arranged and unerringly consultable. Sometimes she rang her up and ran garbled bits of verse past her, and Miriam nearly always knew, could fit the muddled words into their proper pattern of metre and rhyme. And she was good at specialised vocabularies. One day Clare couldn't remember the verb for the Virgin Mary going up into heaven, so she telephoned Miriam. It would come to her eventually, but she was writing a review of Alan Bennett's *The Lady in the Van* and wanted it now. Assumed, said Miriam; she couldn't do it by her own means, she needed help, so it's assumed. Jesus, now, could do it on his own, his own power; he ascended.

If you've got the right words in the right places, then you can feel you've got your life in order, too. For a while.

a measure of kindness

EVEN WHEN YOU ARE MAKING up stories you have no intention of publishing there are certain things you can't write about. Your children's operations, for instance. Clare did once do this, not very long ago, but it had taken her twenty years to be able to manage it, and she made the parents a woman who worked in a credit union, and an upholsterer, simple good people, the voice, though it was in the third person, the woman's, an anxious hard-working woman trying to understand. Not her own clever ironic self-reflexive voice, the voice of the Clare whose head is full of the orts and bits and greasy relics of other people's words, the voice of the woman—she stayed nameless—was humbler, shyer, more innocent. It takes a long time to achieve that innocence, decades have to pass.

This time all she can write down is the words of the doctor to her daughter, on the day they let her out of intensive care.

He gave her quite a tender look and said, Well, you nearly went away and left us, but at the last minute you changed your mind and came back.

You have to wonder: is this cosy doctor-speak, or profound truth? She remembers herself inquiring, all that time ago, (never forgetting the answer, twenty years later giving the words to the woman working in the credit union) about the success of the operation on a beautiful four-year-old child, Clare's daughter and the little girl had become friends, and she used to talk to the mother, who was knitting a jumper for the child, pale green it was, with flowers on it, and the nurse saying, Josephine's parents don't have her any more, and the overwhelming simple sadness of this statement. The grief, so intimately recognised. And also . . . hard to admit, this, an awful irredeemable feeling, a kind of hideous inadmissible relief: if this child has died, the odds may be that mine will live. As she did, that time, and now has again.

At the last minute you changed your mind and came back. That doctor's words imply a choice, a decision. They see the element of will, of spirit, involved. When Geoffrey was dying, he knew that it was Clare's will as well as his own that kept him alive a year longer than expected. And they offer a picture, it is of the valley of the shadow of death, which somehow appears in Clare's mind's eye as a green place, and pleasant, maybe its point is that it's seductive and so the effort of will has to be even stronger, to turn round and come back. She suspects that her daughter was drawn, was pulled, quite a long way through it. And she knows that it would have been the girl's spirit that resisted, that baulked, and brought her back. The textbook heart should have failed at birth. It's not

supposed to be able to function. Which makes commun-
ication with certain doctors difficult—they go by the
textbook heart and not the overriding spirit.

And now mother and daughter smile gleefully at one
another. She has come back. She is safe. Death hasn't won
this time.

Of course we always knew you'd be okay. Didn't we. Of
course.

There is a line in *A Streetcar Named Desire* which is as sad as
anything could be. It is when Blanche says to the white-
coated men who have come to take her away, *I have always
relied on the kindness of strangers*. It's a line that floats around in
Clare's head, along with a whole lot of other small wriggling
pondwater creatures, and surfaces when she needs it, doesn't
have to be trawled for, dredged up, sieved out. *The kindness of
strangers*. It's poignant. And as well there's Blanche's bravery.
Being able to say it, after all that's happened to her. And in the
context of our knowing that these strangers are not likely to
be very kind. As she must, too, but still faces them with this
pathetic courage.

Now the line comes into Clare's head, not as bravery, but
as gratitude, as she sits beside her daughter all those days in
intensive care and watches the nursing being offered. A
commercial kindness, such as you fear Blanche will not
find, but not less valuable for that. Intensive care it is; there is
one nurse for every patient. In ways the room has a medieval
air, if you can ignore the technology, which is so huge
and complicated and intrusive and incomprehensible that
ignoring it is the best thing to do with it. But the medieval air

comes from the silent and monastic way the nurses stand at large sloping lecterns, double folio size, and make notes, recording every detail of their own particular patient's condition.

Recording. Clare sits and holds her drugged-out sleeping daughter's hand. She considers the possibility that this is death, after death, the last judgment, and this place is God's anteroom, and these his angels, recording all the good and bad of the person's life. Any moment now St Michael will come in with the scales. The angels wear simple white robes, their voices are soft, their gaze serene but penetrating, their smiles gentle, their demeanour strict. You can't guess from their expressions the import of their recordings. And you can't tell from looking at the charts, except that they are detailed and highly complicated. Dozens of columns, ruled off into hundreds of little boxes. With figures, and letters, and percentages, and fractions. It's a code that only angels know.

You could suppose, from the way they look at the patients, and the tender manner in which they speak to them, that the news is going to be good, that it is going to be heaven and not hell, but Clare suspects that this is their nature. Being angels, this is the way they behave.

Just as the devils, their fallen siblings, must behave badly, must burn and trick and cheat.

But the angels did keep her company in that valley. Did aid her coming back.

She's never had any illusions about nurses, that they are particularly good people. They're a bunch of employees like any other, pleasant, nasty, friendly, mean, thin, fat, rude, polite. But the ones in intensive care do seem particularly gifted with kindness. They seem able to treat their charges with real affection. The kindness of strangers is not a phrase of almost unbearable sadness, in this context.

Maybe it is the journey they make together, that journey whose every breath is encoded on the double folios of their lecterns.

At the darkest time she was hooked up to:

 7 intravenous drip machines electronically
  dosing her with drugs
 1 cannula into a vein
 1 cannula into an artery
 a bundle of lines through her neck to her
  heart
These lines, plus:
 a sphygmomanometer sleeve
 a finger splint
 electrocardiograph discs
producing
 7 different coloured graph lines and numbers
  on a computer screen for monitoring heart
  rate, oxygen saturation, pulse, etcetera
 a ventilator with a black rubber mask
 a catheter for urine, collected in a sealed
  calibrated plastic box
 a drain for the stomach, collecting blood and
  fluids in a calibrated soft plastic bulb
Was that all? It's all that Clare recalls.

On her fifth day in intensive care, her daughter is sitting in a chair. It's Sunday, only one other patient in the large light room. His curtains are drawn, something's being done to him. Sorry darling, says the invisible nurse.

Sorry darling, repeats her daughter in quite a scornful voice. That's what they say when they pierce some painful part of your anatomy. *Sorry darling*, as they amputate some limb or other.

Clare sniggers quietly, lengthily, behind her hand. She's not sure she should let her daughter see how sweet she finds this scorn.

Don't think that watching television will take your mind off your troubles. On the television women lift their faces and cry with their mouths open and their eyes shut. Their hands fall away, they are on their knees, they weep and howl with this blind anguish that still lifts their faces to where heaven might be, but where certainly the camera is. The camera stares coldly at them. Doesn't even shake. Maybe this is the sign of the indifferent universe. God is dead, and so is the eye of the camera.

It is Bosnia and the war, Turkey and the earthquake, Peru and the mud-slide, China and the flood, Papua New Guinea and the tidal wave. And in all of these the women lift up their faces and weep to the unloving gaze of the camera. They weep for their lost loved ones, their husbands, their children. The pain is unbearable, but it doesn't care, it still has to be borne.

The camera records this unbearable bearing. And the world in whatever safety it has at home watches and measures and grieves, recognises its luck, turns away its eyes.

Clare wonders about the duty of looking. Should she take account of their pain, record it with her own eyes, or turn them away. But her not looking doesn't save their grief from violation. The camera has already seen, already stolen.

In the mall Clare stops to look at the fountain. At right angles to it is a bench, on which a man is sitting, a burly man with matted hair. He is rocking backwards and forwards, with a strict and regular rhythm, as though obeying a metronome in his head. And as he rocks, so precisely keeping time, he is saying something in a slow mumbling monotone, taking its emphasis not from the sense of the words but from his metrical movement. It takes her a while to puzzle out the words. I am not lonely, he is saying. I am not lonely.

Since Geoffrey died Clare has had to rethink the scales of things. It's changed, the whole gamut has been extended. There are lower registers, and higher ones. One result is how trivial some things seem. A book lost. A precious pot broken. The car that they loved because of all the places it had taken them, sold. A friend visiting from New Zealand when Clare will be in Tasmania so she won't get to see her. The lavatory leaking. The dying of an old prunus tree—or was it poisoned, by the neighbour who claimed it dropped messes on his drive?—whose veils of pale pink blossom made beautiful the spring, whose tart fruits were excellent in pies; these for the neighbour were messes. All these disasters have shrunk, are so low down on the scale of significance you can hardly give them head room. What's the loss of his dear old car compared to the loss of its driver? She remembers her father talking about the scheme of things, how our lives are not very grand in the scheme of things; that is how she feels about things that once would have troubled her. At the same time as she knows her loss as so enormous in this scheme of things. And if minor anguishes are low down in a scale that has the beloved's death as its point of reference, still that is not the end of the gamut either. It's as though it has not just stretched, but skewed. As though the weights have changed: maybe a pound of lead is heavier than a pound of feathers.

All the scales we keep separate in our heads at once. St Michael weighing souls in scales and finding them wanting. Last judgment, final reckoning. Scales falling from eyes, suddenly peeled bare, which is supposed to be a good thing, to mean enlightenment, but may in certain cases mean the witnessing of things better not seen, never seen or known, which is why the women caught in that cruel and never turning away cold camera eye close theirs even as they raise them to heaven. What dizzy heights, depths, lengths have their gamuts stretched to? They hood their eyes, but you can never unsee. Naked eyes hurt. But covering them is no protection.

Scales, ranges, registers. There is even a scale for measuring ripeness. A kind of hydrometer, called Baume, after the French chemist who invented it. Used to measure grape sugar, through an associated scale of relative density. The answer is given as degrees Baume. She and Geoffrey tried to make wine out of the mulberries on their disappointing tree, once. They measured the ripeness of the brew on a Baume scale. The wine was horrible, it wouldn't ferment properly, they had to add yeast, and lemon because it lacked acidity; it became terribly alcoholic and disgustingly flavourless. But measuring the ripeness was fun, and so was watching the would-be wine bubble up in an elegant little glass airlock, a pretty device of blown bulbs and pipes.

Imagine death measuring lives on a Baume scale: ripeness is all, you're ready to die now. But if that's the case, death's scale isn't one the rest of us can read.

And you can't measure grief. The scales of the last judgment are supernatural. Are a metaphor. An allegory, a parable, an emblem. All devices to understand and explain. What you want is not measurement, but kindness. Comfort. Forgiveness. Not your soul against a feather, but the ever-lasting arms. Or human ones. Tracing their patterns of love on your willing skin.

Turn off the television. Shrink its disasters to a pinpoint on a black screen. Read a wise book and lay its balm on your soul. *Things are the sons of heaven*, said Samuel Johnson, *words are the daughters of earth.* The sons have been waxing terrible in their aspect, maybe the daughters will be kinder. She calls on them in her hour of need, and they come.

the unquiet grave

CLARE DRIVES HOME FROM THE hospital in that careful, conscious manner that is necessary to re-enter the world. After five hours visiting in limbo. Comfortable enough, but you go glassy-eyed. This mixture of fear and boredom, she told her daughter, you know the other thing it is like? A war. Being in a war. She puts the car radio on; some plaintive jazz is playing, and she thinks of changing over to *Orpheus and Eurydice* on CD. When Geoffrey was alive she liked to listen to words on the radio, to have people telling her things. Now it is music. She leaves the jazz on, it is like languid fingers stroking her skin. It makes her remember lying on a bed, feeling her body spread out and highly strung like that curious musical instrument the koto, while skilful fingers plucked from it taut erotic chords that resonated through its artful frame. Ah, that was then.

It's Sunday, next weekend she will be in Tasmania, talking

about Seduction and Betrayal. Geoffrey's dying seems to have got her making public utterances about sex. Last year in Melbourne it was a panel called *This obscure object . . .* dot dot dot. She wanted them to talk about the kind of desire that art creates as longing for itself. Like *Lucia di Lammermoor* and the lines of melody that weave your heartstrings into their own hopeless passion, but oh what pleasure, it's almost too much to bear. Or *The Pearl Fishers*. But everyone else on the panel talked about sex: about copulation really. And the week after Tasmania she could be sitting on the stage of the booked-out Melbourne town hall talking to Isabel Allende about Lust and Food. But she said no. She's not such a fan of Allende's.

She stops off at the shops and buys a great quantity of cat food, a lettuce, a courgette and a bottle of wine. You can see who eats in our house, she says to the man at the checkout. Always the cat, he laughs.

It would be a crisis indeed, a stroppy cat and nothing to feed her. A human can always find something.

At home she mooches about wondering what to do in that moment before all the things that have to be done, all that has been neglected, start clamouring at her. She rushes round doing the noisiest, then pours a glass of wine. Her daughter said there's nothing on the telly. *Ballykissangel*. Repeats. She can't bear watching it now they've killed off Assumpta so brutally, so cheating, so callous and calculated. Just as she was about to find love in the arms of her priest—and she hadn't even kissed him, they'd just circled one another in an erotic tension for however many episodes—they made her electrocute herself. It killed your faith in the narrative, as well as its heroine.

She switches to SBS. Something about Evita Peron. When she died the streets were banked with great stiff shields of flowers, like targets. Half a million lips kissed her coffin, four people dropped dead, hundreds fainted. There were 20,000 requests that she be made a saint.

The film showed footage of her speaking to the people, massive crowds, pullulating as far as the camera could see, and the increasingly frail Evita drawing their adoration from them. Clare never saw Madonna in the musical, though she tries to picture that healthy gym-strapping girl playing this woman whose death is already carving the beautiful bones of her face, with her great conscious eyes showing that they know it.

Her husband orders her body to be embalmed. It takes months. At first we see her lying, hands clasped, nails long and red in the black and white image of the film. She left instructions to her manicurist to take this off and paint them with colourless Revlon. Her body is dipped in acetate. It takes a year. At the end the crowds pay homage in a torchlight procession. The doctor worries about a spark setting the corpse on fire; it would burn like a torch, would be utterly consumed.

If Evita had been alive she would have saved her people; so much had she made them love her they believed that. But Peron is deposed. Her body falls into the hands of the enemy. Is it really her? Or is she wax? They cut off a piece of her ear, sever a finger. No, it really is Eva, complete with internal organs. She's not just literally flammable, she's potentially a political flame to set the country alight.

The new regime is determined to erase Peronism. A henchman shoots up the glass coffin in which she is sealed.

133

She's stuffed in a wooden crate and kidnapped. A certain colonel, says the programme, was custodian of her body; a perfectly normal man, but with the body he went mad. She was a doll. Intact. As if alive. Not wax. Flesh and bones.

It's sex and death again. Ever since Geoffrey began dying the world has offered her shapely intricate narratives of sex and death. They fall into her pen. They loop and spiral their frail elaborate structures round the central enormous fact of his death. To begin with she thought most of them were unpublishable. They pleased her because they showed her she wrote to understand, not to publish. When she mentioned this a friend said, Oh Clare, I'm sure you won't have any trouble, in the long run, I'm sure somebody will publish them, sooner or later.

No, she said, it's not a publisher, it's me that says they're unpublishable. It's to do with betrayal. They betray not just me, but other people.

But time passed, things change, all writers are tarts in the end, she knows now she will let them go, send them out, after all. She has gained enough self-knowledge in the past months to know that for her to write and to publish have become synonymous; that is why she does it. To understand, yes, but showing other people what she has understood is an integral part of it. The logical and only end of the process.

And one of the reasons is removed, which was keeping them secret from the lover's wife. And the other . . . well, writers always, evidently and inevitably, betray themselves even more thoroughly than they do anyone else.

She emails the stories one by one in a slow narrative to Oliver, who writes to her every day. He is a wonderful reader, so perceptive, he tells her how the stories work, what's in them, things that she didn't know she was doing but is delighted to discover.

After she sent him the fifth one he wrote:

> You asked whether I now saw why your stories are unpublishable. Yes and no. I see indeed why you might indeed think of them that way. But from the reader's point of view they seem eminently publishable. I am aware, of course, of some of the things in them that are direct reflexions of autobiography. But I also know that they are largely fictional, and the uninstructed audience is going to have no reason to treat them, in their entirety, as anything other than imaginative fiction; there seems to me to be a seamless join between reality and imagination. (One could say exactly the same about *Ulysses*.) I can see no reason why a wider audience should not have the benefit of them when you are ready.

One of his charms is a habit of comparing her with James Joyce.

Maybe she'll read one of them in Tasmania. Instead of writing a paper on Seduction and Betrayal. She wouldn't do it at home, but here it may indeed be an uninstructed audience. She will read them The Sins of the Leopard, with its opening line from Dante:

That day they got no further with their reading . . .

Or maybe she won't. Maybe she'll get cold feet.

★

And meanwhile, what of Eva Peron?

It's not really very nice having her standing around in this wooden crate, rough-looking thing, it could contain a batch of garden rakes or ironing boards, and the colonel, what is the colonel doing? Something necrophiliac, we are obliged to suppose. Unspeakable, on the television.

The Pope takes a hand and she is turned into an Italian widow—we see her new name on a black coffin—and sent to Milan, where she is buried upright. The telly offers an image of a marble angel, pretty childish half-smiling decadent creature with a small swag of cobwebs suspended from her ear, across her cheek to her nose, it flutters gently as though she were breathing.

The programme is called *The Unquiet Grave*.

Time passes. The body is returned to Peron and his new wife. Peron and new wife return to Argentina. A miracle, Evita Peron is still intact, fifteen years later. A doll. Perfectly mummified.

The song 'Living Doll' runs through Clare's head. What is Evita? A dead doll?

But Argentina isn't a calm place. Evita may be suffering; the living certainly are. There are rumours that she has been abused, then decapitated. The doctor of the original embalming says not. Her sisters say she is mutilated, her nose broken, her head cut, that there's tar on her feet. The images on television show this.

They get a museum restorer to repair her. This takes another year. Then in the dead of night they buried her, eight metres deep in a marble crypt. Still standing up, Clare wonders, whatever that means. Evita, maybe still miraculously perfect, nearly fifty years after her death.

Except, Clare knows, death is never perfect. It is always the absence of life. Geoffrey, newly dead, with his soul or his spirit, whatever you want to call it, his life, still hovering near, she could feel its energy, the gentle presence of it not in him but not far away, Geoffrey cooling was already not himself. Clare has conversations with her lovers, her ex-lovers, and her friends, about life after death. Most of them are not at all sanguine. Vague, doubtful, or certain not. She likes to think some spirit, some mind exists somewhere apart from their memories of him. But this preserving of a body which can do nothing but proclaim its deadness, its unaliveness, its absolute absence of life whatever orgasms a colonel could animate from it, is too sad to think of. Is immoral and obscene. A betrayal of the woman who once lived.

Clare is beginning to decide what to do with Geoffrey's ashes. One day soon they will take them down in their box from the high bookshelf and scatter them in certain beloved places, and then they will begin to live again. The ashes.

life *is*
dangerous

CLARE WENT TO TASMANIA IN winter and raging seemed a better word than lapping for what the water was doing. Last time had been summer, now it was winter moving into spring, spring being the flowers and blossoming trees believing it was, not the weather. At night she sat inside the warm firelit house with the windows covered to keep out the cold, listening to the roaring rushing pelting noises. She thought the water tanks would be getting full, but no, it was just the wind and the water of the bay roaring, there was no rain. The wind was so fierce it blew through the closed windows. The blinds shuddered, in a movement tight, unwilling, yet obliged.

There were a lot of noises in the night, not just the wind and water and the trees, but knockings and bangings. Once she woke and wondered where she was, and only after a panicky rehearsal of places where she might be fixed on the right one. Someone was knocking on the wall of the house, knocking and wanting to come in. It was not her place to let him in. She went back to sleep, curiously comforted that someone should come knocking on the wall of the house, knocking and wanting to come in. A friendly and safe-keeping knock, it seemed, she did not need to stay awake to do something about it.

In the morning she remembered this, the half-asleep response to what seemed urgent human or maybe ghostly knocking but was almost certainly the wind, and puzzled that it should have seemed so comforting; either it was importu-nate, dangerous, or else it was a sad and shut-out presence wanting to come in, and neither should have soothed her back to sleep. But that had happened, and she was aware of it all day, as some dreams stay through waking hours and make us believe they were greatly important, so that they become part of our consciousness like things that have actually happened to us, and isn't it the case, she said to herself, that they actually have, a dream is an experience we have lived through and can change us.

The day was much calmer. She sat at the table in front of the broad windows and watched the small waves run before the wind which sometimes flurried them white. They hit the shore around the coral-roofed boathouse, that might have been oriental and might have been Venetian but was not very convincingly either. Now and then a small dark squall crossed the water like a fleeting frown, as though a busy person suddenly scrunched up her forehead and said, why did you do that?

There was still a gull crying, the sound plaintive and

stretched out, like a blade pulled from a stone piercing the tumultuous air.

She sat at the table writing, and the pen slipped easily across the silky graph paper.

She had her camera with her, the new one, the other one got lost on the last visit. She hadn't been very upset, it just seemed appropriate that in such a huge loss would be contained a whole lot of smaller ones. The scale of loss had so completely changed that all the old calculations were having to be redone.

The water shimmered, so did the weather, sudden showers of rain flinging from the sky, the mountain disappearing in a mauve mist, then the sun shining, the bay glittering in the dancing cobblestone way that water has. The bare trees sparkled, so did drops of rain on the window, and needles of it pricking down from the sky. Clare was trying to discover if any of these were photographable.

The cathedral of grief was as lofty as ever, but she sat in it, for its comfort, mysterious, perhaps unavailable; cold, demanding, a place of wonder. Still ambiguously splendid. Needing a lot of learning.

The day of arriving in Tasmania was another anniversary. There are a lot when you measure them out in months. Perhaps after twelve of them you can start measuring out in years.

She said to a colleague: Do you ever wonder what will become of you?

The colleague stared. Her eyes were cool. I have been looking after myself since I was fifteen, she said. I've always been responsible for myself.

Clare didn't think that was the answer, but she didn't say so. There are conversations that are doomed from the start. You might as well save your energies for people who want to play. Like her beloved Polly. She gazed at the rain, a bit surprised to find herself thinking beloved, but dear wasn't strong enough.

She gazes through the glittering window and remembers all the times Polly has sat in her house, in the kitchen, in the garden, in the sitting room, drinking wine, drinking tea, serious, frowning, laughing, ready for anything Clare might ask her (though she has never mentioned the lover), Polly fiercely pulling her silvery curls straight in a gesture she doesn't even realise she is making as she pays attention to her answer. She recalls a particular conversation, one evening, sitting in the yellow chairs by the fire, in this last winter that has lasted such a very long time, drinking white wine, Polly wearing her red dress again and making Clare think of parrot tulips.

Life is dangerous, Polly had said. We know that now.

Yes, said Clare. I wake up in the morning, and, well, sometimes, terror is the only word.

What do you do?

Lie there and talk myself out of it. But you know, sometimes I look at people, especially when I'm in Melbourne, on a tram, and you know how dreary and grey Melbourne can be, and I look around me and I think how exceptionally brave people are, what a sublime act of courage it is, simply getting out of bed in the morning, having to go through another day and what terrors it may bring. Because if it's hard for me, who does a job she likes, and is materially okay and all that, so far anyway, how much harder is it for people who don't have those things, who have sorrows and anguish and hardships as well.

When we were young, Polly said. She meant when they were girls, living in the hall of residence. We knew then that life could be dangerous.

Yes, said Clare.

Then they asked the question, What would become of them? What would they become? Would they have jobs? Careers? Would they ever marry? Unspoken, this question. Their relations thought they wouldn't, quiet girls, they thought, serious, studious, set down for spinsters; when Clare turned twenty-one her aunts fussed at her mother over what to give her, nothing for the glory box, that wouldn't be suitable, that would be a reproach. Would they have children? And then at twenty-three they married loving and kind husbands, and forgot that life was dangerous, until in middle age it reared up, and they knew again.

Would they have children? Hostages to fortune. The just-born baby, the delicate hold on life: *If you believe in baptising babies, I would baptise this one*. The sudden intimation of the terror that lies in love. And Clare and Geoffrey did christen her, not because they believed she'd be damned if they didn't, or stuck in limbo or whatever, but because so tiny a life deserved to be marked by ceremony. When he got old enough to realise it their son was mildly miffed that his sister was christened and he wasn't. And so it turned out that sometimes fear could be reassuring. Danger could threaten and then slither away. And all manner of things would be well. Except in Polly's case it didn't threaten, out of a sunny summer day it struck suddenly, and life might have all sorts of good things in it, but would never be well again. Summer, fishing, children, bicycles, a quiet road, an unaware truck, and the world tilts. And forever afterwards that tilting false motion can make your stomach sick. You may forget it briefly, but there's a tremor, it's still rough, your stomach heaves. You don't have to have been there, knowing can do it.

They don't say any of this. When we were young, said Polly. And all these things went through their heads, while they drank their wine and their eyes filled with tears. Clare put more wood on the fire.

The thing is, she said, our fears were the fears of innocence. We were afraid of things not happening. Now we fear them happening.

And you can't even think that the worst has happened, said Polly. We'll be safe because the worst has happened. Because you only have to look around to see that more and more can. More and more, and worse and worse.

Yes, said Clare, thinking of her daughter, to whom more and worse might be about to happen.

Enough of this.

I've done it again, Clare said, leaning back in her yellow chair. This damn Tasmania trip. I'm going to be away in the spring. Again. Every year I swear I won't, I'll stay to see all the new things happening in the garden, and to plant things at the right time, and every year I find myself not here. And photographs aren't the same. I know. I've tried.

It won't be long. Hardly more than a week.

Long enough to miss things. The daffodils will come and go, or be blown to bits by the wind.

Next year, said Polly.

For certain, said Clare.

It's still winter in Tasmania, whatever the blossoms think, and you could suppose them being punished for temerity. But her daughter is all right, that's one worst that didn't happen. There are brief shafts of sunlight, when the rain sparkles on the glass, its silver refracting the gloomy indigos of the stormy afternoon. Carefully she photographs it, trying to work out the light, adjusting aperture and speed, she's new to this and has to go haltingly through it. Maybe one day it will become automatic, like driving a car, which Geoffrey in his deft way taught her to do (though once she burst into tears over it) saying, One day you won't have to think about it at all, it will just come naturally, which didn't seem at all possible, but then it had, and she could just do it. When she'd come back from a trip to Canada, after several weeks of not driving, she'd been zooming up to an intersection with red lights to be stopped at, and suddenly panicked, not knowing which foot to use on the brake, and she'd remembered Geoffrey saying, It will become automatic, and managed to stop thinking, to disengage her mind like the car's clutch and let her feet do what they'd done millions of times before, get the clutch and the brake right, and it had worked. But of course a camera could never become quite so automatic as that, there'd always be some thinking to do.

Geoffrey had liked the beauty of storms. Had liked the sea grey and raging, or pewter-coloured in the twilight. He didn't care for its bright blue under the harsh sunlight. He preferred the evening, when there was a cold inshore wind and all the swimmers and sunbathers had gone home, with only a few holey-jumpered fishermen left. She'd taken photographs of this stretch of water in the summer, when it was blue and sunny, but never seen them, they were in the lost camera. But that seems a glaring and unsubtle beauty, compared with these moody colours and the raindrops now pierced and glittering with the sunlight, now pewter-heavy and gleaming. It's all how you see things, she said to herself. She wasn't too worried about the technicalities of the camera, what was more important was what her eyes saw and chose to make a picture out of. She wanted her pictures to do what her words did when they worked; show people ways of looking at the world which maybe they hadn't seen before, and perhaps make sense of it, but probably not that; at least see that it can be beautiful.

A man and woman are rowing in a small boat across the water which looks calmer now but is still running violently with the tide so you can see the strain of his pulling, the way the water drags the boat sideways and he has to keep countering it. When they get to the jetty they pull the boat up out of the water with ropes, hand over hand, so that it hangs protected under the faded red roof. The wind worries at them, they have to struggle with it as much as with the boat, which lurches in its grip, several times it slips and falls and has to be hauled back up again. Their japaras are plastered to their bodies, she can't see their faces or hear their ragged breathing but she can see the effort it's costing them. When it's finally stowed they walk along the jetty and disappear below the slope in front of the house, then come into sight where the road curves up the hill away from the shore. They are walking hand in hand, tight-clasped, contented.

She watches them, holding close against the wind, and remembers saying to the man who used to be her lover, in one of those long after love-making conversations, Have you ever thought just how dangerous life is? How bleak. How it can hurt you.

He huffed his breath out in a little sigh, meaning he did not think about such things. He kissed her, in the way he had, long, gentle, slow.

All there is, she said, is skin against skin. Bodies touching for a little while.

He held her closer. No, he said, there's more than that.

Yes, there's art. But art takes no account of us.

It does. It speaks to us, intimately. It moves us. Think of the Arnolfini wedding. How you can stand in front of it, and look and look, and there is still so much to see.

But it doesn't see us. It doesn't pay any attention to us. It doesn't care about us.

It's important to us.

Oh yes. But it doesn't know we exist. No, the only comfort is skin against skin. Human beings touching one another.

He slid his fingers over her body, as though to prove it.

That shocks you, doesn't it, she said. Because you have never known what it is to be without it.

He was silent.

Have you, she said. You have never had to be without it. Never in your entire life.

No.

Clare sitting at the table staring out the window has stopped writing. She's stopped taking photographs. There's a limit to how many you want of water running down a pane

146

against a stormy landscape. She turns over the notes in her folder, all the bits of paper on which she'd been writing things that seemed important to her.

We are in the hands of the Lord . . . that was Mrs Ramsay, knitting her sock, looking out at the lighthouse in the dusk, her spirit meeting its long steady stroke. And then annoyed with herself, she didn't mean it, it wasn't true. How could any Lord have made this world, she asks.

> With her mind she had always seized the fact that there is no reason, order, justice: but suffering, death, the poor. There was no treachery too base for the world to commit; she knew that. No happiness lasted; she knew that.

And Clare thinks, there we are, back with the indifferent universe again. No Lord seeing everything. No Father noting the fall of sparrows. Underneath no everlasting arms.

But then . . . she tried to remember the exact words about the sparrows. Automatic again, the text learned by heart at Sunday school. Something about two sparrows selling for a farthing but not one falling to the ground without the Lord our Father seeing. Not doing anything about. Not picking up. Not saving. There's no suggestion that people shouldn't be selling sparrows in the market at two for a farthing. What we are being told is that the Father sees, he knows. He takes account.

It's what we want from our friends, our lovers, our spouses. That they should see us, that they should pay attention. Should know.

Nobody can save us.

Clare could identify with Mrs Ramsay, a woman who sits and thinks the world she lives in into meaning. She'd forgotten about Virginia Woolf's mad exuberant prose, the long disjointing breathless sentences, the images that catch your breath: the old friendship dead but preserved like the body of a young man in peat, still red-lipped. She hasn't read *To the Lighthouse* since she was a teenager, would not have made of it then what she does now. Mrs Ramsay may deny the hands of the Lord, but she knows that it is the work of her body and mind to draw ecstasy out of the simple glorious things about her, the beam of light across the sea as it turns from blue to pure lemon, the joy that rises like the fume from the *boeuf en daube*, the sonnet that is there, *suddenly entirely shaped in her hands, beautiful and reasonable, clear and complete, the essence sucked out of life and held rounded here.*

So Clare looks through the dazzled pane and out across the channel at the mountain slumbering in the shape of Sleeping Beauty, so the locals say, under the indigo sky and reads these words and thinks of Mrs Ramsay: *It is enough. It is enough.*

Art does not see us, she says to herself. But we see it, and can know that it has seen, if not us, our condition. The likes of us. That's something. Maybe enough.

She has the house to herself. She's had to stay another day because of a mix-up with planes, she's done the work she came for, the gruelling exhilarating festival, now she can write and think and read, look at the weather beyond the window, take photos, make herself a sandwich, pour a glass of wine for lunch because this is a day out of the ordinary, not her place, not her job, not her duty, alone in a house not hers she can feel solitude like the smooth poignant taste of the red wine in her mouth, sipped and sucked at, stimulating and soothing together. Why all this alliteration, she wonders. Catches her breath in a small laugh. Solitude isn't something she knows much about. Has never gone in for it. Works alone, yes, but in a house inhabited by the breathing of others, known to be there, available when you need them; Clare managed to live for thirty-one years in her house and only once spend a night alone in it, and that was because she won a prize so didn't go on holiday until a day later than the rest of the family. Not true any longer. She's learning solitude like a child chucked into a swimming pool. She might not be swimming with an elegant stroke but she's dog-paddling away and only occasionally swallowing gulps of water, which is almost making her believe it is a buoyant medium.

Red wine and a friendly swimming pool. A nicely mixed metaphor. Maybe the inner and the outer woman.

She doesn't care for swimming pools much. Too static. The Christmas after Geoffrey died she didn't stay at home but went back to the seaside where she'd grown up, and nearly every day she went swimming in the sea. She hadn't done it since she married, though she'd always known how much she loved it. Now she went in a part of the beach where the waves weren't violent, for it was a summer of rough seas and rips and terrible dumpers, and she gave herself to the lift and swell of these unbreaking waves as she's written them for characters in her books, she'd remembered all those years how they were and been able to write them. The sea being a lover, intense, devoted, caressing, never faithless, always ready to hold you in an embrace gentle, knowing, the everlasting arms, and sometimes rough, fun. Cruel, even, but you could be in control of that; if a lover gets too violent you need to slip out of his arms for a space.

And when you want to stop being anthropomorphic or even pantheistic, sea bathing is a wonderfully solitary pleasure, because all that lover lord business is only in your mind. It's your head inside your vigorous body, and that's it.

It's an odd thought, that Geoffrey's death may have given her the gift of solitude. The cathedral is a place of immense stony contemplative calm.

At the festival in Tasmania, when she read her story called The Unquiet Grave a woman at the back of the room said, That's a poem, you know. 'The Unquiet Grave'.

Is it. Ah.

Yes. A folk song. A ballad. People still sing it.

Clare nodded.

The thing is, said the woman, it's got a year and a day in it. The girl sits on her lover's grave for a year and a day and mourns him and he complains that he can't get any peace. He wants her to go away and leave him alone.

Oh, I see. I didn't know that. I mean, I knew it was a phrase, a saying. I'd love to get a copy of the poem.

There's plenty around. There's one in the Norton Anthology.

The Unquiet Grave. A year and a day. It all seems too serendipitous.

She has to wait until she gets home to look it up. It's not

quite as the woman in the audience described it; interesting
how our memories select and shift.

> 'The wind doth blow today, my love,
>   And a few small drops of rain;
> I never had but one true love,
>   In cold grave she was lain.
>
> 'I'll do as much for my true-love
>   As any young man may;
> I'll sit and mourn all at her grave
>   For a twelvemonth and a day.'
>
> The twelvemonth and a day being up.
>   The dead began to speak:
> 'Oh who sits weeping on my grave,
>   And will not let me sleep?'
>
> ''Tis I, my love, sits on your grave,
>   And will not let you sleep;
> For I crave one kiss of your clay-cold lips,
>   And that is all I seek.'
>
> 'You crave one kiss of my clay-cold lips,
>   But my breath smells earthy strong;
> If you have one kiss of my clay-cold lips,
>   Your time will not be long.
>
> ''Tis down in yonder garden green,
>   Love, where we used to walk,
> The finest flower that e'er was seen,
>   Is withered to a stalk.

'The stalk is withered dry, my love,
So will our hearts decay;
So make yourself content, my love,
Till God calls you away.'

So it is the girl buried and the man who sits weeping, and it's not until the twelve month and a day that she asks who's not letting her sleep. One kiss doesn't seem much for a lover to want. Except of course that it is a token. Clare wonders why the man will be doomed: because a kiss from her so long dead will be mortal, or because of some more supernatural danger, that by kissing her he will share her fate? And if their hearts will decay, does that mean that love will die with it? Hers doesn't seem to have yet. Whatever, it's good advice she gives him:

So make yourself content, my love,
Till God calls you away.

It's what she's trying to do, make herself content. She just has to work out how.

She rings up her daughter, who's been listening to the news headlines.

Listen to this, she says. A man, in Wales, has one diseased kidney and one healthy one; he has an operation to remove the diseased kidney and after it's over they realise the doctors've taken out the healthy one.

Her voice is soft with horror. She feels a terrible affinity with bad hospital stories.

On no, says Clare. That's a terrible story. She's shuddering too.

What's he going to do, says her daughter.

Die, I suppose, says Clare.

The poor man. The poor man.

It's the perfect horror story. Succinct, dense. Roald Dahl could use it as the twist in one of his tales, but it needs no more words, The man, Wales (Wales the only detail, a neat little anchor), the kidneys, the doctors, the wrong one.

She often thinks of this story, for the pleasure of a narrative so small yet perfectly formed. Her favourite kind; a few spare words, and everything else provided by the reader.

.   .   .

Teacup. Teapot. There's a certain clarity in the way these words form themselves in the mouth. They have a freshness, a dryness, in the way of unsweetness. They chime with the pure notes of silver spoons and thin china. There is orderliness in them: *teacups*, *teapot*, a life in which they occur will be ceremonious and fine in its detail. Like the curved spout which shapes the tea itself into an arc of steaming gold. So it seems when your mouth shapes the words *teacup*, *teapot*. Manners and morals will stand to attention.

Clare back from Tasmania is making tea for Polly. The cups are shallow, in bluish-thin porcelain, washed with a brown flushing to orange under faded-garish pink and green transfer roses. They are Victorian, they belonged to her grandmother who was born in 1872, they are quite possibly hideous, and she is very fond of them. She places the strainer over a cup and picks up the teapot, her fingers fluttering over the knob of its lid though it is well made and won't fall off when she tips it.

She feels like a picture out of a *Girls' Own Paper* that belonged to her mother; Victorian too.

The Cup that Cheers but not Inebriates, she says.

Polly gives that wonderful snub-nosed little chuckle that sets Clare off too. Polly knows these things, and she has cups like these odd little brown ones, only hers are green, and have more gilt, and are posher. They don't know much about them but think they must be nineteenth century Japanese imitations of English china. Or maybe Austrian. Acquired it is likely in some early ambitions of upward mobility.

Lips that touch alcohol will never touch mine, says Polly.

That's not a picture. That's a temperance slogan.

Yes, not my scene really.

Polly was brought up a good Catholic girl in a country town, Clare a nice little Protestant in an industrial city, but they share all sorts of curious Victorian–Edwardian remnants of culture, and take delight in exploring them.

Now there's a lot of gossip to catch up with. Hardly any of it cheerful. Like the story of Lily, who's been organising going to Melbourne to live with her lover.

She must have left by now, says Clare.

It was all fixed up, says Polly. Her furniture had gone. Her piano, everything. And suddenly he says, Don't come. I don't love you any more.

What! But they were absolutely besotted with one another. You only had to look at them. They were radiant.

Well, I thought so.

What a shit.

They were so handsome together; maybe that deceived them.

How is Lily?

Not good. I don't think she's stopped crying for a week.

The cups chime against the spoons. The silver milk jug is beaded with water drops. I suppose the tea table has always been the place for telling tragic tales, says Clare.

Watching Polly's long fingers holding out her cup to be refilled she hears her father singing as though he were in the next room. *Pale hands I loved beside the Shalimar*, she says.

Polly obliges by warbling the line, very prettily, her voice quivering with the musical emotion it seems to require.

What comes next, asks Clare.

I don't know that I've ever known.

You don't need to really. The whole story is there. The beautiful woman, pale hands are always a beautiful woman, the lost love, the exotic setting. Where is it, the Shalimar? India, or Persia? It is a river, isn't it?

I know it's a French perfume. In a curvy little Persian sort of bottle.

That's a lot of help.

Hang on, is it *loved*? Are you sure it isn't *love*? Pale hands I love, beside the Shalimar.

Oh well, then, it's a completely different story. Not lost love at all, but love requited.

Or maybe not, maybe he hasn't declared himself yet. Or this is it, and she'll say no.

Or yes, and they'll live happily ever after.

Speaking of perfect one-line narratives, says Clare, How's this . . . and she tells her about the man in Wales having the wrong kidney removed. Polly gasps.

Oh, she says. Oh. It's the fates. Blind fates. One eye

between them, and the one with the eye never the one with the scissors. Or the scalpel, in this case.

Some people would wreck that story by turning it into a narrative forty pages long, says Clare. But the sentence is all you need; the reader does the work. Odd, though, the place is important. You need the place.

Like Shalimar. Pale hands I love beside the Molonglo: you can make it scan but it doesn't have at all the same ring.

We have to find out where it is.

They get out all the dictionaries and such but can find no entry for Shalimar. Then Clare gets an atlas, and there it is: *Shalimar Railway Station* is the reference. Polly's snub-nose chuckle sets them off again. And when they look up the map it turns out to be on the south west edge of Calcutta, opposite the Kiddepore Docks, on a river called the Hugli. (It's a detailed atlas.)

It's the British in India, says Polly.

There must be something else. Why Shalimar Railway Station? Does it go there, or come from it? Why isn't the place on the map?

It must be all there is.

They can't help laughing at the idea of a young man serenading his love's pale hands beside a railway station.

If only we knew the rest, says Clare. Maybe it's a comic song.

No no. Has to be romantic. She warbles the line again.

Who can we ask? Who knows about antique popular love songs?

Maybe just about only us.

Not yet, surely.

The phone rings. It's Polly's youngest son, guessing where she is. Her face goes solemn.

Oh my goodness, she says. Oh my goodness. She says to Clare: Francis Hepple has died.

Clare doesn't know Francis Hepple but she knows who he is. He's the kind of very senior public servant who talks to the prime minister. She heard him give a speech once, in the sense that she was present, but failed to make herself listen. His wife Marie is a colleague of Polly's.

Yes, she says on the phone, yes.

Clare asks: An accident?

No. A heart attack. At work. His secretary found him. At his desk, pen still in hand, the words trailing off . . . kind of classical, really. Almost a quotation.

What they call a good death.

Good for the person dying. Bloody awful for everyone else.

How old was he?

Middle fifties. Marie is fifty-three, he was a bit older.

Too young, says Clare. And Marie too young to be a widow.

Oh yes.

The obsequies of Francis Hepple are attended by grandeur. The nearest the city has to a cathedral. Numerous eulogies. Children fly in from overseas. Mourners come from all over the country. Distinguished people are photographed for the television news: politicians, diplomats, mysterious bureaucrats. Marie in a black suit and a face entirely devoid of expression is only glimpsed. This is not the glamorous television funeral-as-entertainment, when the country can feast on its popular grief for heroes of disaster, firemen incinerated, policemen shot, helicopter pilots crashing on mercy dashes, or for pop stars suiciding or maybe just snuffing themselves out practising unsafe sex, or sporting stars expiring in the fullness of time and honours. Funerals with tons of flowers, extravagant tears, quavery-voiced idolatry. Francis Hepple's funeral is the hieratic culmination of the life of a public servant, good and faithful, and probably the most public event of it.

Quite strange, really, said Polly, who went. Marie and the kids didn't seem to be much part of it at all. I mean, they were there, there was quite proper formal recognition of them, but it didn't belong to them.

The property of the state.

In death as in life, you might say.

I saw Marie on the television.

That face. You can tell she doesn't know what's hit her. At least you had a chance to get used to the idea of Geoffrey dying.

Oh yes, I know. I know how important that was. But also you know it didn't help, afterwards. Remember how I said there are no rehearsals for grief.

I remember. But there are for the moment of death.

Not at all like the real thing. And the point is Marie is still in the early part. When there's so much to do, that's just inexorably got to be done. It's later, when the ceremonies and all that attention are over, and it's just you and no husband . . .

It makes me think of that hymn: *The tumult and the shouting dies* . . .

Lest we forget. Not much danger of that with you.

Would you want there to be?

Perhaps, beware of hagiography.

Clare looked at Polly, she frowned, as though listening to the echo of the word.

Hagiography? Do you think . . .

I didn't say . . . I just meant, beware.

I don't think I'm making any kind of saint out of him. Just missing the person he was, even his flaws and warts and all. Not that I'm thinking of warts, really . . .

Should I say, exactly.

I'm pretty robust about him. Remember that time we were meeting Miriam and David in that restaurant and they arrived two minutes early and we were already there and they said, You're early, you're never early, and I said, That's because we haven't got Geoffrey to make us late, and they looked rather stunned and then laughed like mad.

Yeah, you're okay. Marie now . . .

She'll be okay. Eventually. As ever one is. People say to me, You're so wonderful, you cope so well. And I think, well what the hell else can I do. I suppose I could stand in the middle of my life and howl, but where would that get me? I bet everyone I knew would move well out of earshot. People say, In your place I think I would go to pieces, and I want to say, have you noticed, people only go to pieces when there's somebody around to pick them up.

Well, says Polly . . .

I know, some people do go round the bend, lose their marbles, etcetera. But I am pretty bloody rational. Too rational for my own good, I sometimes think.

Clare knows she is lucky to have Polly for a friend. She can say anything to her. Just about anything.

Hagiography? She knows Geoffrey wasn't a saint. It's not

saintliness that she misses. Rational, she says to herself. Too bloody rational.

When she embarked on an adulterous affair she might not have seemed to be behaving rationally. What I like about you, the lover said, is that you are ruled by your emotions. You let them show you how to behave. Ah, she said, I take notice of my emotions, but in a rational way.

Well, that was then. This is now.

In one of her novels the heroine realises that she has been reading a primer of women to help her to work out how to live her life. Some are alive, some dead, some friends, some a matter of history or repute. Her character thinks that by examining their lives (*the unexamined life is not worth living*, said Socrates, which she put in another novel) she will find clues for living her own. Clare liked that image, the primer of women, the idea of all the lives a person could read to work out her own. But then after all you just have to go about it, and your own life becomes a part of the primer. You hope not a cautionary tale: don't do it like this. Avoid that at all costs.

But it was quite a few years ago, that book. Now the power and the strength of the women offering themselves for examination seem always in danger of being overwhelmed by sadness. Now her life seems more like living in a Greek chorus. Finding words, and you hope they will be shapely, memorable, poignant words, for grief, death, disaster. Turning terror into a poetry of beauty and dignity, whose only comfort is its own grave self. Dancing with light feet that belie the heavy hearts that move them.

.   .   .

She got the Tasmania photographs developed. The raindrops on the windows pictures turned out very well, she was pleased with them. Photographing great scenery doesn't interest her, it's this unexpected small detail that charms.

She didn't see Polly for a while. She hadn't been one of Marie Hepple's closest friends, but now Marie was needing her. Recognising however obscurely Polly's gift for looking after people. Then one day after work she called in with a small sheaf of papers. Clare was again sitting beside her fire reading, creating her small ceremony of comfort and control in the cold spring afternoon.

I've found it for you, said Polly.

Sit down, said Clare, I'll get some wine. What?

Shalimar. Not a river, but gardens. Water gardens, with fountains and pools, Mughal gardens.

Ah, Kashmir.

Yes. On the edge of the Himalayas. Srinagar, it seems. Built by the son of Akbar, called Jahangir, which means Seizer of the World. Famous for his gardens too, and Shalimar is the most famous of them. Polly reads from her paper: *Shalimar Bagh has an air of seclusion and repose, and its rows of fountains and shaded trees seem to recede towards the snow capped mountains.*

I knew it had to be more romantic than a railway station.

And so it is. We've all seen those gorgeous tourist pictures of Kashmir and its water palaces, all those domes and lacework and slender columns, that Mughal style. Lots of fountains that fling tiny drops of water in the air, so you walk around in a rainbow mist. Well, that's where our hero is. And what's more, here's the poem.

No! You haven't found that too!

Yup. It's one of the Indian Love Lyrics. 1902.

Of course, of course. We had the music of them at home. And of course it's Edwardian. Where on earth did you get all this?

Off the Net, said Polly smugly. Then she gave a hoot of laughter. Did a search on Shalimar. And you know where I found it? The poem? On a site devoted to P. G. Wodehouse. Designed to cross-reference everything he ever mentions.

Read it. Read it. Clare is opening the wine.

Okay. It is *loved*, by the way. You were right. Written by Laurence Hope with music by Amy Woodforde-Finden. Not exactly household names. Or not any more.

Polly reads the poem, properly, not hamming it up. Reads it well.

> *Pale hands I loved beside the Shalimar,*
> *Where are you now? Who lies beneath your spell?*
> *Whom do you lead on Rapture's roadway, far,*
> *Before you agonise them in farewell?*

> *Pale hands I loved beside the Shalimar,*
> *Where are you now? Where are you now?*

> *Pale hands, pink-tipped, like Lotus buds that float*
> *On those cool waters where we used to dwell,*
> *I would have rather felt you round my throat*
> *Crushing out life, than waving me farewell!*

> *Pale hands I loved beside the Shalimar.*
> *Where are you now? Where lies your spell?*

Oh wow, said Clare. That is good.

Isn't it.

I especially liked, what is it, the pink-tipped fingers . . .

Like Lotus buds . . .

Crushing the life out of him. Serious stuff. You can imagine that electrifying Edwardian drawing rooms. The young man just happening to have brought his music case with him, fixing his lustrous eyes on some conscious young woman.

It's got a kind of roughness, a sharpness, that's a bit of a surprise. I thought it would be frightfully sentimental.

So did I. I wasn't sure I wanted to know how it went. And it's so economical. Just the hands, and the rapture, and the farewell, than which he'd rather be strangled. Nothing explained, it's terrific. And Shalimar; gorgeous word.

I wonder did they live on a houseboat, says Polly. Those cool waters where we used to dwell. That's why it's beside the Shalimar, on the lake beside the gardens.

If you're going to wonder there's a huge number of things to wonder about. That's what's wonderful. Who are they? He? She? Are they English? Kashmiri? The lotus buds and the strangling are maybe the passionate terrible East. What parts them? Perfidy? Parents? Fate? Race? Etcetera, etcetera. And of course, the garden as an image of paradise.

That's what the word actually means, you know. The Greek word *paradeisos* means just that, garden.

Really? So that's what you and I are doing, grubbing about in our back yards; we're making paradises. I did know that Muslims imagine paradise, as in the afterlife, as a garden. And that's what these Mughal gardens are about, creating it on earth. A sort of preview glimpse of the next life's attractions.

And maybe the lady with the hands is the houri in it.

So there it is, our fragment of a narrative. And the whole vessel imagined from a shard.

The fire burns up, their cheeks are flushed by its heat, the wine is dry and cool in their mouths, they are playing their old games. They gaze at one another smiling with the complete pleasure of all these things.

It is enough. It is enough.

Mrs Ramsay might have said so. Virginia Woolf . . . ? Well, who knows.

flights *of* pigeons

CLARE TEARS OLD A4 SHEETS OF paper into quarters and uses the blank side to make notes. Sometimes she imagines them becoming an archaeological problem, as some latter-day scholar comes across them and tries to decipher the messages on both sides. What sort of semiotic sense will they make of one another? Which side will be valued? Maybe her scribbled deep thoughts will seem insignificant beside the typed or printed fragments of messages on the recycled discarded pages.

When she shakes out her doona a sheaf of these little pages rises in the air and flutters to the ground. You can believe you hear them cooing like the wood pigeons in the tree outside.

I am cold. Come to my bed and warm me.

Love me. You do not need to make love, to love me is enough.

Loving, of course, is huger than making love, warmer, longer, harder. It lasts beyond the grave. To an extent.

Geoffrey and Clare were never cold. They always warmed one another. Never slept with an electric blanket, or hot water bottles. Kept their hot doona for guests and bought a lighter one and even so had to stick out their feet and arms for coolness sometimes, so warm did they grow together.

I am cold. I want you in my bed.

These pages have been nested safely in the doona for several days. They come from a night when she was cold as she doesn't remember being in all her life with Geoffrey, not since she was a girl living beside the sea and everybody believes you don't need much heating beside the sea so you are cold a lot of the time, the winter gets into your bones. On this night her bones were cold, and she got up and put on woolly socks and a long-sleeved nightgown that anybody else would have tossed in the Smith Family box years ago because they hadn't worn it for years before that. But still she lay and shivered under this feather-filled doona which mostly was too warm for her. Much later she supposed that it must have been fear that made her so cold. Fear of another death that crept in through some crack in her being and spread its noxious chill through her blood. She'd known the fear was there, but not that there was some crack, some wound, some entry place within her that would allow its virulent attack. She thought that she was strong. Had fortified any weak places.

That night of cold was when she wrote her notes to Geoffrey. Remembering the shape of him in the bed, his smell. How touching him warmed her. His side is still there, she sleeps on her side, not the middle or his side. His side has sheltered her little oblongs of paper. *I am cold. Come to my bed and warm me.*

On the back of one slip are lines of a menu . . . *plings, crushed peanuts, 8.50. chili jam garlic aioli $8.50. Galette, avocado 12.50, 18.50.* She can't remember what restaurant that would have been. Another says, *for more information please contact. Re Council working party. Meeting July 26.* And, this one takes her back, a pale pink sheet exhorting her in French to vote for the local Communist Party. Which got elected, she remembers, that very bourgeois suburb of Paris believing that the Communists were the best lot to ginger up the government. They didn't want them running the country, just keeping on criticising the party that was. In those days Geoffrey was very much warm and lively in her bed. Their bed.

There's also a heavy card, an invitation to Government House, a Children's Book Council thing; the backs of such cards make good note pages, they are so thick and smooth to write on. This note says, *Mrs Hand and her Five Daughters*, an expression she was recently much taken with, never having heard it before. Where have you been, her colleague said, telling her how her parents scrimped to send her to a private school at the age of five, and how the first thing she learned was to masturbate. If they'd known, she said. All their money for that. She found it so good, so rare, so secret and setting apart she believed she was an angel.

Don't you write that, said her friend. That's mine. But Clare knows that all writing is betrayal, or rather that you have to choose which betrayal it will be, your friends or your art, and masturbating yourself into angelhood, well, you'd be an idiot to let that slip. And it's still her friend's to make something of. She's just mentioning it in passing.

It hadn't occurred to her to try masturbation to drive out

fear. Calling on the ministration of Mrs Hand and her five daughters. Good women all. She knows that sex is a help when there are terrors lurking. Passionate love-making sex. She remembers how they made love at the time of other operations. As though this love which had given a child life in the first place can somehow keep her from losing it now. She thinks that you need two people. It's the love, as well as the making of love. Pleasuring she thinks isn't likely to count.

She had conversations with her recent lover about the way all sex ends up being an affirmation of loss because the lovers must part. Maybe only to sleep, to wake up in the same bed knowing that they will sleep in it again the next night. But in the metaphysical way that sex is the desire to become so united with the lover that you become part of him, it's always doomed. However nearly you get there, you have to stop, and come back. You can't fuse, you have to part. A man who turns away instantly he comes so insists on this it is heartbreaking. But if he stays locked close and continues to kiss you, and express his desire for you, it's a consolation. Next time, you might manage the fusion. Of course deep down you both know you won't, but desire is saying you're keen to have another go. That you can allow yourself to believe that this time it'll all come together. You want to know that the assuagement of desire isn't the end of desire. That's what good lovers do, they stay an hour, a night, continuing to love you. And good husbands. They stay a lifetime.

On one of her paper fragments, this one a flyer from a cultural studies conference, she writes about fear. How sometimes you can control it, as though your will is a medication for it, a powerful antibiotic that fights the infection, and eventually it passes (cured by circumstances, in fact, in her case the operation having eventually worked), but how you remain convalescent, still rather frail with the memory and the weakness of it. You've known it and you can't forget it. You have a susceptibility. Like tuberculosis.

And there are lots of notes out of Arthur Schnitzler. She has been reading him because of going to see the Kubrik film *Eyes Wide Shut*. She found it riveting; she knew it was long and found herself sitting in the cinema watching herself watching this long slow-moving morbid movie, and being riveted. She talks about it to everybody she knows, and discovers that it is a film that polarises opinions; a lot of people hate it, don't want to talk about it. Others are fascinated, as she is.

The basic premise is the problem. A man's wife gets stoned and tells him of a fantasy she had once, to make love to a young naval officer. They were staying in a hotel in the summer and she saw him in the lobby. She tells her husband that she would have given up everything, him, her children, her rich apartment, her comfortable life, for a night of love with this stranger.

Schnitzler wrote this in 1925. Kubrik sets his movie in late nineties Manhattan. So, doesn't this make the subject anachronistic? Frederic Raphael the writer of the screenplay said something like this to Kubrik. Haven't relations between men and women changed since then, he asked. Do you think they have, said Kubrik. I don't think they have.

Clare wonders about this. She thinks that betrayal may have become more complicated. Less absolute. Perhaps even more manageable. A confession of a fantasy, from a stoned wife: the women she knows have forgiven so much more. Her lover's wife, for instance. Herself, once. But the thing is, it's not the point, that's what she argues when people like, it has to be said, the former lover, claim that the basic premise is ludicrous. Ludic, maybe. It's a trope, a construction that stands in for a betrayal; accept it, willingly suspend your disbelief—she did not need much will to suspend hers—and the movie works.

There was a scene where a number of women stood in a circle and dropped their cloaks to reveal themselves naked except for g-strings and high-heeled shoes. And masks, enormous elaborate masking headpieces. Later the g-strings went too, and revealed pubic hair trimmed into heart-shapes. Clare was moved by the nobility of the women. Their hieratic quality. True, they conformed to an image that was itself an unnatural construct, so tall they were, so small in the waist and curved in the buttocks, so jutting and firm in the breasts, they weren't real women but images of an ideal whose premises were flawed but whose expression was gorgeous. They were noble, and they were proud, but they were not erotic. They were hieratic, denatured, grand. So men have always made art of women. And as well these were terrible in their masks, like dangerous goddesses.

The men were entirely ignoble. At first they were sinister in their cloaks and head coverings. Some wore plague masks with bonnets and great curved bird beaks, and you thought, yes, this is wise, they are in the presence of disease. Then, naked, they became ferrety creatures, scampering about on all fours, poking in and out of the women like wood-pecking Russian toys. Poor forked creatures, entirely without courage, though they were men of immense wealth and power and with death easily in their command. And so feeble were their imaginations, this was their idea of fun. Of ultimate pleasure and the quintessential expression of desire. And the viewer can only think, how pathetic. The women noble, even bent back over tables, and the men able only to peck at them.

No, says Clare, I do not believe it is misogynist. The men may be so, the film isn't.

She hasn't managed to get hold of *Traumnovelle*, the story on which the movie was based, but she has found some other stories of Schnitzler's. They are all about desire. About how desire goes wrong. He is very good at expressing desire through weather, hot weather, burning sun, white flimsy dresses with no underwear, languid afternoons beside lakes and distant shrouded mountains, inside dim shuttered rooms. His women know what their bodies are telling them, even when they think they ought not to be saying such things, especially when their husbands think their bodies ought not to know such things. There's a lot of foolishness; it seems to be the endemic human state.

Schnitzler wrote plays too. She discovers his most famous is called *La Ronde*, which she and Geoffrey saw years ago as a French film, the Max Ophuls version. The play was first printed in a run of only a couple of hundred copies, since he knew it would enrage people. Later, after the war, it was performed, and it did enrage, it was denounced as a plot against the German people, against all that was good in the German way of life, on the part of sinister Asiatic invaders—that is, Jews.

It's a series of sketches, of couples, beginning with a whore and a soldier, then the soldier and a parlourmaid, the parlourmaid and a young gentleman, the young gentleman and a young wife, the young wife and the husband, and so it goes, until it gets back to the whore again. She remembers the merry-go-round music of the movie. Each sketch contains a copulation, which appears as a line of asterisks in the text. All the women in *La Ronde* want the men to stay with them, the men who have mostly persuaded the women to fuck them by lying that they love them, and these men having got their way and fucked want to go on to the next thing. The women are often quite hypocritical too, in their case pretending that they don't want to fuck, never do this kind of thing, are being persuaded against their will, but when they succumb they want to believe in love, some little love, they want to believe that he has not divested himself of desire along with his semen. Leaving him empty and satisfied, and her full, of him and of longing. Frustration.

The women are gentle, they don't want the man to go but they know that he will, all they ask is that he not go with too great haste. They want him to tarry a little. *La Ronde* isn't some crude subversive racial tract, how could anybody think that, it is about loveless love-making, about lust that does not bother even to pretend it cares, once it has slaked itself.

Clare is becoming addicted to this moving plain translated prose. It feeds her own obsessions. She makes little notes about them on her torn-up oblongs of paper, writes down phrases and sentences, ideas. The story called 'Casanova's Home-coming', for instance, when the famous lover is old and poor and trying to get let back into his native Venice. His lechery seems as lively as ever, though, and he bribes a young soldier called Lorenzini to let him sleep with his lover of so far only one night, a pretty young girl who is clever too, a philosopher in the habit of corresponding with famous mathematicians.

The men have been playing cards, with a marquis whose wife's been having it off with the soldier, and Lorenzini loses a lot of money which he can't pay, which will mean his dishonour, his ruin, the end of his glamorous soldier's career, the end of his life as he knows and loves it. The marquis will see to that, it is he who's owed the money, he will demand every jot and tittle of his cuckold's revenge if the young man does not pay. Casanova offers Lorenzini his own winnings from the same card game, in return for this night of love.

She ponders this, so much hanging on one night of love. Casanova evidently believes that one night with a woman and he has possessed her. Does not realise what all continuing lovers know, that possession doesn't last, that it does not even really happen, that it is an illusion. That you can try again and again and not, never, possess anyone. That even when a woman gives herself to a man, she has inevitably to take herself back. A woman or a man, two women, two men; always the self has to be taken back. Though it can be given again. But you can't possess by taking, only by being given. In the dark of night she writes on one of her slips of paper: *And that this is the wonder and the terror of sex.*

Casanova has his night with the fresh lovely intelligent young woman, who's called Marcolina, and Schnitzler makes you believe it is something pretty special in the sex stakes. She doesn't notice that he isn't the gorgeous young soldier. Wouldn't he smell different, feel different, the young silky fresh-fleshed young man, from the flaccider, more lizardy, more bristly, probably rancid old man? Old: between fifty and sixty, but worn out you suppose by dissipation, and in more aging times. Skilful still, but definitely not the lovable body that once he was. But Clare who feels sure she could distinguish between one man and another even in the pitchiest dark, would never not know a lover from a stranger, assumes that this is also a trope, and one often used in literature. Shakespeare does it. It's always a sneaky nasty trick. And usually backfires, though not because the woman twigs.

Marcolina only notices it's not the expected lover when the man in her bed falls brutishly asleep and she opens the shutters. Which he was supposed to be alert and in control of. She is scathing, furious, beside herself. So he leaves, wrapped only in the other's cloak, no shoes or clothes to give him away, but with his sword. He is, even starkers, a gentleman. As signified by the sword. He makes for a waiting carriage, but Lorenzini accosts him. Challenges him to a duel. With a naked man? So Lorenzini takes off his clothes too. Both naked. They fight in the pale dawn. Casanova kills Lorenzini. So he's ruined, after all. The youth lies on the green grass like a flower in the early summer morning. Casanova puts on his clothes and goes on his way, pleased that he has had his desire, he has possessed the lovely young woman. She's done. Notched up. No more to be had there.

It's clear to Clare that Schnitzler is showing that the world's greatest lover doesn't know the first thing about love.

Loving is huger than making love, warmer. Longer, harder. It remains when the lover is gone. Clare gathers up her paper pigeons and makes a nest for them under Geoffrey's pillow. Now and then she writes another. Little flights of love letters, kept under the pillow. You might think she is not sustaining the image too well; birds under a pillow can't fly, could suffocate. But paper pigeons with words on have special powers.

love potion

THE NAMES SOUND LIKE THE characters in a novel. A Proustian sort of novel. Madame Alfred Carrière. Madame Isaac Pereire. Zéphirine Drouin. It would be nice to write a novel with a character in it called Zéphirine. But difficult, names are such a delicate matter, you could run the risk of being thought precious. Or overly French. Lucky French, who can manage much more glamorous names than English. Who can put fairies in place names and be taken seriously.

Albertine: that's perfectly Proustian. Armandine. They have a curious music, these names, a grave and stately music. Not to be abbreviated. Not Mandy. Not Bertie. They are as they are. And they are men's names made female by those extra leisurely syllables.

There's Martin Frobisher too, and Mrs Herbert Stephens and Cécile Brunner; Clare and no less than four of her friends discovered only last year that this wasn't the man's name Cecil but the feminine version. Except Elvira, who'd known all along.

Of course these names aren't characters in a book, but roses in a catalogue. Everybody seems to be talking about roses these days, ordering them from nurseries, comparing. Clare has had some men dig out the hideous self-perpetuating roots and trunks of the bloodtwig dogwood, the bloody bloodtwig dogwood, that dates from the days when the garden grew nothing higher than a paspalum stalk, and any green was grateful. It pushed densely up against the bedroom window, in front of the house. Now there's a good dug-over composting space, she is planning what to plant. A quince tree, Smyrna is the one, so she can make quince paste, Cotignac, carnelian-coloured; cooking it is like supping with the devil, you need a long spoon, it sputters and spits. And quince jelly. And quinces are good just to put in bowls, so their ancient yellow smell fills the house with memories of autumn.

A quince tree, and as well some roses. Polly said she must have Madame Isaac Pereire. Clare wasn't sure, it was awfully puce-coloured in the pictures. It's the smell, said Polly, you can smell it right across the garden, it's so heady, so swoony, put it in the house and you might faint.

So perhaps Madame Isaac. The roses she plants must be fragrant, she doesn't like scentless roses. The catalogue puts a row of fat little bottles after each of its listings, which indicate intensity of smell. She's going for the five-bottle rating. Presumably they are perfume bottles. She and Geoffrey bought a car from a shop in the Boulevard Pereire once. In

Paris, that is, a long time ago. She wonders if it was the same Pereire. The boulevard not one of the great Hausmann constructions, but over beyond the Arc de Triomphe in a dull bourgeois area that seemed to have no beauties at all. They had been going to do without a car, but it was too hard, with small children; they rang her father and borrowed some money (was it $400? She can't remember) and bought a Peugeot from the man who'd sold Geoffrey a Renault Dauphine when he was a student, a decade before. She remembers going on the metro to pick it up, the long journey, the stolid streets, everything grey. Boulevards and roses: seemed likely they'd be the same person. Except that the rose was the wife, there were a lot of roses named after wives but always with the husband's name.

The year she was married she had her photograph taken at an embassy party and published in the *Sunday Telegraph*, herself and two friends, all looking about eighteen, their innocence sinister, she thinks now. *Mrs Gerald Laman, Mrs Dieter Wimmer, Mrs Geoffrey Charllot*, said the caption. Mrs Gerald Laman is Polly, and the other woman, called Leisl, she hasn't seen for years.

When in Geoffrey's last year they had an area in front of the house paved so they could bring the car close to the front door for him to get in and out more easily, paved with old Canberra bricks in rosy terracotta colours with sometimes a bluish tinge, she planted a small citrus grove in tubs, where the sun-warmed bricks in winter would have a slight *orangerie* effect, and some roses. Lordly Oberon smells good and has long pointed pale pink flowers; he seems to be outgrowing his tub, become long and straggly, so maybe she'll put him in the ground and give him a trellis to climb up. But the other she keeps in in its pot, it's happy there. Love Potion.

It has a marvellous deep crimson smell. She bought it because of the label, from the local nursery. The label said it was a small robust bush, and that its blooms were a rich lilac with slightly ruffled petals. But what persuaded her was this sentence: *Though its bush is small, the exquisite colour and the intense perfume provide the reason for its name . . . Love Potion.*

She looks it up in her book of old roses but it's too new to be there. Madame Isaac Pereire is, along with twenty-one other Madames with their husband's names—but only eight Mrs something. Madame Isaac is supposed to have huge flowers, of a deep magenta-rose, is strongly fragrant, and blooms over a long season. Maybe she will order one, plant her beside Lordly Oberon; the French bourgeois matron beside the king of the fairies.

She'll have to watch the possums. The roses will grow on a trellis up as high as the roof where the possums disport in the small hours of the night, running long galloping races the length of the house, thundering across the tiles with the heavy tread of speeding wombats. Sometimes they sit in the trees making those guttural visceral hissing noises that are so terrifying when you first hear them, make you think that the beasts are about to engage in mortal combat, raking soft furry bodies with sharp claws, until you discover that they actually mean sex. Irresistible cries of love. Possums are fond of roses. Nissa in Melbourne has to cover her Sainte Thérèse de Lisieux (white, pink-blushed, fragrant, fragile) with a net to stop the possums eating her, and if a saint isn't safe what hope for a wife.

Love Potion flowered and she picked single blooms and put them in a tiny glass vase beside Geoffrey's bed. Now she puts them beside a picture of him. Of both of them, eating what looks disturbingly like ice-cream sundaes in a nightclub in Katoomba. She remembers the occasion, how they ordered champagne, Australian bubbly, and the waiter opened three bottles, each of them flat. So they gave up and drank sparkling rhinegold. It's odd how you can't remember what things tasted like, but only the pleasure they gave you, or didn't. She remembers their disappointment that the champagne failed, but that they enjoyed the sparkling rhinegold, and suspects she might not now. Of course, the state they were in, nothing could have worried them for long. Bliss blesses all around it.

Geoffrey knew about love potions. The medieval kind. How they saved you from the sin of adultery.

Like Tristan and Iseut: Tristan is cured of a wound by this beautiful daughter of the king of Ireland. He tells his uncle the king of Cornwall about her, and is sent to woo her for him in marriage. When he's bringing her back *they both unknowingly partake of a magic potion and become enamoured of each other*. They are on a boat sailing back to Cornwall. It's hot, they see the flask that has been given the lady-in-waiting by Iseut's mother, for her daughter and King Mark to drink on their wedding night, so that they will love one another. Tristan drinks half of it and gives the rest to Iseut. So their passion is not their fault. It is not the deep sin their adultery would be if deliberate.

Geoffrey and Clare were in a car driving to their weekend in Katoomba. Not *a* car, *his* car, that he bought so he could come and visit her, he said. He lived practically on campus, but she'd moved to a distant suburb. She remembers the night, the storminess of it, the darkness, how the rain hurled itself against the windscreen in great fountains of water that burst and sparkled in the lights from oncoming cars. Like *jeux d'eau*, he said, water games, in the gardens of Versailles. It was a dangerous drive, on a winding road in a storm in the dark, but she felt safe. Not knowing it was the beginning of a lifetime of feeling safe with him.

He told her about Tristan and Iseut, his voice full of affectionate irony when he described the love philtre. How the smitten pair tried to behave well, but were overwhelmed. About King Mark spying on them while they played chess, and discovering that was not what they were doing. *That day they got no further with their chess-playing* . . . He talked about Tristan running mad in the forest. And about Mark finding the lovers lying asleep, their lips not touching, with a naked sword between them. How Tristan, realising their love was doomed, and worried about the adultery after all, married another Iseut, named Iseut of the White Hands, to distinguish her from the Fair. And most terrible of all, of him lying wounded, sick to death, and his wife sending for the first Iseut, who'd shown herself so good at healing him before, and then the wife, attacked by jealousy, telling him the ship that ought to have brought her had black sails, meaning she had not come, when in fact they were white, meaning she had. So Tristan turned his face to the wall and died, and when the Fair Iseut came to him she held him in her arms and died too.

Clare sort of knew these stories, but liked hearing them again.

His original name was Dristan, said Geoffrey, but writers

changed it to Tristan, because of the association with *triste*.
That means sad, you know.

Yes, I know, she said.

When they'd had enough of old stories they told one
another their own, their childhoods, their parents, their
educations, what they liked. Their voices in the dark warm
space of the car touched and plaited together as their bodies
could not, in a grave and blissful dance which she perceived,
tremulously, on that slow and dangerous progress through the
storm, might last their whole lives. And so they got to
Katoomba, and found a guest-house called Emoh-Ruo, a
ramshackle old warren of a place that offered them a
bedroom wallpapered in yellow roses, not blowsy Edwardian
flowers but stylised Jacobean invented blooms that Geoffrey
said resembled French wallpaper, oddly matt and chalky to
touch. Later, when she read Oscar Wilde's dying witticism
about the yellow wallpaper in his French hotel—One of us
has to go, he said—she remembered the roses in the guest-
house in Katoomba.

And so they began making their own stories that they
never tired of telling one another for the rest of their lives.
The flat champagne, the sundaes—can they really have eaten
ice-cream sundaes? The ultraviolet light on the dance floor
that grabbed her white dress and his shirt and turned them
into isolated suggestive shapes. Staying in a guest-house called
Emoh Ruo. The best stories are the old ones, as children
understand, the ones you know and desire to hear again, but
every now and then you need to brave a new one, which can
then become old and beloved too. Part of the repertoire.
Their voices always happy to move in that familiar graceful

dance, even though their bodies could not touch. Even when they could, the words still having their place.

No problem with bodies touching in the guest-house narrative. The creaky bed, their naked skins, their eyes absorbing one another. Spending a large part of the night upon one another. In a room like a very tall box, a very deep box, lined with imagined yellow flowers.

Then there was the story of the curry. Later this, they were married, buying a house because it was cheaper than renting. A hot night, and they'd gone to bed straight after eating it, and made love, their bodies wet and slippery with sweat, and suddenly they smelt it: the dusky mysterious scent of the spices they'd used in their cooking. They still smelled of themselves, but themselves aromatically overlaid. They began making love all over again, intoxicated by the exotic odours their bodies were producing. Remembering it, they embroidered the narrative: It was like Conrad, they said, sailing into some tropical port, his nostrils snuffing the humid oriental night with its spice-laden air. And later still they said, Man is born to trouble as the sparks fly upward. *Pass the bottle.*

Geoffrey took a photograph of her, naked. In that new house, sitting on a borrowed chair, the sparseness and bareness evident around her. The wooden floor. A yellow plastic radio, bookshelves made of bricks and planks, an ugly wedding-present lamp. She'd recently found it, looking in a box of papers for her marriage certificate. The certificate wasn't there, but the photo was. Black and white.

She's sitting on one leg, the other, slightly raised, is touching its pointed foot to the floor. She's looking at herself in a small mirror, framed in cast bronze flowers, her other hand holds her hair back from her face. Not from her body. As a nude photo it is a deception, or perhaps a suggestion. She is the least bare thing in the room. Part of one breast is visible, otherwise the heavy curtain of wavy dark hair—she must have been wearing it in a plait to make it undulate like that— completely conceals her. In another picture she's sitting back to front in the same ugly old tapestry chair, leaning slightly over the arm, playing with the cat, and again her hair falls in a curtain, just touching the floor, leaving only her legs visible.

There's another in this series, in the album, also playing with the cat, her hair equally evident, but she's buttoned up in a long cherry-red wool dressing gown. This for the album, the others not for public display. Geoffrey would have liked the photographs to be of her nakedness, but she resisted, was too shy. Now she's sorry, she'd have liked to see again her twenty-three-year-old body. She remembers him lifting her hair back, drawing it away so her flesh could be seen, and how she'd felt a kind of terror, of being caught forever like that, of being seen, being exposed, no longer in control of herself, subject to the eyes of people she knew nothing about, from the man who processed the films to who knew what lascivious critical indifferent gazes.

People do it all the time, said Geoffrey. People are always photographing their wives and girlfriends without any clothes on. It's not an odd thing to do. But she spread her hair out, and hid behind it.

Later still, when there were children, put to bed, they'd find themselves on the floor in front of the fire, their clothes off, making love on the silky wool of the Persian carpet. You just had to hope the children didn't wake up. Though the sofa would have protected them from view.

And so you plant roses, and grow children, and one of you buries the other.

Horace says, his Latin so much shorter and sharper than the English she needs to know what it means:

Tecum vivere amens
Tecum obeam livens

With you I love to live, with you desiring to die.

On that night drive to Katoomba they learned about loving to live with one another. Dying didn't come into it. There seemed enough life ahead to make mortality irrelevant.

There is that lifetime of gentle growing together, inter-twining and inextricable, towards some light that pulls and warms without needing to be named or even understood. You can keep the metaphor going: the old wood, the new wood, blooming on whichever, dieback, the pruning, the water-shoots, the worm-i-the-bud, and rose bushes with separate roots but their branches so plaited together that there is no possibility of unentwining them, no one could uncurl each tendril and make them separate, the old soft shoots have grown into strong hard branches, thick and woody, shaped and fixed to those entwinings. Trying to part them would kill them. Until one dies, and the branches wither, and can be clipped away with secateurs, damage to the dead not being relevant.

And then, adultery. The sudden lover. The dark journey into the erotics of grief. Oliver who is playful in his names for her sometimes calls her *schöne lustige Witwe*, which she had to look up in a German dictionary. *Schöne* she knew meant beautiful, and *lustig*e she thought she could guess, but was wrong, it didn't mean what it sounded like, but happy, cheerful. Merry would be the best translation. And *Witwe* was clearly widow. Reminding her that widows are famously given to lively behaviour, for which read sex. Clichés always have their reasons. Merry widow, lusty widow. Lust is the word here. The couplings are short, urgent, they cannot wait, there is not a lifetime, desire overwhelms its subjects. Not time even to unlock the front door; there on the table in the courtyard, not even her knickers taken off; thrust aside. Who'd have thought she'd be so athletic, her hips on the edge of the garden table, her legs around his neck. And afterwards falling into laughter at the urgency, the immensity of it. Laughter excited, delighted, slightly ashamed. Or getting inside her door, just, and starting there. This is the first time, she said, I have fucked in overcoat and scarf and gloves with my handbag still slung over my shoulder. It was interesting, all that.

But then she said, No more table fucks, we have to pay attention, it has to be splendid, or not at all. And when suddenly it was all over, and they were not supposed to be lovers any more, when they were one day sitting drinking wine in a small suburban cafe, a dim gloomy distant place, but not so dim that anybody they know, had they been there, could have failed to recognise them, she remembered that setting of rules.

I was wrong, she said. There was something splendid about our table fucks. I wish we'd had more. Sadly she thinks of the times she said no, not now, not here. All a mistake.

We could do it here and now, he says. Like the joke.

She manages a wan smile. Polite. She wants passion, if not the fact then its memory in words, not a joke.

You know that joke? He is stroking her fingers, his eyes sparkle.

She shakes her head, but when he begins she does know it, her son told it to her, her and Geoffrey, once, years ago, but she'd forgotten.

There's this couple, he says, they've been married for a while and their sex life's no good, doesn't exist really, no spark. They think about getting divorced. But they decide to go and see a psychologist, see if he can help them.

He takes a pull at his wine. He makes his jokes last, does this lover. He embroiders, he decorates, he adds diversions and red herrings, anything to spin out the narrative. The upshot is, the psychiatrist . . .

Psychiatrist?

Psychologist, whatever . . . tells them to try the old tricks, have a good dinner, a delicious meal, candles, wine, conversation, music, look into one another's eyes, the full romantic bit.

She looks into his, but he is spinning his tale.

Well, a week later they're back at the psych's again. What's the matter, he asks. We did everything you said, says the wife, great meal, candles, music, the whole thing. And, says the psych, so, what happened?

There's a woman several tables away reading a book. She sits tranquilly drinking a cup of coffee, voluptuously—maybe not voluptuously, but why not—turning the pages. Clare wonders what the book is.

Well, says the wife, it worked, just like you said. Instantly. He grabs me, bends me over the table, the glasses and plates go flying, he fucks me, one of the best fucks we've ever had. The psychologist looks at them. So? What's the problem? The wife hangs her head. Well, don't you see, we can't go back to that restaurant ever again.

The old lover shouts with glee. Clare laughs, a small ha-haing laugh, the best she can manage. She's never faked an orgasm, but she's faked a few laughs in her time.

She looks up Pereire in *Le Petit Larousse*. It's the name of two brothers, Jacob and Isaac, who were bankers, parlia-mentarians, developers of railways. Born at the beginning of the nineteenth century. She wonders which one the boulevard was named after. The rose is Madame Isaac, this gorgeous carmine creature filling a garden with her scent, and you could consider this a kind of immortality. Rather second-hand. If she were Zéphirine, now, Albertine, Cécile, Lorraine Lee; we wouldn't know any more about her but at least we'd have her own name. Was she beautiful, to have a rose named after her, or was it just because her husband was important? Maybe he bought it for her; the naming of a rose would be a pretty present. Except it's his own name he's perpetuated. She is just the wife. The female incarnation of his nominal significance.

.   .   .

Oliver would be interested in the photographs with the veil

of hair. He liked her hair, always wanted her to wear it entirely unconfined. When she was with him he would pull the pins out so it tumbled heavily down. That was another thing that made her shy, because women didn't, it wasn't until a year or two later that they started to let their hair flow free. But she could have been ahead of her time. A bit daring. She remembers her mother saying once, sharply, impatiently, Silly thing that I was. As she'd have spoken about somebody else altogether, as though that younger self was not her, and the silliness to be judged harshly. As though she was the mother of that young self, giving herself a little shake, a push, speaking with vehemence. Scolding, even. Kate said, meeting Clare's mother for the first time when she was over eighty years old, You should feel good, looking at your mother, she's so pretty in her old age, you can expect to be too. But Clare thought that she hadn't been as pretty as her mother when she was young, why should she be when she was old? Her mother had been famous for her rose-leaf complexion, which of course meant the flowers, not the spiky green leaves, her skin like rose petals, soft, silky, faintly flushed with colour, unblemished.

Her mother was vain. At some point, in the fifties, or the sixties, she cut the bottoms off old photos because of the twenties dresses she and her friends and sisters were wearing. Why did you do that, her daughters shrieked. They were terrible, those dresses, she said, they made you look like the side of a house. They were lovely, said her daughters, what you have done is vandalism. Fortunately she missed some, so there is still a record of the small pointed strappy shoes and the straight low-waisted dresses, tucked and flounced and embroidered, and no they don't look like the sides of houses, though maybe not quite so slender as their bodies were, underneath.

Clare thinks of vanity and sex. How you dress yourself in silk underwear and lace-topped stockings, in clothes that shape the body, concealing and promising. With necklines that offer glimpses of round breasts, and skirts to slide away across the knees. How you sit and stand and move with grace, hold your head up, your stomach in, shoulders back, how you offer your best angles, most charming lines, all the while doing your best to hide the flaws, the bulges, the blemishes. And then you manage to get alone at last with your lover and you tear your clothes off or he does and you cast vanity aside with them, or maybe it evaporates with the heat of the passion, and you grasp and pull and wrangle, scrunch yourself up, offer all the rawness of your nakedness with perfect trust in the desire of his gaze. Safely knowing that these eyes that devour you, stare avidly into your own, that glitter with the absorption of their own self in the body of you the other and their desiring to possess it, or crinkle in gleeful pleased laughter, because sex is funny, these eyes that lose themselves in yours in a simple wide stare, these eyes do not judge.

And then after all that you put your clothes on again and smooth them down and stand stretching tall and offer your most elegant and fetching angle to the eyes of the lover, like a mannequin in a shop window, seeming to forget what folds and crevices and deep slitted passages have opened and been penetrated, have been touched and tasted and flowed with juices.

And maybe it is a kind of madness, this desire to possess and be possessed, which makes two usually self-possessed smoothly ironed thoughtfully turned-out people fall on one another and tear the clothes off and invade and open their bodies to invasion with a kind of holy delight. Violating one another with complete trust. Maybe that is why you need to see it as the effects of a philtre, even though readers or listeners would always have known that Tristan and Iseut could fall in love all by themselves and that the philtre was a slyly ironic metaphor. Oh yes, we can all blame passion on this utterly random external agency, but our hearts know we do it all ourselves. We may lay our sins on this scapegoat the magicking drink, but we understand that it is a metaphor that compels our belief even while we know that it isn't true.

It would be interesting to write a new version of the story of Tristan and Iseut. Classical procedure, each generation writes the old stories for itself. In this one they don't get to drink the potion. The lady-in-waiting brings them some cool spring water instead. The philtre is safe, Mark and Iseut drink it on their wedding night. So then what happens?

Ah, that's the game the novelist plays with herself. There are all sorts of possibilities, you'd think. But consider: the most likely narrative is the exact same one. After all, King Mark got interested in Iseut because Tristan was keen on her, described her so enthusiastically. (Foolish boy.) Tristan wasn't a king, but he was a hero. Mark was a wimp and a coward, so the stories have it. The men of Cornwall were like that, the Newfies, the Belgians, the Tasmanians of their day. Famous for cowardice. Perhaps unfairly, but not in Mark's case. Tristan was always fighting his battles for him, Mark ran away, or waited at home. Iseut fancying Tristan knew what she was about.

Of course, the philtre might have been a placebo. (Leaving aside any scepticism about its potency anyway.) Designed to have a psychological effect, to make those who drink it believe they are in love.

I doubt it would have worked for Iseut and Mark. She had gazed on Tristan, she had nursed his lovely body back to health, her blood had learned what her eyes and fingers had taught her. Their passion might have had its mindless moments, but in the mind it began. They knew one another, not in the biblical sense, as people so pruriently say, but in the mental sense, which is so much more devastating. As lovers they were fated to love one another, and if this also doomed them, they had their moments, such moments.

And if immortality is being thought about by other people, that they have.

Love Potion is producing a profusion of blooms that begin crimson and fade to purplish pink and fill the brain with their dusky scent. Smell, says Clare to the former lover when he brings her back some books. Mmm, very nice, he says.

She picks a couple to put in a small glass beside the Katoomba photograph. The bottle of sparkling rhinegold, the possible ésundaes, and she's often thought thank god she wasn't pretending to wear a wedding ring as sometimes she did; her finger is appropriately bare. She is glad Love Potion bloomed before Geoffrey died. She remembers giving a flower to him, and his smile as he breathed it in; she did not need to say, it smells of desire. They smiled with dreamy lips, long-learnt smiles of promise and expectation. Their gazes hooked together, and they knew. The flowers perfumed their blood, as Shakespeare said of wine, not roses.

her silken layer

AFTER GEOFFREY DIED CLARE lost weight. In his last year she had prepared food to please him, which he ate delicately, and she enthusiastically, because she ran around a lot and was always hungry. Then when he died she found herself often not hungry, or if she had any appetite it was for crisp raw foods, salads, vegetables.

Her friends said, You've lost weight. You look wonderful. How do you do it? She replied: Grief.

Like a lot of truths, it was part.

Her friend Kate said, Why does that work for you. It doesn't for me. When I'm unhappy I eat. I get piggier and piggier. The way I eat, the way I look.

Well, said Clare. Grief can take away your appetite. And then there's anxiety. I think that changes your metabolism.

Grief meaning you don't eat a lot, but anxiety meaning that the little is all gobbled up by this incubus with the voracious appetite to feed its nervous energy. The heart beats faster, it falls in the body, there are obstacles in the windpipe so that air has to be sucked in violent sighs, it is impossible to be still, the mind won't let the body rest but makes it jump up and bustle about the next thing. You sit in a chair, lean back, relax, cross your legs, but before many seconds have passed you are jumping up, after the next thing to be done.

Her friends say, You've lost weight, it suits you, you look good.

Grief, she says, anguish, anxiety.

All truths, but still part.

She noticed her appetite had shrunk, that she didn't care for rich and meaty foods, and cultivated this distaste. Chose not to, made such fat and greasy heavy edibles not an option. Trained herself to follow her desire for the fresh, crisp, light, for vegetables and fruit. Hardly ever cheese, though it used to be one of the delights of her life. Their life.

I don't know why I'm so hefty, says Janet. I go to the gym all the time, I walk every day, take the dog up the mountain, but I can see I'll never be as slim as I was, not even ten years ago, when I thought I was fat.

Why should you be, says Clare. You're a mature woman, aren't we allowed to look like mature women?

I think my husband would like me to be slimmer.

How do you know?

Oh, you know these things.

He doesn't say so.

No.

I think he likes you as you are. I've seen him nestle his hand in your neck. You're happy, that's what counts. Your figure is comfortable with it.

Clare wonders what Geoffrey would have made of this slenderer self. He would have liked it, of course. She's thought like Janet in the past. My husband would prefer me to be slimmer. Not that he ever said so, didn't even hint. Clare herself was very brave about not bothering. One has to be true to oneself, she said. If one is fat, one is. But she would have liked not to be. Slimmer equals sexier, not in the eyes of the world, necessarily, but in the way you feel about yourself, in the clothes you wear, the way you walk, the way your body bends.

And here is yet another irony this widowed state throws up at her (lucky she is a connoisseur of irony): the person who would most have enjoyed the fact that his dying has turned her back into a more slender creature is the one person who can't know. At least, that is what you believed, she says to Geoffrey. Maybe you are wrong, maybe you do know, are somewhere chuckling. Nibbling on this tasty morsel irony.

No wonder people believe in life after death. You can't bear to think that there'll be no more conversations. You can't bear to think you'll never be able to share the jokes.

She realises she can look at food so coolly as she does, so unseduced by its charms, because it was so much part of her life with Geoffrey. Even before they were married. Their first date was her inviting him to a meal—was it, can that be true? Truly the first, or nearly. He came in the bus and was annoyed with himself for not bringing wine; she had most of a bottle of cooking wine and they drank that. It cost 4/6 a bottle, appallingly dear for something calling itself Cooking Wine. Very rough white it was, by Penfolds. And when they got married she had a vision of a lifetime of meals, one or two or maybe three a day, all cooked by her, as was the case with wives in those days, and she understood that meals had to be interesting, had to be an idea, have some mental as well as physical substance, otherwise they'd be a chore. Looking back she thinks she can say that they didn't eat many bad meals, and most of those accidental. The meals were often simple ones, basic even, bread and cheese, pâté on toast, rare grilled lamb chops with mint and garlic, onion sandwiches for supper when they played 500 with her parents, but always she paid attention, good ingredients, real bread, tomatoey tomatoes. Meals were rituals, sometimes simple, sometimes complicated, but always having a meaning. They were part of being married, and now she isn't any more.

You're so much thinner, say her acquaintances.

It is because I have given up conjugal eating, she says.

Once when they were living in Paris she went to a conference in Bergen. She'd never been to a place where food was so absent. You could walk down streets, into cafes and hotels and shopping centres, and never see any. There didn't seem to be any shops selling it, no fruit to be seen, or meat. The woman organising the conference made them a meal which was important, and grand, of reindeer, and a dessert of cloudberries, that her family had climbed a mountain to pick at just the moment they were ripe. A rare and splendid meal. The lunches were sandwiches of donkey salami, or some pale cheese, and there seemed to be a lot of blandly sauced fish. Though breakfasts were copious, and they all got into the habit of eating them as if they didn't know where their next meal would be coming from.

It made her remember Ford Maddox Ford writing that civilisation begins where garlic starts, somewhere south of Paris. Fortunately missionary fervour has spread garlic further these days. Not quite to Norway, it seemed. Norway made her think about Paris, of shopping twice a day, and going into the bakery to get the bread, and spread before you the great displays of cakes and tarts and confectioneries and chocolate, the *charcuteries* and the vegetable markets, all the different kinds of mushroom and potato and lettuce, the yellow chickens and tiny long-necked quail, the slithering slopes of fish, and she thought, the satisfaction of this is a lot to do with visual pleasure and a kind of intellectual awareness of it, as well as trust in its being there tomorrow, you see it but you don't have to buy it, you know it is available so you don't need to choose it, this moment, this day. She never bought cakes, perhaps twice in a stay of six months, three times perhaps, but she loved looking at them, choosing them with her eyes but not her words. She thought that you could become very greedy in a place like Bergen, entirely preoccupied with finding food, so fearful of its absence. But in Paris the eyes are dazzled by the perpetual feast, the senses can graze upon such wonders that actually ingesting them isn't so important.

Of course, you eat. You have a Bresse chicken, or a black pudding, some *girolles* with a bit of veal, a little *pâté de campagne*, some medium-sized oysters, *brandade de morue* from the good place. Comfortably and sparingly you work your way through your list of favourites. Keeping a sharp eye on the seasons, of course. Saying to Geoffrey, Shall we have a little pork roast today (that being the cheapest) and when will we have some foie gras, and let's go over to the Auvergnat shop and get some fresh Cantal, *tome de Cantal*, and make an *aligot* . . . asking for the right kind of mashing potatoes, with cream and olive oil and a great deal of garlic. Paris the most truly thrifty place she knows. No need to buy too much, to stock it up and throw it away. Buy what you feel like and eat it now.

Now she eats a pot of low-fat yoghurt for lunch, and an apple. She can't even remember her hunger for strong savoury foods in the middle of the day. At night she has some appetite, uncorks a bottle of wine, makes a salad, maybe cooks a cutlet, or a potato, slices onions, chops garlic, cuts up tomatoes. Oliver asks can she make a successful omelette with olive oil. You're not supposed to, but he'd like to, and seems to fail. Oh, I think I can, she says, and gets out Geoffrey's solid little metal pan, he was the omelette maker in their household, he'd learnt in France as a student, but she watched him often enough, he taught, explained about sliding the cooked egg back so the surface liquid runs under and is in turn cooked. You put chives in, or mushrooms, a little tomato perhaps, turn it over and out it slides, its middle still runny, self-saucing is a way to describe it. You never wash the pan, just wipe it out with paper towels.

I have made omelettes with olive oil, she writes. But these days I put in a knob of butter as well.

She falls in love with omelettes all over again. Maybe it is the pleasure of using Geoffrey's pan, his method. One day she made one with six eggs, to be eaten in the garden at a small marble table, with sour dough toast. Elizabeth David was right, she said, you should make two omelettes, two of three eggs, six is too many, but she wanted them both to eat together. It worked well enough, though she waited a minute too long to cut it in halves and serve it, there was not much runny sauce. But it was moist and tender, the coffee was strong, the garden was admired: A charming wilderness. A bit chilly, perhaps.

One day in the middle of winter Clare went to Miriam's for lunch. She was feeling very strange, shouldn't have gone, not ill so much as remote, choked up, closed down, as though her body didn't function any more, her brain numb as well, but thinking maybe lunch out would make her feel better. But she couldn't really eat any, not David's green chicken curry or the salmon mousse that came before it, until the dessert. Miriam had made mango ice-cream from fruit she'd puréed and frozen in the summer, when there was a glut of them. It was a faintly creamy cool light essence of the fruit, and eaten with a small flat silver spoon it slipped across the tongue and down the throat in a self-contained comforting refreshing way. And that wasn't all. Miriam had made two desserts. The other was mandarins segmented but still in their shapes and caramelised, which meant covered with a melting toffee, and decorated with strips of candied orange peel. Its tart slightly crackled sweetness was wonderful.

Clare who didn't usually care for desserts ate both of them and felt better. It's very clever of you, she said to Miriam, to know exactly how to make me feel better. You've made a healing dessert. David was playing a CD with songs her father used to sing in the shower.

So kiss me my sweetheart
And so let us part
And when I grow too old to dream
I'll have you to remember
When I grow too old to dream
Your song will live in my heart

She bent her head over the sweet food, the sweet song, and her eyes filled with tears that were a soothing lotion to her tired eyes.

One of the reasons for the greater slenderness—let's be clear about this, she says to herself, you aren't thin, you aren't slim or slender, certainly not lean, you wouldn't have a hope of fitting into the clothes of even fifteen years ago, you're just less fat, but she's too busy enjoying the difference to take much notice of this carping self—one of the reasons is the hectic life she's been leading. Early on she realised that sitting in front of a white page was too hard, she didn't write, she thought, and the thoughts got into her chest and swelled and blocked it and this made her jump up and start doing something to shake them down. They were like a huge rich disgusting meal she couldn't digest, that was giving her heartburn, she had to exercise herself to use up the terrible fat excess of them.

So then she said yes every time anybody asked her to go anywhere or do anything. She spent a lot of time in aeroplanes and even more in airports, wrote papers, shaped panels, all with edgy nervous deadlines. She liked this life, though she complained about it too; she found it exciting though she knew she would gratefully give it up soon.

She started going back through her own books for the material for these papers. At one conference she read a bit about a woman at a market weeping before a stall crowded with olives. The woman is remembering how all her life she went to markets and bought little packets of food and brought them home and unwrapped them before her husband, and how he shared her pleasure, how it was a gift she was giving him as well as food for both of them to eat, and he would open wine to drink with them, he is a man good at wine, and now she won't be doing this any more, she has lost him, not to death in this case but another woman but he is still lost and is grieved for, or rather, she is grieving for herself who has lost him. She looks at the olives and weeps for him. Black olives, green, cracked, peppery, hot chili, small, wrinkled, fat. *And the large violet ones from Tunisia.* There is something surprisingly poignant about that line. *The large violet ones from Tunisia.* When she reads it she feels and knows her audience feels that all the heartbreak of the husband's loss is in that line, and all the more so because it is mysterious that it should be.

In Adelaide at a festival of food writing she goes to a session called Murder in the Kitchen: Killing and Cooking. One of the panelists says that if we are to eat animals it is important that they have a good death. Don't we all want that, mutters the woman next to her. Nick Nairn whom they've all seen doing it on television talks about the pleasure he gets from hunting. Which is better, he asks, shooting a rabbit through the head so that it dies cleanly and instantly, or keeping hens in a battery for the whole of their miserable lives. Of course, there is only one answer, and the audience knows it.

But the star was Cheong Liu. He looked as though he'd

just stepped out of a painting on silk of a sage. Earlier Gay Bilson had said she thought he was one of the two most important chefs in Australia. He is a man whose intellectual engagement with food is matched by the lucidity of his technique, who cares for its philosophical and spiritual elements as well as the pragmatic and practical. These rather grand words are Clare's, she's framed them in response to speakers who pretended to engage with the serious questions they were meant to be examining but were actually saying, I've got this shiny new cookbook just published why don't you go and buy it.

Cheong Liu likes to cook pigeon, and if you are cooking pigeon for a lot of people you need a lot of birds. He described how he kills them himself. He cradles them in his hands, and he showed the gesture, a bit like Picasso's child with a dove, but more enclosing. He cradles the bird, presses his thumbs on the bird's neck and gently squeezes until it dies.

He related how one of his apprentices said to him, If I am going to cook pigeons I need to be able to kill them, too. So Cheong Liu showed him, as he described it to his audience. How do you know when it is dead, the apprentice asked. You feel the life go out of it, said Cheong Liu. You feel the moment when the life goes out of it, and it dies.

The audience was silent. There was a small solemn moment of respect for the life of this bird and all the other animals that die so people can eat them. This was a gift that Cheong Liu gave them, that they must know what they do and do it wittingly and with respect.

Food and death. You can't get away from it. Clare may not care to eat meat very often, but she is totally carnivorous. *Pay attention to what you do.* She and Geoffrey once found that inscribed on the capital of a column in a small town in France. Not fortuitously, they'd read in the guidebook that it would be there and searched for it. *Gara que faras* were the actual words, in the late Latin that turned into French. It could be a motto for most of your life; all of it. She thinks of the wood pigeons that coo in the trees outside her bedroom window, and flutter up from the grass when she walks in her garden. And the pigeon breasts she ate in a restaurant two nights ago, red-rare, juicy, tender, because they were cooked with the care they deserved. A good life, and a gentle attentive death. Afterwards treated with respect for the delicate nourishing entertainment they offer.

Eric Rolls in one of his books celebrating food says the best thing to do with endangered species is to eat them. To breed them, nurture them, sustain them. They will continue to exist, and we to enjoy them. He's speaking specifically about Wonga pigeons, which have lost so many feeding grounds that now they're protected. We should breed them for the table, he says, because most of the pigeons we eat are squabs, killed at thirty days, before they can fly and toughen their muscles, and since they don't eat wild food their flavour is domestic. Wonga pigeons have exceptional flavour, and breeding them to eat would ensure their survival.

Rolls also recommends cooking feral pigeons in olive oil, barely simmering them, for ten hours.

Once she and Geoffrey had gone to a barbecue at the property of a hobby farmer who'd had some Galway cattle; he crept up and shot one to butcher and barbecue it, the creeping and shooting being because that way it wouldn't die in fear and so its flesh would not taste of fear. All this was explained beforehand. But in fact the beef tasted horrible, and privately they'd wondered if they were used to the taste of fear, that their palates were trained to it and liked it, and the taste of a beast happy in its life and unsuspecting in death was horrible to them. But Clare decided the problem was that it was too fresh, too newly slaughtered; it had been shot on Saturday and eaten on Sunday, not being hung at all, not aged. Their friend gave them some hacked up chunks of meat to take home—he was a kind killer but no butcher—taking them down from the tree branches where they'd swung in the shade, covered in sheets and thick with flies, and although she didn't like the smell of them she put them in the freezer. Later she thawed them out and smelt them again and threw them away.

Clare knows a man who became a vegetarian out of intellectual persuasion. He read a book that convinced him that eating other animals is wrong. At first when she invited him to dinner she made meals of vegetables, but she realised this was not what he wanted. He enjoyed meat, and liked to be obliged by politeness to eat it. Whereas her nieces are truly vegetarian. They can't stand meat. Once their mother made a caesar salad, in the classical manner, beating a raw egg with oil and vinegar to make the dressing. She put in cos lettuce, added Parmesan, and fried cubes of bread with garlic in olive oil to make croutons. When it was all tossed together her daughters tasted it and said, Yuk, chicken, we can't eat this. Though in fact they normally ate eggs, were not vegans, ate cheese and even fish sometimes, but the raw egg gave the salad a taste of chicken and they couldn't stomach it.

★

On her own panel Clare talked about one of her favourite topics. How we can be charmed by the dangerousness of food. How we like to play on that thin knife edge that separates delicious from disgusting. She mentioned the pork kidney that Leopold Bloom eats, early in *Ulysses*, faintly deliciously smelling of urine. Or a urologist of her acquaintance who always ate kidneys for breakfast; clearly he had a real interest in them, alive or dead. And of how, when she goes to France the first thing she always eats is *andouillettes*. Fried tripe sausages; you can see the pink furls of intestines when you cut into them, and yes the taste is rather visceral. Her children would never touch them and Geoffrey wasn't fond of them, they would eat *steack frites* while she had the crisp-skinned sausage with mustard and some chips too. And she loved it, but also knew she was being brave, that she was playing with her fear that it might be too visceral, that it would make her palate and stomach heave. It never did, she always enjoyed it, finished every bit, but each time she was aware of the possibility. It's living dangerously, she said. Like flirting with a violent man. And added to the *andouillette* she always ate tripe at yum cha in Chinese restaurants, with black beans perhaps, and tried chicken feet flavoured with star anise in the same spirit, and now always ordered them. And on this panel she went on to describe Philip Searle's banquet (he was the other cook, along with Cheong Liu the greatest in Gay Bilson's mind) in the 1980s that pushed its diners far along this path: the great glass aquarium (specially made) filled with turgid and murky green gunk, like a stagnant pond in which lurked indescribable creatures (the guests' faces a study in doubt), which when served turned into a most sublime and delicate fish jelly with rare morsels of seafood encased in it; the sausage of goose liver like a great turd on a plate; the quails cooked in bladders that were cut open with scissors and waiters with gloved hands pulled out the pale pink bony birds with limbs dangling, in a parody of a caesarean birth. He made his diners face up to the most horrid realities of what they might be eating, and rewarded them with flavours so rare and refined as to be close to a spiritual experience. Well, she said, the whole thing was over the top, the language has to follow it.

Food and death. Food and birth. Pythagoras wouldn't even eat beans, because the souls of the dead might have been reborn therein. Our souls transmigrating into vegetables.

Once at a dinner party they'd played a game about what sort of vegetable people would reincarnate in. Who would be an asparagus, who an artichoke with a prickly hay inside, who the humble essential potato. Clare said she fancied being an onion, so many layers, so delicious, so indispensable, sweet sometimes, sometimes sharp and strong.

What did they say for Geoffrey? Now she thinks he could be grapes, not spectacular, quite humble-looking, on the vine, but turning into wine. Perhaps the most sublime substance you can put in your mouth. She remembers kissing him. Kissing like sipping at the other's being. How it continued to be delicious. She never tired of the taste or the feel, never thought she'd had enough. And this would be why people say kisses are like wine. You want to sip and sip. And they are intoxicating.

When Clare got back from her zipping about the country she asked the old lover if she was thinner or fatter than when she left. Maybe fatter? said the lover. But she didn't think this was true. Her clothes fitted as they had before, that is, a lot were too big, she could still comfortably get into old ones she hadn't been able to wear for years (being thrifty she hadn't thrown them away), and the closer-fitting new ones were fine. She likes her body as it is now, not thin but well-fleshed and an okay shape. She finds a quotation from Naomi Woolf, that fat is sexual in women. Ah. The Victorians referred to a woman's fat as her silken layer. She lies in bed smoothing her fingers over the satin surfaces of her silken layer. Her fingers like the feel of skin, her skin likes to be stroked; this is a fortunate collusion.

And were it to be other fingers . . .

She takes one of her quartered slips of paper. There's a fine black felt pen to hand as well. She writes.

She pleasured me with her fingers.

She looks at the sentence. The letters are small. The fine black pen has shaped them so that in the their smallness they are round and full of curves.

She pleasured me with her fingers.

It's compressed. It's tight with meanings. It will resonate, if the reader listens.

Her breasts jostled softly against mine.

She thinks of Queen Victoria not believing that women made love to one another, because she could not imagine what they did. In a period which could come up with a phrase like *her silken layer*, and name it after the age . . . and the queen. Poor Victoria. Half a life spent lamenting the death of sex, and no imagination.

It is interesting to think how men's flesh is different from women's. Men may be heavily built but there is a lean hard sinewy quality to their bodies. And their tummies, even when they are pot-bellied, are tight and hard. You could play a tattoo on them. Practise a drum roll. There's resonance for you.

Whereas a silken layer should be smooth, not bulgy, and not too muscley, it should be soft. It mustn't ripple or bag or droop, should be cushiony and plump but not take over in its own enveloping way so that the bones can only be guessed at. It's a pleasure to feel the fine sharp bones under it.

Clare ate a large lunch, in a restaurant, with wine, so tonight a salad, with maybe a courgette sliced and quickly cooked in almost no oil with a lot of garlic. Will she ever again become so happy and calm that she grows fat and comfortable once more? Hard to imagine.

.   .   .

You are greedy, says a wife to her husband. Greedy for food, greedy for books, greedy for CDs, greedy for sex. You want too much.

She says this because he has been what they call philandering.

I just want to experience as much as possible, in the short time left to me, he says. You're a long time dead.

Clare doesn't think she wanted too much. Just to keep what she had. Not wanting more. She's never been greedy for experiences; just a few, and savoured.

Dante had his gluttons in his next circle down from adulterers. Gluttony not such a bad sin, a sin of the leopard too. But it is *a ruinous fault*, its perpetrators suffer *eternal, accursed cold and heavy rain*.

When you get to hell, whose gate is wide—remember, narrow is the way and strait is the gate leading to salvation, but the path to hell is easy, it's comfortable, pretty, a primrose path, and the gate wide and welcoming—you are met by the monster Minos who winds his tail round his body, one coil for each level down. The gluttons are two circles down. Dante doesn't say much about them. Mainly that they are swinish and sodden, broken by this endless rain, that is hail and snow as well as foul water. It makes them howl like dogs, and they are guarded by the ghastliest dog of all, Cerberus, who's fed a nasty and foodless meal; Virgil throws handfuls of the stinking earth into all his mouths to make him shut up. The only glutton mentioned by name is Ciaccio, which means pig, but the reader doesn't find out much about him. Clare would like to know just what he did to be sent to hell for gluttony. But it's mainly Florentine politics that is the subject here, ancient internecine feuds (not foods) that nobody would remember if it weren't for Dante, and even then don't bother much. Just enough to give a little bite to the reading of the narrative.

There's a small joke in one of her novels, that some olive oil comes from a particular slope in Tuscany, and while the label doesn't actually say that Dante used it, it implies that he might have. People laugh when she reads it. Though it's a mild joke. And there is a brand of olive oil called Dante. It comes in four-litre tins, with his picture on, the hawk-beaked profile crowned with bay leaves. The oil is not extra virgin, and it comes from Spain.

Clare is writing a novel about a woman who cooks, but she isn't a glutton. She's small and childish in figure, her cooking is a mental activity. Paying attention to food isn't gluttony. It's ritual and ceremony, and a shared life. With husband, lover, family, friends. Or if you are a chef, with anybody who chooses to come and pay.

Food is love. In fact food is quite like sex. (Remembering the gluttons are the slightly worse companions of the adulterers.) There is desire, and its assuagement, when desire dies, until it arouses again. But always there is disappointment; the desire so full of hope, that this time, this time, there will be the perfect connection with the desired other . . . and it never quite is. Nearly, sometimes, a state of almost perfection, but never quite. That is why there is such pleasure in feasting your eyes in Paris food shops; you are never disappointed. The omelette is never too dry, the sauce too salty, the chocolate cake too sweet. No fishbones, no calories, no chance of salmonella.

And the desire for food is like the desire for sex. You can possess it, but only for the moment of eating it. The consummation is the end of it. Of course, food may stay with you in all sorts of unwelcome ways, as indigestion, repetition, flatulence, fat. As well as the perfect idea of itself. Like a lover, in fact.

A fairly new friend, who lives in New York in a loft with a photographer called Alice, is coming for dinner. Eliza, whose life follows a quite other orbit from Clare's, but they touch now and again. Touch, and gaze upon one another. Clare has to stop writing and go to the market. She doesn't know yet what she'll find to cook. It's necessary to shop with an open mind. There will be champagne, and red wine. White if she chooses something fishy. And the conversation will tingle with desire. Will sparkle with desire. Like two wine glasses, gently clinked together in a toast, chiming with a faint crystal music. Too hard and the fine bowls would break, falling into dangerous sharp shards on the table, spilling the wine, spreading red stain. The toast must touch gently, so the glasses faintly chime, the faint vibration sparkles from fingers to flesh, the wine remains in the glass, and nothing is broken.

Nothing spilled, nothing broken. Just sips taken.

the weirdo's kitchen

POLLY SITS AT THE TABLE IN
Clare's kitchen, as people do, the table long, Welsh pine, very
battered, filling the space of the extension they had done ten
years ago. Don't regard it as a kitchen you eat in, see it as a
dining room you cook in, said the architect. They discussed
how they avoided the term *farmhouse kitchen*, but knew that
was a subject. He grew up in one, in Italy, it was where the
family lived. It's great for making dinner for friends when you
are a woman on your own. Clare did not think of this at the
time, Geoffrey was in perfectly good health, but they both
knew that a kitchen separated from the dining room didn't
suit them, either they had to prepare meals in advance, and
they didn't often want to spend the time, or one was in the
kitchen listening to the waves of laughter from the living
room. They said, We have to get the eating and the cooking
together. This kitchen is the solution, tall, full of light, with

211

french windows into the garden, people can sit or stand, eat and drink wine, and all the conversation is happening right there. Some people say they can't make food while there are others about, and it is true it slows you down, but how does that matter? Others like messes hidden, but Clare doesn't find food messes unsightly.

So the kitchen works well in this new life. The perfect set-up for a woman on her own, says Clare. When Janet and Bill are renovating their kitchen, she tries to persuade them to take a wall out, so it opens to the dining room. Don't forget, she says, it's highly likely that one of you will be alone in this kitchen. Leaving the guests to themselves while you're shut away in here. But they choose to remain shut away.

Polly sitting at the kitchen table has a story to tell about her granddaughter going to school for the first time. She comes home, relates Polly, and first thing she says is, I found out what a weirdo is at school today. Oh yes, says her mother—you can imagine, says Polly, not all that thrilled, this is what school's going to be like, loss of innocence etcetera—okay, what's a weirdo? The child says, A weirdo is a woman whose husband has died.

Well, when they've finished laughing at that, Clare says, And this is the weirdo's kitchen, yes, that's right, that's what it is.

Sounds like the title of a book, says Polly.

Polly the only person who gets this anyway near right, ever, prognosticating books, subjects, titles. Not very, but a bit.

Yeah, says Clare. *The Weirdo's Kitchen*. I'll work on it. But she doubts she'll get far. It does sound rather sinister.

a year
and a day

WHEN CLARE PUT THE FUNERAL notice in the newspaper it had at the end *Garden Flowers Only Please.* This was because she didn't want wreaths or formal stiff arrangements, but loose natural bunches of flowers. Her friend Jane who was organising the food for the wake told people that it meant Clare wanted flowers to plant in the garden, so a whole lot of them brought plants growing in pots, and others when they noticed this thought it was a good idea and brought plants later.

Some people in funeral notices put *No Flowers By Request.* A curious phrase; Clare always wondered why you needed to say by request. It made it very peremptory. You could say, *No Flowers, Please*, and that would be a request, and quite polite. Families in such cases often wanted donations given to medical charities. Clare wanted flowers.

Wonderful bunches of them. They filled all the vases and

jars she could find, and the fish-pond, which didn't have any fish in it because it leaked, she hadn't realised how badly until she found it nearly empty and Willy and Nilly belly-up and stinking. It was one of the ways in which life got out of hand. Now the fish-pond full of flowers was a gladdening sight. The funeral parlour men—can you still call them waits, asked Polly—had given her the flowers from the casket, a great spread of white and cream and pale greenish blooms that had hidden the ugly coffin—all coffins were ugly, the fancier the uglier the more expensive, which was why she'd hidden it under flowers—and when people left she gave them a handful each. The rest she put in water and slowly they died until finally there was a small cluster of white roses remaining, which yellowed and dried and didn't fall; a year later they sit in a vase on the bookshelf, wrinkled, papery, but still roses. There were some lovely blowsy ones from people's gardens. A former student brought floppy scented pink old-fashioned ones and with solemn eyes told her the names, which she's forgotten. Her daughter collected the petals that fell and spread them in a shallow basket. She didn't make pot pourri out of them, just spread them out. They have dried and crumpled, but they still smell faintly of themselves.

Sentimental is a word that comes into Clare's head, but she does not believe it. This is ritual; these are small invented ceremonies to hold Geoffrey's memory.

. . .

She gardened quite a lot in his last year. It was easier than doing her own work. Words did not easily come, not the kind she could make use of. Sometimes he'd sit for a while outside with her, other times she worked where he could see her from his window. In the spring the camellias were covered in blooms, huge perfect flowers, probably all the cow manure she'd given them, so he could look out and see the garden full of colour. She hung a basket of birdseed from the eaves outside his window, and king parrots and rosellas came to feed, squabbling and fluttering and observing quite strict hierarchies which occasionally one would try to subvert, sometimes successfully. She told herself she was getting the garden in order for Geoffrey to enjoy, and so she was, but she was also bending it to her will. Geoffrey's life and health were also the subject of her fierce willing, but she knew she would lose this battle. With the garden she might win.

She advertised for a handyperson and got a big strong young man. She'd imagined him as an extension of herself, weeding, planting, tidying up. But he was a bit heavy and plodding, his huge boots stomped on delicate plants if she let him near the beds, and anyway it was clear that he knew what he liked, which was large-scale chopping, slashing, clearing. So he got rid of the privet that seeded everywhere, and in a corner that had become a wilderness he cleared away the thigh-high clotted mass of ivy and a whole lot of rogue bamboo. She and Geoffrey marvelled at how much bigger the garden looked, now that this corner was clear. They discussed what to do with it. At first paving seemed a good idea. Make a formal garden, around the silver birch, with geometrical patterns and plants in pots. She always thinks she's better at plants in pots than in the ground. But when she grubbed around in the soil it seemed rich and friable. A pity to ignore it under paving stones. In a book she found a picture of a woodland garden, with random clusters of rough greyish rocks and drifts of small plants among them. Geoffrey liked that. And they have the rocks, hidden under the ivy were a dozen or more of them, from some forgotten intention of a rockery. So she strews them about in a casual fashion, the effort of course not casual; most of them she can't lift and has to roll with her feet. She orders a teak bench to set against the luxuriant green wall which is all that is left of the ivy, to turn slowly silver in the weather. She parks Geoffrey in the chair, she sits on the bench, and they plan what might be grown. Polly brings special plants from a trip to Victoria, some Chatham Island forget-me-nots and crimson candelabra primula.

But nothing much got planted, though she tried to keep the soil tilled to stop weeds growing, and Geoffrey didn't go out to the garden in the chair any more and the cultivation of this area like all the rest of their lives was suspended. Except the conversation, the conversation was full of incident, of events that had happened, might, ought to, could. Including the plans for the woodland garden. It filled the time while they were waiting. Clare marvelled that Geoffrey was so calm, that he could so courteously and with such kindness talk about things he knew he would never see. They considered how the fish-pond might be made waterproof in a way that wouldn't harm the fish and whether the greengage would get fertilised, since the other sort of plum they'd planted to be its mate seemed to flower at quite a different time. (It didn't, but this year the tree is covered in tiny green fruit; will they ripen or be pecked off by the cockatoos, or simply stay dull and hard and pellety?)

And now it has become a memory garden, planted with the *Garden Flowers Only*. Her brother-in-law offers a medlar because it is a medieval tree, so she and her sister go and buy one. It flourishes, and in the spring almost a year later it is covered with small flat flowers like enamellings in a manuscript. The star jasmine flowers then too, and she cuts bamboo stakes to make a pyramid for it to twine around. The hostias come back bigger than before and she fights the snails for them. The campanulas, the ajuga reptans, the creeping thyme cover the ground, and there are small spots of nearly black heartsease. The aquilegias are spreading, and the geums. The lily of the valley is a small green spike. The dozens of bluebells don't seem to have come to much, but they were put in too late, she left them in the crisper drawer of the fridge long after they should have been in the ground; that was because she was away travelling a lot, it was her year of saying yes to everything, going to Tasmania and Melbourne twice and Geelong and Wagga and Brisbane and Adelaide for a month. Maybe next year for the bluebells; they like to naturalise, anyway. The camellia she moved because its leaves were dying, turning brown and dry, seems to be happy here, and is putting out leaves as though it is as keen as she is to lose its old spindly shape. The acanthus in a dark and hidden corner is hanging on, it's supposed to like full shade. Polly gives her a tree peony, which is terrifying because she knows how difficult they are to grow and what a lot of negotiation and travelling afield even acquiring this one involved. Polly is not like Clare, grateful when humble plants bloom, she is ambitious, she wants to grow grand rare difficult things. And succeeds, as often as Clare does with her common ones.

She leaves the peony in its pot over winter. It disappears. But then with the spring it comes back again, taller and bushier, so she plants it in the ground, in the same place. So far it is happy.

When Elvira comes to visit she brings several pots of small geraniums. True geraniums. Not to be confused with pelargoniums. There's *Geranium cantabrigiense*, specially appropriate, which is a cross between G. *dalmaticum* and G. *macrorrhizum*, with aromatic leaves, G. *clarkei*, the variety called Kashmir purple, G. *maculatum*, good for woodland gardens. They are all pinkish purple colours.

I've marked their names on them, because I know you won't remember. You can call them cranesbill if you like, which is quite charming.

This is a reference to Clare's hopelessness at remembering botanical names. Elvira is always deploring it. Mental laziness, she says. She always uses the true Latin names.

But it's your field, says Clare.

You're the gardener, that's the field.

Elvira is in town on business. She's staying her last night with Clare, otherwise the Hyatt is just so handy for clients. Elvira is slim and dressed wonderfully powerfully, a little red fitted jacket, a short black skirt, black stockings and shoes with real heels. Elvira flies business class and orders limousines instead of taxis.

Nunc est bibendum, she says, as always, so it's one of the bits of Latin that Clare knows. Now for drinks. She's brought Veuve Clicquot. The Widow for the widow, she says. You should drink nothing else.

Of course, says Clare.

Remember what la Veuve said: she drank it when she thirsty, and when she wasn't, with meals and between meals, when she was happy and when she was sad. Etcetera.

I visited Champagne once, says Clare. They seemed to be still doing the same thing. And believing it doesn't make you drunk.

You know, says Elvira, you're lucky. Your husband is dead, you can grieve, whole-hearted and with real tears. But what if the sod is living on the other side of town with his new love, and they are doing all the things that you planned to do, travelling, and spending a year in Rome, and sailing round the Greek islands, all the things you were going to do when the children went and you had enough money. She empties the last of the champagne into their glasses. And are you supposed to stop loving him, just because he's stopped loving you? Can you hate him, wish him dead, ill, dying? Or are you supposed to rejoice in his happiness with his new love, this *boy with the lovely body*? Who's probably a better wife than you were anyway, more wifeish, in the way none of us are any more. The church ought to canonise you if you're that saintly. You feel like a monster if you hate him, another kind of monster if you love him still. And yet, he is still the beloved husband that you've lost. How you could have grieved for him if he'd died, instead of gone off. Rejoice, my dear, that you are saved from ambiguity.

She gets the other bottle of champagne out of the fridge. She always brings two, one for now, one for later, and later is usually now. She raises her glass.

To death, and widowhood, and the absence of ambiguity.

Clare's sip of champagne turns into a gulp. She looks at Elvira, and sees tears in her eyes. She takes her hand.

Oh, admit it, she says tenderly. He did you a favour.

Maybe, says Elvira, flashing four inches of black lace stocking top as she shifts in her chair.

Maybe. She loves the life she's made herself, the business, the travel, the grand hotels and little dinners, the frequent fallings in love. So she tells Clare. But wouldn't she give it all up to have stayed plump and comfortable, married to her childhood sweetheart and teaching Latin to schoolgirls?

Nonsense. Of course she wouldn't. Been there done that, fun while it lasted. Now on to the next thing. She's got grandchildren in most of the capital cities, it seems, flies in, hugs them, dandles them, talks to them, is more fairy godmother than granny though that is what she likes to be called. Why would I want that old life back? What would be the point? Sometimes she has dinner in a restaurant with her former husband. She tells Clare that one of her daughters describes him as a good person to dine with but you wouldn't want to live with him. He doesn't bring the boyfriend, for which she admires his tact.

The lovely boy makes pickles, says Elvira. And jam. From their own fruit trees. His cumquat marmalade is a sensation. And his Christmas pudding has to be tasted to be believed. What's more, he grows blackcurrants so he can make his own cassis.

Entirely admirable.

The good life, dictated by the seasons, says Elvira. Sounds as though he invented it.

· · ·

A year and a day was the space in Clare's mind. Before anything could be settled. Before she could even think what might be, for instance the plans of the lover in his palmy days, whatever. The space of the fairy stories, which have their own wisdom. Though she's not sure what she expected of it, that's the point, that something slightly magic might happen. The garden's known what to do with it, the new plants have grown and flourished, none of them has died, even some that seemed to disappear have come back again. But Clare is less sure about herself. There was one potent morning, more than halfway through, a Sunday, when she woke up and thought, I can manage this life, I know how to do it, and she lit the fire and sat reading a book, for the first time not overwhelmed by the anxiety of all the things she had to do. But this was a simply practical thing, of managing money, paying bills, keeping the house going, a kind of husbandry she knew to be within her achieving. It wasn't to do with how she might live.

Grief has flourished, and she did want it too, has cultivated it, though the kind of happiness that she thought might shelter within it seems rather sickly. Grief itself endlessly surprises, and this is a kind of delight, the way it catches you, and you marvel that it should have such shapes, such resources. For instance when she was in Adelaide, and suddenly realised with an exquisite sharpness that she could not telephone Geoffrey, he was not just in another city, not just absent from her in that old normal surmountable way, but not in life, nowhere she could ever talk to him again.

So even the habit of his death isn't certain. Sometimes she forgets he's dead, expects him home, thinks, when I see him, and realises with a sickening little jolt that she won't again.

And she holds these words in her mind, *not again, never again*, and wonders at them. They have no resonance, they are not believable. She doesn't believe them. It's a trick, a not very good joke, of course it isn't going to be like that. And there's another thought that comes sometimes; Geoffrey what have you done, leaving me like this. It is so unlike you to be so careless. As though soon he'll notice and come running back to find her.

And sometimes grief vouchsafes moments of grace. This is one of her pigeon papers:

> You turn over in bed one morning and there is your young husband lying beside you, his thirty-year-old self, his hair dark red, his face on the pillow turned toward you, looking at you with love in his eyes and— yes, probably—sex on his mind, and the moment is as sweet as if he had leaned forward and kissed you, his soft lips opening and his tongue finding yours, and for a long time, days, perhaps, he stays with you, his head on his pillow, his eyes gazing at you, with that quizzical light of love, and the touch of his kiss on your lips.

She sits in her garden sometimes and reads. Books offer strangely apposite messages. And maybe she chooses them for this. Jim Crace's *Being Dead*, for instance: *Grief is death eroticised*. And he describes sex as a kind of premature death, a trial run, where you actually leave your life—*shuffle off this mortal coil* is the expression he uses—and fall into a post-coital afterlife. Which is only putting into more words what is already in the phrase *little death*. And how the shock of a death sets adrenalin flowing, and adrenalin cannot discriminate, so that at first people feel invigorated and erotic. A friend whose wife died when they were young, not quite thirty, and he's married again since and had a number of children, but still he remembers the grief of his widowing, he tells her about his wife's good friend taking him home after her funeral and fucking him, and how important that was, and how he ran about the town where he lived for months and that was what he did, he needed to do.

She's always known about the energy that keeps people going though funerals, which are the one thing in life which happen to us without our choosing the time of them, unlike weddings or even birthdays, which you can plan for.

She looks around the garden and remembers Geoffrey's wake; the after-the-funeral was at one in the afternoon and it was one in the morning before the last people left; some had gone away back to work and then returned. Everyone said how Geoffrey would have enjoyed it. She ordered two dozen bottles of wine, and her children said, Not nearly enough, so she got another dozen and a half (thinking that people would stay until three perhaps, maybe four, and wouldn't drink much in the middle of a working day), and that still wasn't enough, they had to send a nursing mother out for more, and then later still for pizzas to feed people, late in the evening. The nursing mother being the one sober enough to drive. People sat in the garden and wandered about and talked, there were old people and her contemporaries and her children's friends and small children and babies, and they talked and laughed and she moved from one group to another and it was a wonderful celebration of Geoffrey in his house and his garden.

And the next morning—she was lying in bed, it was a bit after eight, she didn't have to get up, nothing to get up for, when she heard the noise of a truck outside, its engine running while it was parked. It sounded like a delivery of some sort. Not for her. And then she remembered: the clothes drier had packed up, it was more than twenty years old, had simply stopped functioning, and her sister had just bought a new one and done lots of research into the best kind so she rang up several shops and ordered the same machine from the one offering the best price, she might have to do without a husband but she was bloody well not going to live without a clothes drier. The truck would be it. She was just jumping out of bed when the knocker thundered. Found dressing gown and slippers and hurried down the stairs as fast as possible; two surly men on the doorstep.

The laundry was full of empty bottles and even a couple of full ones swimming in the melted ice in the tub. The men looked around, and sniffed. While she moved trays of glasses from the top of the washing machine, so they could put the drier on top of it. You're installing it, aren't you, she said, and they grunted. That was it, they just put it there, she could plug it in. She said, You have to take the old one away, too, and took them out to the garage for it; it was big as well as old and hadn't fitted in the laundry. On the back terrace their feet crunched broken glass. They looked at the debris, the glasses whole and smashed, the fish-pond full of flowers, the messy aftermath. Looks like quite a party here last night, said one of the men. Their disapproval was so sour, so sneering, that she said, Yes, we had a funeral. She didn't trust them to know the word *wake*. And not telling them that it was her husband's.

Afterwards she turned it into a good story to entertain people, the terrible dour critical sniffiness, the positive disamusement, of the delivery men.

She looks over the orderly garden. No sign of the party now. Except every now and then a spike of glass. And still in a pile, round a corner, the shards of a pot full of basil that someone knocked off the terrace. The basil replanted and dead now too, only the pieces of terracotta remain.

.　.　.

Elvira comes visiting again. How are all our cranesbills, she asks, and Clare takes her out to see the true geraniums growing. Not quite lustily, but delicately and well. They sit on the silvery bench in the grieving garden with mosquito coils wafting scented smoke about them. With a bottle of the Veuve Clicquot that Elvira has brought. Some habits are greatly comforting. After a bit Elvira stands up and delicately on her high-heeled sandals makes her way to the geranium plants, pouring a little champagne on to each. Clare looks at her with scandalised delight. Veuve Clicquot, poured on geraniums.

A libation, says Elvira. You always have to use the best wine for libations. She brushes her nose across a medlar flower. The diamond earrings she bought from a little jeweller she knows in Bangkok flash discreetly, but precisely. You have to wait until medlars are bletted, before you eat them, she says.

Sleepy, says Clare.

What?

Bletted. Sleepy.

Oh. Yes. Apparently they can go from the point of perfect ripeness to disgusting rottenness in a minute, so people used to wait up all night with a candle and a plate and knife, watching for the moment. I read about that in a novel. Elvira pulls a yellow leaf off a camellia. You are lucky, she says, you can grieve.

Maybe I am, says Clare to herself. Geoffrey didn't leave her, didn't betray her, didn't prefer another person, another sex. Though sometimes she has reproached him, directly: Why did you leave me, how could you be so cruel.

The hardest thing, says Elvira, for a person like me, in my situation, is hanging on to what you once had. Believing that when you were in love, once, you were. I've not always been very good at that.

It was true, says Clare. It still is true, of then. I remember how much he loved you. I was there. I remember when the children were born, how he looked at you.

Oh, the children. He was always besotted with the children.

And you. He loved you. You don't fake that.

Ah me, sighs Elvira. *Eheu, eheu*. Oh yes, I do believe it. I tell myself to do so. You can't let the present taint the past. But it is another country.

But the wenches aren't dead. We're as lusty as ever.

And still committing fornication. She snorts into her champagne and nearly chokes.

Do you ever have affairs with married men, asks Clare.

Only when it's safe.

Safe.

When I know they won't get some stupid idea of leaving their wives and coming and living with me.

Ah.

Mind you, it mostly is. Thoroughly safe. The thing about most men is, they're faithful to their marriages, they're just not faithful to their wives.

Is that a paradox?

Not at all. They want to be married, they want to stay married, the woman they're married to is a nice habit. They just want to fuck other women but not leave their wives.

But sometimes they do leave.

True. And you'll find it's nearly always because they've slept with the wrong woman, some female who decides she wants to be the wife and inveigles him into giving the other the shove. Exceptions, of course, some really bad marriages, deeply unhappy people and all that, which is why I said you've got to watch that it's safe. But it's pretty generally true. That's why you see second marriages that are no better than the first. Worse sometimes.

But what if it's the women leaving? That's supposed to be more common.

Oh yes indeed and that's a whole other matter. I'm talking about nicely married men sleeping around.

Faithful to their marriages but not their wives. Positively epigrammatic, says Clare.

Feel free, make it your own.

Two women, sitting in a garden that one of them has made, one in a black linen shift dress which you know is fabulously expensive but not why you know, with evident diamonds, the other in leggings and an old coral-coloured clinging silk shirt, neither quite offering glimpses of skimpy black lacy bras—Elvira's first rule of underwear: it's for the wearer's benefit, no one else's, and Clare suspects that one of Elvira's little wisps of lace costs more than all her underwear put together—decadent women, dissolute women, desirable women, guzzling champagne and secrets, women who had they been their mothers that age would have been considered elderly, though they suspect now that maybe their mothers didn't quite believe it either. They just went along with it, and these women don't. Age is a figment of other people's imaginations.

In fact, says Elvira, it's the present that's another country, it's here that we do things differently.

Elvira's good at change. She turned herself from a blue-stockinged (literally at times, under large woollen skirts and bulky pullovers) teacher of Greek and Latin into an expert on computers, taught herself by reading books and magazines, anything she could, so that they went from being incomprehensible to a language she spoke intimately, and from then to running her own custom-made software business, turned herself from a plump contented wife to a lean and glamorous woman of affairs.

I saw the writing on the screen, she says. Didn't take genius. Four Latin students and none at all in Greek were pretty soon going to add up to redundancy.

She read an article in a newspaper, long before computers were household objects, saying that Latin scholars made the best computer programmers, and off she went. But could still be teaching in a school, had Bruce not decided to come to terms with his sexuality.

Besides, she says, doing something for a while is enough. You don't have to do it for always.

Yeah, I know, says Clare, I think that too. But I'd like to have gone on living with Geoffrey a hell of a lot longer.

Ah yes, yes indeed. She stares into her glass, then wriggles and crosses her legs, no stockings today, a lot of slim tanned leg (fake, the tan, says Elvira) and Clare notices again that she often moves abruptly when there's an unpleasant thought about, as though sloughing it off. Ah well, she says, no point in repining. Needs must when the devil drives. She stretches her arms over her head, the shapely well-muscled arms of a woman who goes to the gym. One day I'll have a garden again, she says.

I thought you did, your gorgeous rooftop creation.

Clare has visited her apartment in the city; it is the top floor of an old wool store, and has several enormous terraces with formal beds, trees in tubs, box hedges, gardenias scenting the night air, iceberg roses trained as standards.

Garden. That's not a garden, that's a *parterre*. I wander in it like a Louis XIV whose Versailles has shrunk. I don't do anything in it. The people who installed it come and tinker with it from time to time. I wouldn't dare touch it. Even the watering is automatic.

Install. Tinker. It sounds like something on a computer.

Yeah. The nearest you can get to a virtual garden and still have real leaves. You might wonder, it's all so perfect, but I know they're real. The young woman who maintains it comes and washes the city grime off them, every so often. And if something isn't flourishing, it's discreetly removed and replaced with one in good nick. How's that for a metaphor for our times?

Clare shivers. Everything disposable. Nothing irreplaceable.

No, says Elvira, one day I'll have a real garden, and grub in it and get dirty, and let chaos reign.

The other night, says Clare, I was watching the gardening programme on ABC and there was a marvellous garden in Western Australia, in the desert. The woman who'd made it pointed out wisteria and blossoming fruit trees and oh all sorts of things that would be wonderful anywhere, but in the desert . . . stunning. Especially roses. The interviewer said, Tell me, what is the secret of your roses. Well, she said, I dig a hole eighteen inches deep and in the bottom of it I put a dead animal.

Wow, said Elvira.

And the thing is, he didn't ask her what sort of animal, and whether she killed it especially, like a sacrifice to the gods, or whether she often had dead animals around. Does she catch possums? The neighbours' cats? Does she slaughter a cow? Mice? I've been wondering ever since. How can I possibly emulate that handy hint?

Elvira laughs. Stick with the blood and bone, my dear. Nice and sanitised, in a packet.

It is time for her to go. Her car is waiting. Tonight she is dining with a lover. I must go and bathe and perfume myself. And put on my new dress.

No, says Clare. Not a new dress! I don't believe it.

Sarky bugger.

Who this time?

Colette Dinnigan. I wondered if I was too old and then I tried it on and decided I wasn't.

Beware of the mutton dressing as lamb.

Oh, I do, I do, never fear it. This one's black, with faint brown roses. Pink, now, I might have drawn the line at pink.

They hug one another for quite a long time before Elvira gets in the car. Remember, keep on drinking la Veuve, she says.

I'll have to write a best-seller first.

Well, okay, any decent bubbly.

Clare goes back to her garden and sits on the bench. A blackbird is trilling. The light is falling greenly through the leaves. She can have a green thought in a green shade. There are words that the mind gathers and lays like balm on the heart, believing that they will heal, but still the heart aches. Surely a little less? Maybe for a moment.

She wonders whether it is because of the movie that she thinks of Elvira as a tightrope walker. A movie she saw when she was young and in love and will never watch again in case it is not as good as she remembers it. Elvira stepping along her high wire. Such poise, such talent, such skill, but above all such will, to keep going, not to fall, never for a moment can the will flag or she will be lost, all her skill will not avail her and she will tumble ungracefully down, splat, limbs all jangled, no safety net to catch her, the Colette Dinnigan split and blooming with blood jelly roses. Of course Elvira has no regrets, they might sap her will. She moves swiftly, agile, as if dancing, not letting herself look back along the tightrope of her life, so clever she makes it look easy, and only a fellow *funambule* knows how hard it is.

The coils are burned out, the mozzies are biting, the evening is chilly. She winds some more of the star jasmine around its pyramid of bamboo, gathers bottle and glasses and Persian cushions, and goes inside. The bottle isn't empty, and she stoppers it. You can have enough champagne, even the Widow.

remarrying

THERE'S AN ARTICLE IN THE
weekend paper about John Bayley and how he is getting
married again. So soon, is the implication, after his devastating
loss of Iris Murdoch, which he wrote about so movingly, so
freely. Months after her death her medicines were still in the
fridge, her clothes lying about. People thought that the rest of
his life would be a footnote to his forty-three years with her.

He's going to marry their old friend, Audi Villers, whom
he has known for years; she and her late husband Borys and
Iris and John used to holiday together. Later the widowed
Audi would help him shower Iris. Friends seem to be saying
that they are so much in love, that it is a marriage made in
heaven. Bayley says, It's a question of having started out as
four, then three, and now we are the two survivors. So we are
just doing what's logical for survivors.

A spokesman for some national bereavement council says

people often think the widowed remarry too soon, on the rebound. As if there were only one way to grieve. In fact, he says, an early remarriage can be a sign of great love for the dead spouse. That elderly people often remarry quite quickly because they are so used to being married the death of the partner leaves a void that they can't stand. Whereas people who are married less time, who are widowed at a younger age, often never marry again. He also says that people do not understand the utter devastation of bereavement, unless it happens to them.

(You could consider here Ethel Kennedy, pregnant when Bobby was assassinated, thirty-four years later still not choosing to be a wife again.)

It's often children who object to a parent's remarrying, says the article, but Bayley and Iris never had any. Furthermore, she had been ill for a long time, he had been getting used to the idea of her death. The article finishes by saying the ghosts of the past will not trouble the newlyweds, the past is what they have in common. Far from never talking about it, it is probably what they will do, most of the time.

Bayley is seventy-four, the age of his wife-to-be isn't mentioned. Apparently he wrote that he and Iris were never much interested in sex, even at the beginning. They used to like kissing one another's arms. So you can speculate that maybe sex won't have much role in the new marriage. Maybe it will be mainly friendly, and not totally and utterly erotic, as was the love of Iris and Bayley, from the moment he saw her riding past on a bicycle, and fell in love with her, and stayed that way all her life and after. Never needing children, just Iris.

listening to herself living

YOU WILL SOON FIND ANOTHER lover, said the man who had been that. The light leaking round the edges of the curtains was pewter grey and cold, the room warm and yellow lamplit. She sighed.

You will soon find another lover, he said.

Would you be jealous, she asked.

This was when they were still lovers. They were in bed, having one of those conversations full of the curiosity that belongs to such moments.

Oh no, he said. I would like you to tell me all about it. I think I am a voyeur at heart.

Not even a little bit jealous?

I don't think so.

She thought she could feel put out by this, but then remembered that jealousy wasn't part of their affair, she was not jealous of his life with his wife, this was their own small

234

illicit moment of adultery, secret, private, and when they went out of it they went out into another world (not the real world, she said, this is the real world, but this was a remark that only could exist in the small illicit space of the adultery) and became quite different people.

Ah, she said to herself, not to him: another lover; when that happens, if that happens, I shall not tell you about it. But she wondered if she meant it. She would not know until the moment came. She was reading her life like a book that someone else was writing; not until she turned that page would she know what she was going to do.

This was her year of being wicked. So she described it. All those years, decades, of being good, of being a good wife, no eye or mind or body for anyone else but her husband, but being good as well, and now she is being wicked. Which is why she was in bed with this man.

Being wicked. Another way of putting it is accepting new experiences as they offer. The good person would have said, no, not proper, not a good idea, not right. This one says, I wonder what it would be like? And goes ahead and finds out.

And then writes it down. Transcribes the stories that her life offers as she turns its pages. Maurice Schwob says poets listen to themselves live and sing what they hear. In her case, she said to herself, the singing is for me, nobody else will hear. Or read. She will not publish these stories, her grief and the expression it's found in making love will remain as secret and as private as the adultery. Which means that she gave them to her lover to read. They delighted him. It was like making love twice, once in the flesh, again as these other people.

But then the wife found out about the adultery, and it stopped.

But there were still the stories. She wrote them and her lover read them. Keep them safe, she said. They are a secret. One day the wife found them and she read them too.

They are love letters to you, says the wife to the husband.

But I am not the person in the stories, he says.

What nonsense.

I am not. They are fictions.

That is special pleading. It's a lie.

Moreover, the wife does not like the portrayal of herself, and tells the mistress so.

The mistress says that in these stories the wife is not her. The wife has no name. The mistress has a name, but the wife doesn't. She is left as a kind of lay figure. The mistress could write a story in which she tried to capture the nature of the wife, gave her form and character, but she thinks that would be taking liberties.

You think it's okay to sleep with my husband, but not make me a fully fleshed character.

That was life. This is art.

Art. It's not very nice to read all this detail in a story about your husband.

You weren't supposed to read them. How would you? I was never going to publish them.

But you wrote them.

I'm a writer. That's what I do.

How could you do such a thing? I don't mean the writing, I mean the . . . other.

It was meant to be secret. For comfort. And for grief. For

a little while. Illicit, not known. It would have stopped and stayed that way. Not known. Not existing any more.

Until he started leaving me.

Ah. I had not thought of that. That was never my idea.

But you went along with it.

I did not think it would happen. And you see it hasn't.

You'd have been pleased about it.

No. No I wouldn't. I wouldn't have known what to do.

Have a nice time. Enjoy yourself.

He's your husband. I don't actually want to live with your husband. Different habits.

Sex. It's some of the best writing you've ever done about sex.

Not really.

Pretty explicit.

I'm often that. All my books have sex in them. I put in something you told me once, remember? Making love under the willows by the lake. With that man you nearly left your husband for. I've always written about sex. But these are about mourning. About grief.

The other woman looks at her.

It's hard to explain.

Yes.

But it's important. It's the hard things that are important. It's because it's hard that I have to try to do it.

And what you've ended up with is love letters to my husband.

I think if you look carefully you will see that they are love letters to my husband.

★

237

Or so the conversation might go. Something like that. Maybe not so neatly, but that the gist of it. It's the mistress that's writing it. Ending up with her saying that she has let go. That's the phrase she uses. She has let go, stepped back, turned away, and the stories are a way of doing that. The wife is a remarkable woman, and when she has said these things, the various versions of them, chooses to remain friends. The lover wants it, the mistress wants it, she will want it too.

The writer thinks of writing it all down in detail, this working back to the friendship, as a kind of tribute to the wife, and as well it's a terrific narrative, but decides not to. Decides to leave her the lay figure, not a personality, not a person. This is something of a sacrifice, because the wife has achieved this marvellous degree of unstereotypicality, she would make a good character, but writers cannot always be cannibals. So they tell themselves.

Clare has usually felt strongly irritated by writers who write about being writers. She's always avoided it herself. Who wants to read about what it is to be a writer writing about being a writer writing about being a writer, like the old Uncle Toby's oats packets which if you could only squeeze yourself small enough you could walk into forever and make yourself a master of infinite space, only the wrong way round. Infinite smallness. But now her life has begun throwing up stories, they fall around her like pages of a book, and when she picks them up they find their own order.

Ah, but do not underestimate the writer in this; the vasty subconscious that knows what's going on even if she doesn't, the imagination that sees how to do it.

The wife is quite clear that the writer ought to stop this

writing. But they are what I do, says the writer. She thinks that the wife has the husband to herself in every important way but she has the pleasure of finding words as she wants them. As she wants them, not as they are. The wife has the marriage, she has the stories. Of course these stories are not the wife's version, or the husband's, though it is possible that they would be closer to his. If the wife doesn't like it she can write her own. Except one of the nice things about the wife is that she doesn't want to be a writer, and since almost everybody else the writer meets does, this is a great charm.

Clare is in a state of nervous excitement over what her life is offering her to think about. A whole lot of things that hadn't occurred to her before. She'd always known about the pairing of sex and death, from Alfred Deller singing, *I weep, I die, I die for love of thee*, to Georges Bataille pointing out that after sex the only thing left for people is to die because once they've reproduced themselves they're redundant. But now there's this discovery of the merging of grief and sex, how the sex doesn't only comfort the grief, it intensifies it, so she can live in it and desire it. She has learned that grief is like desire, that she needs to feel it as she feels desire. Grief isn't sadness. Grief is a kind of passion. Pleasure, pain, a whole panoply of experience. A gamut. It is ambiguous, paradoxical, counter-existing. Splendid.

And all these things she has already written in stories.

And now these stories that she always told herself were unpublishable. Because she would not have the wife read them. They were written for herself. And she could show them to the lover, because he shared the secret they were about. Maybe she would put them with her papers in the National Library. When everybody is dead, they could be . . . resurrected may be the word.

But—and here's the irony, an exquisite one—now the wife has read them and knows the secrets they contain, they are no longer unpublishable. Now the wife has read the stories she has given to their author the possibility of publishing them.

When she wrote her first story ever she didn't imagine anybody reading it. She wrote it because it was there to be written, a marvellous narrative, that she could form and shape and find her own words for. She gave herself all the freedom she needed in following her imagination. She was thrilled when it was accepted but then when it was published she was astonished by the result. Of course the story, though a construct, a fiction, got its elements quite directly from people and things that had actually happened, first stories usually do, and she was naively shocked to find readers observing the connections. She had imagined the story, but not its readers. Not even the man on whom it was based, her old professor; it had never occurred to her that he might read it. That was almost a criminal innocence, she thought, looking back. Not because he might not have liked himself, she thinks he might have been flattered, but because she ought to have foreseen it. Innocence is not always virtue.

When he died, some time later, her words were quoted in his obituary. The archivist from the university he'd worked in rang her up and asked her permission to put it in his files. But it's fiction, she said, it's a story. Oh, said the archivist, you put it so well. We all know it's him.

240

It had always disturbed her, that response, the obituary, the archives. It was fiction. She'd made up names, events. It was as much about her as it was about him, the ignorant schoolgirly student, it was about her own education. She had offered it to the world as her own narrative. You could draw parallels between it and real people, real events, but you couldn't say the story was them. If she'd been asked to write an account of her relationship with this man she would have done it quite differently. Marked fact from speculation. Not invented.

It's not history, she said to the archivist. You can't let people think it's history.

Can you hear a shrug at the other end of a phone line? I suppose I could mark it as fiction, if you like, he said. But people know it's him. You catch him so well.

She wrote another story, a sequel, after the old prof's death, finishing the narrative of his life, with his suicide, in fact, and it an entirely factual story, no inventions, but discussing her speculation with the reader, wondering what could be known, telling the reader she was imagining him dead in a squalid boarding house with a bag of oranges rotting as the hot summer days passed. The oranges documented in the newspaper report, the rotting her idea. Discussing the way she had turned him into fiction in that long ago first story. Redressing the balance, putting the earlier one in perspective. She's learned sophistication in her writing, and how to play with narrative forms, how to use her own voice.

Sometimes she writes essays. She knows the difference between a story and the sort of thing that claims to be non-fiction. Take *Villette*, she says. *Villette* is a fiction. Maybe you can say that Charlotte Brontë based it on her own falling in love with a professor in Brussels, but you cannot say, It is the story of her life. It has autobiographical elements, but it is not her autobiography.

She is surprised that it should be necessary to keep on spelling out these things.

The other thing she learned from that first story was that a writer writes to be read. This is what she does. The work does not achieve its existence until it has been absorbed by another set of eyes. And of course it is what she has been wanting all along. No matter how much she told herself it was a kind of therapy to get her through a bad time, and that was true at first, she wrote as a gardener might mattock up hard earth, or a confectioner make elaborate cakes or a window cleaner polish glass to invisibility, because that is what you do and when you are unhappy you do what you do with energy and conviction, so maybe you will be tired and forget, but at least you are doing. When being is unbearable. But she's known for a while that since the only valuable thing a writer can do is find words for things so other people may know them too, so she has wanted her stories to be read. And now they can be.

This is the gift of her lover's wife.

Once upon a time . . .

There was that time, quite short, when her lover thought that he was going to be able to walk away from a marriage that had ceased to be interesting, to him or his wife, in an amiable, it's been great, have a nice future, we'll always be friends sort of way, not denying affection or connection, If she were ill, he said, I would go and nurse her, and it was at this time that Clare, a bit dizzy from the sudden move from sex nicely enclosed in the tight little box of adultery to lifetimes together, said that she would have to wait a year and a day before she could know what would be right for her. The fairytale length of time, the year literal, the day figurative, meaning a year plus a bit more time. From Geoffrey's death, she meant.

The year and a day was a ceremonial space, for mourning. Something that was owed. The least, you could say.

But it is also necessary as a time for understanding. For coming to terms. All her writing of stories an attempt to achieve that, and she hadn't yet. Might not have done so, in the potent ceremonial lapse of time. But she certainly hadn't yet. She was in no fit state.

She suspects a lifetime and a day might not be long enough.

If a good fairy were to come and offer her a wish? Once she'd have said, perfect eyesight, all the time, all my life. Followed by eating as much as she liked and staying slender. But now there is no question. Any offer of a wish, she will choose being unwidowed. She will ask for Geoffrey back. And she wouldn't be like Swift's foolish Struldbrugs, organising eternal life but forgetting to mention eternal youth. She'd have him in brilliant health, not necessarily a lot younger, maybe her own age, and in health and vigour for another couple of decades, at least. No point in being modest, with wishes. Firm and clear and spell it out.

Not forever of course. Death eventually is essential. But they could do it together.

But the thing here is, being widowed is so much part of her now, is so important to what she's become, could she undo it? She certainly doesn't want to as things stand, it's hers, it's priceless, it's taken enormous work and concentration and anguish to achieve. She likes the clarity it's given her, the awareness, the insights. Likes having become a harder wickeder more selfish person. Could she go back to being the wife she was?

Oh yes. For Geoffrey she could.

Well, good fairies are not known for being good at putting people back together from ashes. She's never heard of it. She's heard of good fairies but only in old books, no recent sightings. *That leg which was lost in America, that arm in Africa*, so Donne describes not just the resurrecting but the reassembling of the body . . . but it takes the Last Judgment to put those together. It is not Geoffrey who will unwidow her.

Clare is a naturally optimistic kind of person. Her Pollyanna instincts are highly trained. She may be myopic, but is hawk-eyed when it comes to searching out silver linings. No luck so far. The best she can do is consider blue skies rather harsh: clouds may be a comfort, even grey, even indigo. Perhaps a dull pewter colour.

Still, she went on searching her life for positive ideas. There weren't many. Only one that had any legs at all, as they used to say in her bureaucratic days. And they were pretty tottery. But could be trained to support her, maybe could be walked on, could even manage to dance, one day. That idea was being her own mistress. That was good. Of course being somebody else's mistress was very nice too. But you could still go on being your own as well as somebody else's mistress, which might sound like a paradox but could be a given. But being a wife again, a wifeish person. No, Geoffrey was the only man she would want to be unwidowed by. But a man in her bed, and in her life sometimes, to have conversations with, a man who read the same books, what a treasure.

Once she bought a book at an airport because she'd read everything she had with her. Ann Tyler, *The Patchwork Planet*. Oh yes, her lover said, I read that a couple of months ago. Very good, but the ending rather disappointing. Arbitrary. Ostentatiously confounding, somehow.

Oh yes, she said, exactly what I thought. And did you see, it's dedicated to her husband, who's just recently dead, and it's full of sad old widows with nobody to bury them.

Yes, he said.

And he bought a copy of Irving's *A Widow for a Day*, and let her read it first; she loved it because it was about writing. The widowing wasn't very sad, either.

A man in her bed, in her life. Accidentally or on purpose reading the same books. A man to have conversations with. But a man in her house. No.

Well, it was all theoretical now. It wouldn't happen. Not with this lover. Former lover. He was happily staying where he was. Clare suspected that he let his wife find out so that she would call him back to her. Suddenly finding change too dangerous. The workings of the human heart are hidden in murk and quite bloody. Or as Ted Hughes says, *What happens in the heart simply happens*. So he is safely called home, to comfort, a constructed past, and the hope that compromise may be done with integrity. She wishes him well, both of them well, it is the right suitable proper thing to do, she would have it no other way, and if at moments she regrets he isn't choosing his old world well lost for love, they both have read enough books to know that it is always a disaster and death its only logical end. The only moment of logic involved.

And anyway she's always understood that its illicitness was its power. Something that you can hardly ever have, that has to be . . . she was going to say snatched, but is that the word? Greedy children snatch toys, or food; there seems to be something bumbling and obvious about snatching. Public, even, if you're a bag snatcher. Body snatchers are more secretive, and planning, so are baby snatchers. But all rough. Whereas an affair is delicately plotted, and its givens are always somebody else's. That is its wickedness, and when it works, its delight. It thrives on parting, separation, unprivate meetings where good behaviour must be sustained. It hides behind veiled eyes, bored conversation. This creates longing. It fans desire. You don't need languid afternoons in shuttered rooms to feel the heat of desire. It is stoked by its own impossibility. If it could happen whenever it wanted to it might not want to.

Actually, they were never good at bored conversation. Even now, when they are friends, their conversation is full of passion.

There are different kinds of love making. There are the plotted voluptuous adrenalin-fired dialogues of adultery, and the long slow luxurious murmurings of marriages.

She remembers the image of herself as the koto, the beautiful long wooden finely crafted musical instrument, and the tense erotic chords that can be drawn from it by skilful fingers, practised learned fingers. But even without the music, it is still a beautiful intricate instrument; the music is mute, but is still present. The koto always contains its music, whether there is someone to play it or not.

Hang on. This is a metaphor. Stock in trade of the writer.

Very nice to illustrate, or illuminate. But do you want to live one? Its maybe dismaying implications? You don't want to live a metaphor, but a life. She's not a koto, but a woman, and quite capable of playing her own music. She thinks of the pianos in old movies, with their own hands to play them, and giggles. No. Not like that. Like a person who lives in her own body and her own head, and hears her own music, and makes it up and writes it down. As Marcel Schwob said, who listens to herself living, and sings what she hears.

You'll soon find another lover, said the man who had been that.

Maybe she will. Maybe one day he'll be another narrative.

The wife, the lover, the mistress, the husband.

It is time to give up the language of fairy tales. Stop claiming the archetypes, hinting at modish Greenaway mysteries. The lover, the ex-lover, the man who was her lover, its periphrasis is starting to sound portentous. Call him Henry, that's what she called him when he rang up and it wasn't private. Hello Henry, she'd say, and he'd know that others were listening. Another game. Henry, the married man. The fairytale is over. She is Clare, and the wife . . . well the wife is not to be named, she is still in her fairy story, has gone off to her happy ever after. Time for Clare to return to the named, the concrete, the particular.

But she won't give up the year and a day. Clare can hope its space is magical, she knows it is ceremonious. She will wait and see what other pigeons have come home to roost by then. If not in her life, then her pages.

★

When she meets him for coffee one day Henry says to her, I've been thinking, and I have to say, I've come to the conclusion that, I don't think, I mean, I'm not too happy about those stories of yours being published.

Clare is suddenly dazzlingly angry.

I. I. There is no I about this, she shouts inside her head, but not aloud, she is folding in on herself, like a desert plant, offering no surfaces.

This is the man who read the stories with small secret smiles, who did not say much but whose eyes shone when he looked up from her words. This is the man who said, when he wanted to run away with her, It'll be my claim to fame. I like the idea of going down in history as the lover of the famous novelist.

Oh history, she'd said. Fame.

Certainly. Both. And me part of it. He'd kissed her as though offering fresh material, that would be beyond any she'd already imagined.

The thing is, he says now, they're, well, they're intimate. I've been thinking, would I want my children reading this, knowing these things.

Clare looks at him with wide hard eyes.

When he was about twenty, she says, my son went to the coast with his girlfriend, you know how he's always had exceedingly beautiful girlfriends, and this one was, and it rained all the time, and they were in this tiny tent on the beach, and they spent the time, well, some of it, with him reading my stories aloud to her, it would have been my first collection. He hadn't read them before either. When he came home he said, Wow Mum.

Another coffee, asks Henry.

Mm, she says. He said, Wow Mum, and his eyes were shining. I had to think what was in those stories. They weren't particularly autobiographical, no more so than anything a writer writes, you know I've always said that you write fiction but at the same time it's not possible not to be auto-biographical. But the thing is, he was pleased. He looked at me with—and I thought about this—intrigue, and pleasure, but most particularly with respect. And after all, why not. Why shouldn't your children see you as human, just like them. As sexy, for god's sake.

I just thought, there are some things that should be private. I just think, I know how . . . I think it would be better if they weren't published.

I again. The tricky I. The lying I. But still she doesn't say anything, just looks at him with those wide hard eyes.

I hope you don't mind me saying this.

I'm sorry, Henry, she says, in the voice of one who is not sorry at all, though she is a bit, for him, but he ought to know that the messenger always runs the risk of being shot. He looks like a messenger, no longer the hero, the lover; a middle-aged man, portly, nervous. I'm sorry, Henry, she says. They are my stories. What I do with them, well, I can't possibly let you tell me.

Well, yes. It's just that I . . .

She wants to say, Shut up, just shut up. She wants to say, You are a shit. She wants to say, Do you know what you are doing here? But she's not going to be so friendly as any of these protests would sound. Instead, she says in a strangled voice, You disappoint me.

She stares down at her cup, eyes even wider to stop tears falling out of them. You've got to let me have my stories, she said. And stood up and left the cafe, leaving him to pay.

She doesn't let the tears fall. She walks around the square and across the road to her car. That Geoffrey bought so they could go travelling. She says to herself, He doesn't even know he is breaking my heart. And she resolves that she must never let him do that again. She presses a button, and the voice of Elisabeth Schwartzkopf singing the second of Richard Strauss's four last songs fills the car. *The garden is in mourning* . . . This is what matters. Art not quite making sense of life, but offering its heart-stopping beauty.

She knows that conclusions aren't come to just once. They have to be come to over and over again.

her own
mistress

WHEN CLARE TOLD ELVIRA SHE
was going overseas for a month, to England and France, Elvira
said, Oh good. I'll tell you my cure for jet lag.

Nunc est bibendum? says Clare. The Widow, again?

That too, in moderation. But mainly water, for drinking.
Buckets, really buckets. But that's prevention, not cure. No.
This is cure, and brilliant. Sex. You get off one of those damn
dawn flights into Heathrow, straight into the arms of your
lover, who whips you off to an okay hotel—the Hilton will
do, he can push your luggage on a trolley through one of
those endless walkways, it's quite easy—and you fall on the
bed for a good fuck, and I mean good, a lovely how-
wonderful-to-see-you-after-all-this-time fuck, and then a
nice cuddle. After that a shower, fresh clothes, and a car into
town, and you can be in Harrods when it opens at ten. Or the
merchant bank of your choice. Fresh as the proverbial daisy.

Mm, said Clare. What if you take your lover along with you?

Nah, said Elvira, doesn't work. He has to be there, waiting. It's the circadian rhythms, you see, he's there, he's in harmony, and you catch the rhythm from him. Fucking a local makes you a local.

Rubbish, said Clare, looking at Elvira to see how straight a face she was keeping. Elvira stared back with limpid serious eyes.

You reckon it works?

Absolutely. Every time.

How many times?

Now Elvira's face did crack a little. Every time I've tried it. It's a controlled experiment, you see. Sometimes I've done it, sometimes not, and I tell you, there's no comparison.

Well, said Clare, and she heard her voice sound waspish, maybe there's a nice little business opening. Lovers waiting at major airports to cure jet lag. People could book them at the travel agent, along with their tickets. You choose your agent not because they're good at travel bookings but by the sexiness of their clients. Businessmen can make it a tax deduction.

Clare! That's prostitution. Do you see me as the madam of an international string of brothels? Her face cracked again. Don't think I haven't thought of it. But I reckon it's got to be a real lover. Not a commercial transaction. You've got to arrive dizzy with lust for a special person, as well as jet lag. That's what spins the circadian rhythms round.

Honestly, said Clare.

And it's such fun. Such an achievement. Getting yourself all beautifully washed and perfumed and clean-knickered in one of those tiny little aeroplane lavs. Gives you something to do, which is after all the problem of long-distance travel. I tell you, I recommend it.

Thanks, says Clare. Okay for you business-class travellers. But it evidently wouldn't work in economy: even tinier lavs.

Not really. You'd be surprised at how similar they are. Both absolutely exiguous. No, it's a matter of will, that's all.

The trouble with Elvira is that she's nearly always right. Whenever Clare has been able to check. And the other trouble, much more serious, is that she's easier to admire than to emulate.

. . .

There's a nice irony here, which is that she is meeting a lover. In a way. Oliver her first ever lover and perfectly ardent correspondent, who has been emailing her all year, from whom she has a volume of correspondence larger than an epistolary novel. An epistolary novel in four volumes, she said to him, not entirely a joke. She's thought of publishing it. It would need a lot of editing, of course. It could be a joint project, going through this mass of paper (she has kept it all on paper, he on disc), deciding what to put in, not censoring, anything but that (though maybe some of her more malicious remarks about the living would have to go) but some are more quotidian and dull (not of course to the correspondents, but to a public reader) than others. What fun they could have. She's even mentioned publishing to him, quite seriously, a bit nervously, but more brazenly offering him everything about her, including this writerly cannibalism that sees the narrative value in private letters. He wasn't fazed, he liked the idea. They'd start with the very first, on paper and posted, letter, that he'd described as a belated love letter, *delayed* was the word he used, remembering, she thinks not quite accurately, telling her father he wanted to marry her, and her letter written back—she'd kept a copy of it—a calm letter, even a little cool, with her version of her father's response. Geoffrey was well then. She hadn't told him about the letter coming from Oliver, or her writing back.

After he died she wanted to tell Oliver about it, not from any particular expectations but because she had to find things to do with herself that involved writing down what had happened to her, so she wrote and they have corresponded ever since. Writing to him makes her consider what her life is about, in the passing present moments but also in all the years of her marriage when they had no contact. She likes his idea of love, that once it has been it goes on, however circumstances change. He is married again now, and happily, and one of their main conversations is about beloved spouses, but the fact that they were lovers once is something that is still happening. Being in love with somebody once is something that can last forever.

She has talked to him about whether it is a good idea to meet. There's an Elizabeth Taylor short story, about a middle-aged woman meeting a writer she has corresponded with for years, beginning with a small note of admiration, and developing into, for her, a significant part of her life. She invites him for lunch, and it's all a disaster. She buys lobsters, but the cat gets them, it's hot, she's flustered, the wine's not cold, the food is a failure, and so is the conversation, with none of the delicate wit that illuminated their letters, they find no charm at all in one another and he leaves with them both knowing that they will never have anything to do with one another again. She has lost this most precious thing.

We are not characters in an Elizabeth Taylor story, she wrote to Oliver. Are we?

They both believe not. They are under no illusions about the passing of a lifetime since they saw one another. She is not a tremulous spinster. They have communicated with utter frankness nearly every day and several times some days for nearly a year. Nevertheless there are moments in the long dreary flight when she wonders if this is a dangerous enterprise, if there is not something which might be lost.

She is not seeing him until some days after her arrival. They don't have the sort of relationship that will pluck her off the plane for a fuck. Nevertheless she doesn't suffer at all from jet lag. Maybe it was all the water she drank. Neither have her ankles swollen. They are comfortingly narrow above her soft black boots. In which she walks all about London. Down Piccadilly. Across St James Park in all its frigid midwinter beauty. Herself happily warmly dressed against this second winter, coat and scarves and the silk-lined leather gloves Geoffrey bought her years ago at Monoprix in Paris. Through the squares of Bloomsbury. Around Regent's Park and into Camden Town. Trafalgar Square, Shaftesbury Avenue, Jermyn Street. On a boat down the river to Greenwich, past the London Eye as big as a sixteen-storey building overpowering the skyline, and the Millennium Dome belying its name with ugly ladders of scaffolding puncturing its mighty curve. Through the great galleries: Van Dyck at the Royal Academy,

Bloomsbury at the Courtauld and the Tate, and Tracy Emin's bed, recreated as witness of a disturbed period in her life (a disappointment this, not nearly grotty enough, the dirty tissues and condoms and rusty knickers, the vodka bottle, all too neat, too lined up, somehow, even the sheets with their skidmarks too tidily grubby, Clare thinks she could do a better disaster bed than this). Botticelli's mystic nativity at the National Gallery catching the heart, and all the old favourites like the Van Eyck Arnolfini wedding. And plays.

Interesting, these plays, in their references to herself, her preoccupations, in the things she can learn and use from them. *The Lady in the Van*, with its two Alan Bennetts arguing over art and life and how they should relate and where the writer's responsibility lies. It's a brilliant device this, to have the author as two characters in his play, especially one where the plot has no surprises: the cranky old lady who parks her van in his front yard for fifteen years is a narrative that Bennett has been telling for nearly as long. Clare's been wondering how he would make it work, since anybody who is interested in his writing knows the story, and it isn't a dramatic one: the old lady parks the van, lives in it, stinks, is grumpy, demanding, a complete pain in the neck, mad, she dies, he can get rid of it. As a narrative it's plain enough, as a piece for the stage, what can it offer? But having himself in it twice, played by two different actors who both look amazingly like him but also quite different from one another, so that he can argue with himself over whether it is timidity that leaves her there, or squeamishness, or kindness, or the desire of the artist for material, that secret terrifying cannibalism that all writers recognise in themselves sooner or later, and how significant is it for his relationship with his mother, turns it into riveting theatre.

Then there's Noel Coward's *A Song at Twilight*, about what's publishable and what isn't, or shouldn't be, and truth and biography and what matters in a writer's life, and what connections there are between a writer's nature and personality and his work. Coward's last play, written in 1966 and not performed since, quite different from what people think of as vintage Coward. It should come back into the repertoire, it has powerful things to say.

Even Alan Ayckbourn's *Comic Potential* which is mainly very funny, she and her companion clutch one another and laugh all the way through, is about love and art and the nature of humanness, and gives you seriously to think even while you're laughing your head off.

When the immigration officer at Heathrow asked her the purpose of her visit she said, vaguely, because she hadn't prepared an answer, oh, seeing friends, going to some plays, and galleries. And that is exactly what she's been doing.

She bought a postcard, or rather two because it's a very wide picture, of Botticelli's *Venus and Mars*, from an exhibition at the National Gallery of not just painting but furniture, ceramics, objects generally, from one decade in fifteenth-century Florence. It's awe-inspiring to see what was produced in that short period in that small town, in the space of the 1470s. In this painting Mars, on the right, *a young man with a lovely body*, lies sleeping, entirely relaxed, abandoned even, mouth open, head fallen back, utterly asleep. Small chubby satyrs climb around him, playing with his armour; one holds a conch shell to Mars' ear. Venus is ostensibly reclining, but in fact is sitting sharply upright and has a look on her face that speaks volumes, if you give it careful reading. A complex expression: a little disappointed, perhaps, slightly critical, deeply thoughtful. Thinking a complexity of thoughts that could include: Is this all? Tired already? Better make the most of it, I'll have you awake in a moment. Certainly nothing languid about her, or satisfied, none of the small secret smiles of a woman who's been satisfactorily fucked. The conch may be her doing, in a moment the satyr will blow a blast in Mars' ear. And he will wake to its battle call, and see Venus with her enigmatic smile, which maybe he will know how to read.

Back at the apartment Clare writes some notes on her torn-up quarters of paper. The counter narrative of these has changed hemispheres, and may make another set of puzzles for the literary anthropologist: a fragment about a conference at the Tate on Bloomsbury and Modernism, in which Heroism and Housework is one of the topics; price lists from Fortnum and Mason, *Salmon Dressed with Quails' Eggs, Beef Wellington* (fancy that still going), *Traditional Fish Pie with King Prawns*, from a flyer picked up because everything was so wonderfully expensive, but now torn up you get either dishes or prices, not both; some information about Provincial Booksellers' Fairs. She looks at Venus's cool gaze at sleeping Mars, and writes:

One thing about sleeping by yourself is that there are no expectations to be disappointed. He is not sleeping peacefully while she lies awake, wanting the day to begin. Or sleeping noisily, while she lies awake, wishing she were asleep. Is not jumping up for a pee and a shower while she wants to lie and be cuddled.

In a love affair, there is one person who sleeps and one who is slept at. Even Venus couldn't manage any better, says Botticelli.

In a marriage—maybe that is the definition of a good marriage, that you sleep together.

Otherwise, you might as well sleep on your own. Wake in the morning, stretch, stroke your own breasts. Your own mistress.

The Botticelli offers its enchanting images on the postcards before her. There are other ways of looking at it. She's been reading Alec Hope's poetry again. There was a time when he would take her out to lunch and at the top of his voice tell her tales of copulation. He was very deaf and she had to talk in a loud voice too. The whole restaurant would turn fascinated and sometimes appalled faces to them. She enjoyed it a lot. Though it didn't make for very subtle conversation. He was quite elderly at this time and talking about fucking to a much younger woman seemed important to him. She didn't mind, she'd been a fan of his poetry since she was a girl. Knew it well, which was a reason for revisiting it. It had been important to her when she was young because of the sex, the engagement of his intellect in it, and the physicality, it made her body open up in hollows and hot places she hadn't suspected were there. This was a long time ago, when girls could not easily come by vicarious experiences of sex.

She knew that a lot of people thought he had a dreadfully male-centred vision of love, even misogynistic, that his women were objects with no minds or feeling of their own, and maybe that was true, but when she read the poems she was caught up in their sexuality in a way that was neither mindless nor objectified. For the space of a poem she would be one of his women, her body responded and so did her emotions and especially her intellect.

Some poems intrigued her in a different way; these were the ones where the woman was voluptuous and voracious and destroyed the man, squashing him, swallowing. Even a sugar-and-spice milk-toothed Little Red Riding Hood could swallow the Wolf in a single delicate gulp of *her minikin mouth*. Botticelli's Venus is hardly a huge white woman who will roll over on Mars and squash him so flat she will to turn him into a bedside mat, but maybe there is something . . . She is dressed with a certain demureness, her gown seems transparent, but you can see nothing through it, though it shapes her round breasts with gold-embroidered braid and falls between her wide thighs. (Round breasts, wide thighs, slender waist, very A. D. Hope.) Only her feet and hands and a little of her neck are bare. As Venuses go she is cool, more elegant than fleshly, not one of your lusty knowing pneumatic goddesses, and yet perhaps that thoughtful gaze appraises, maybe Botticelli is seeing her ready to open her delicate mouth and gobble Mars whole, maybe Mars is feigning sleep to postpone the apprehended moment of his devouring.

She prefers her version to this putative Hopish version.

But then, gloss this with his poem about the Countess of Pembroke's dream. This is a much later work, it was not around in her youth, in fact she has just read it for the first time. How this beautiful intelligent cultivated young noblewoman loved to watch stallions mating, and wished for such power to be unleashed on her. She doesn't want to swallow anybody, she begs for a man to batter, master, crush her, as befits a man, that's her idea. So Hope has it, following Aubrey in his Brief Lives. But no man comes near to achieving the power she sees in the stallions.

She dreams she is a centaur.

Does everybody know that centaurs have two sets of genitals? One human, one equine, to match their double nature. The Countess dreams she is a centaur coupling with her brother, Sir Philip Sidney, in the same form, first of all in the human way, when

> . . . *each in love and gratitude conspires*
> *To mount the other's ladder of desires.*

This copulation is ecstatic, violent in its way, they lose themselves in the blind locking and rearing and swaying of their bodies, but the terms are human, and they finish by gently pressing together and kissing. But then suddenly they realise that they are horses and the *brute fury* rises within them and *demands its due* and they gallop off and couple in the manner of stallion and mare. As the Countess watched them through the peephole on the stairs at Wilton. Hope describes their loosing of seed as a prayer from Nature and from Zeus, whose presence blends the natures of god and man and beast, and is the source of heroes who will renew the world.

Maybe the problem with Mars and Venus is that they are both gods.

And maybe she is reading them quite awry. Maybe Botticelli is being a bit thoughtful himself, giving the goddess of love a pensive rather than a sexy expression. Or maybe he simply painted his model, and at that moment she happened to be thinking about something quite everyday, like what would be for dinner, or which style to have her new dress made in.

Later she finds a line in Kenneth Clark's book, *The Nude: No doubt it is the strength of Venus that her face reveals no thought beyond the present*. Not Botticelli's; Clare can read pasts and futures, disappointments and possibilities in the face of his elegant Florentine.

She takes the underground and sits in that crowded public solitude watching people. Regarding them closely (Clare, don't stare, said her mother) while pretending her eyes are idle. Opposite is a fat young woman doing her homework. Conning it. Her lips move as she reads the words meaningfully clumped on the pages in front of her. Her face is anxious. Clare imagines her future hanging on getting this right, some course, some diploma, some job. She eavesdrops with her eyes, and reads the words: *Save your life again*.

Save your life again? Have you nearly lost it once? Several times?

When she looks at the words again they say, *Save your file*. Save your life, save your file. Two letters transposed and you are in different worlds. Or perhaps not.

The doorway next to her building has an awning over it, and leads to an establishment called The Gaslight. One night she comes home late after the theatre and there's a bouncer standing outside. Wearing a fine navy blue cashmere overcoat. Good evening, he says, politely, with a faint accent that might be Italian, and when she has trouble with her key he helps her to open the door.

The Gaslight is a gentlemen's club, but not the usual St James variety. It offers naked ladies dancing. All credit cards accepted. And after that, whenever she comes home late, there is the bouncer, courteous, inquiring after her health, her day, chatting about the weather. She sends a postcard to Elvira. It's what every girl needs, she writes, a bouncer at the door to protect. You feel so safe, coming home late, knowing there's a man at the door whose profession is the protection of womenfolk. Whatever your profession.

One day she went to Oxford, to see an old friend. She took her to evensong at Magdalen, the chapel dim, high, very quiet, the choristers all children, none of the men singing, their voices so pure and gentle and yet so filling of that ancient space that she remembered the cathedral of grief and how it makes everything more poignant, more important, more full of its own savour. She'd been feeling nervy and overexcited that day, full of babble. The singing of the children saved her. And when she got home, late, catching the bus and then a taxi from Victoria, looking forward to the comforting presence of the bouncer, and had her conversation with him, she told him all about the children singing, and he seemed interested.

Not that it's a rough neighbourhood. The pavements outside its elegant shops are decked with terracotta pots stuffed with cyclamen and other extravagant flowering plants, and nobody ever seems to steal them or vandalise them. Imagine Canberra, she writes to Polly, they wouldn't last two minutes.

At an antique market in St James churchyard with clusters of small stalls and some knowing customers—one is looking for a Stilton spoon—she wanders round solitary looking at the wares, for a moment buying each object that takes her eye, for a moment becoming the person owning this thing, taking it away, making it belong to her, changing her life imperceptibly with its butterfly wing, until she passes on, saying to herself, of course you had no intention, but for a second she did, for another second she passed from intention to ownership. What she does buy is teaspoons. She has suddenly seen them as good presents for friends, small, light, unbreakable, belonging to this place. They are Georgian silver, 1818, 1823, 1826, say the hallmarks, as deciphered by the stallholders—the knowing customers can work them out for themselves—the spoons themselves worn, frail, their rims thin, their bowls wafery, in one case pitted, all the hands which have touched them, used them in the humble ways of teaspoons, wearing their silver away, so now they are a kind of etherealised essence of teaspoon, and yet at the same time the hands and years have given them weight and substance, so that their frailty contains this solid lengthy life. They are polished to a moony gleaming splendour, and the friends for whom they are intended should delight in them.

And then it is time for Oliver to come. His voice is tinny on the intercom. And before she can look at him he has wrapped his arms around her and is kissing her mouth.

They go shopping, and buy wine, and bread, and a truss of tomatoes (costing considerably more in pounds than in dollars at home, and it's not a kind idea to convert because the dollar is worth hardly more than a third of a pound) and some highly artisanal Roquefort. They sit at the little dining table and talk. She has brought photographs and they kneel on the floor at the round coffee table like children hunched over them together while she tells him their stories. They sit on the floor and talk. They sit in a pair of idiosyncratic armchairs— this is one of the charms of the apartment, all the furniture is full of character and some of it has a certain shabby grandeur which is her favourite thing with furniture, being once good but now worn—and talk, and go out for a meal, an Italian restaurant somewhere in Soho, walking quickly and briskly through the cold air, and she asks if she may take his arm, partly because she likes walking along holding a man's arm, spent thirty-five years doing it. But also because when you want to move swiftly through crowded pavements it is better to do it as a unit, to make a single space in air with its own single rhythm. Afterwards they come back and talk more. It's as though all the decades since they've seen one another are no more than a source of conversation. When it's time to go to bed he wraps his arms around her.

When they were first falling in love he came to her room in the student hall of residence and said, Have you ever slept naked with anyone? It's nice. I don't mean making love, I mean just lying together. The words the classical seducer's trick, but he meant them, that's what they did. And it was nice. As this now is nice. It's sweet and comforting and gentle and loving, and when it is time to go to sleep they push their

265

beds together from opposite sides of the room so they won't lose touch in the night. All night he is there. She can touch him with her foot or her hand. He is not sleeping at her.

In the morning he looks at her. Ah, your smile. Your smile. It is still the same.

She can feel it on her face. That smile. She knows what it offers and accepts. But feeling a smile does not mean that it looks like that to someone else. He says it does, and she smiles at him.

He makes coffee, and they sit at the small table and eat toast and tomatoes. And smile at one another.

It feels like a kind of Garden of Eden smile, she says.

If I weren't married, I'd ask you to marry me.

She looks at him. Her smile fades, her face grows solemn.

But maybe you'd say no. Maybe you don't want to be married again.

And indeed that is what she has decided, in her year and a day. That she will not marry again. Have lovers, yes, perhaps, but not marry. She has been married, it cannot possibly be done again. But at this moment it is difficult to consider all at once this so severally hypothetical question. *If I were not married* . . . Henry said the same thing. If I were not married. If my wife were . . . translated. Both these men think they know the misery they would suffer if they lost their wives, but she knows they don't. They can try to imagine, and maybe at times they whiff the hot breath of that loss. But briefly; immediately they are taking deep steady lungfuls of the fresh bright air of their happy marriages. The stink of loss the faintest waft, never the miasma it is for her.

Two men—Clare is clever at choosing uxorious men, men who are the marrying kind, good at it—two men, both saying, Ah, if I were not married, I would want to marry you. Meaning it. And they go back to the fresh soft air of their comfortable housekept lives. To a woman they love, who knows them well and cares for them. Possibly better than Clare would, now, in her selfish widowed state. As she cared for Geoffrey. You are brave, these men say to Clare, you are tough, and she looks at them with clear eyes, and is alone.

As now she looks at Oliver. Maybe I would, she says. Her mind is crossed by a brief comical Victorian memory of politeness: a lady should always thank a gentleman for a proposal of marriage, even if she has no intention of accepting.

She does not say, this is the second time you have conditionally proposed to me, the first even including asking my father for my hand, both times saying, If I were not married . . . well, the first was rather, When I am not married. But that didn't happen, not for twenty years or more.

Not being married.

But he is. Both times.

Maybe I would, she says. After all, the situation is not arising. It is a kind of game they are playing, solemn, but a game. But where would we live, she says. Here, or there?

And the second day passes like the first. With talking, prattle, conversation, exchanges of stories. They go out briefly, to buy food, and in the evening to an Indian restaurant round the corner. There's far too much to eat, they take some home with them.

She is happy, hardly even sad. There have been no promises between them, except of love and friendship. They will go back home and continue the multi-volumed epistolary novel they are writing to one another, via email, continue to pay one another attention. That is a definition of love, says Clare, to be seen by another person. Truly seen.

How well we fit together, he says. It's so comfortable walking along with you. It seems as though we have always done it.

She says, Isn't it odd, to be here, so simply ourselves. I mean, normally we come with houses and gardens and furniture and books and cars and wine cellars and kitchenware and ornaments and pictures, we have people we live with, children, family, friends, jobs and duties and pastimes and habits, and here we are with nothing, just the clothes we are wearing, just simply stripped back to ourselves without all our belongings, encumbrances, the things which to the casual and the loving eye too define us. Just our words.

Isn't it good, he says.

And maybe this is why it doesn't seem to have been a dangerous enterprise, of the Elizabeth Taylor variety.

(Except that later she checks up on the Elizabeth Taylor story and realises she has got it wrong. The lobster, and the cat, yes, that's how it happens, they have to have a tin of sardines instead, and a whole lot of Rockingham cups and saucers come to a bad end in the cat's stealing of the lobsters (the precious china a glossed-over loss, she won't care, not in the scale of disasters, but its presence poignantly signifying her spinsterhood: the cups would not be hers, would have come to her from some richer domestic life) but the meaning of the story is quite different from Clare's memory of it. They have no time to get beyond stiff conversation because the awful sticky-beaking risible neighbour (we are a booky family, the frightful woman says, of course we don't read the books but we read the reviews) turns up and is appalling whereas in the letters she was wonderfully comical, and the novelist realises what a consummate artist his correspondent is, turning this life of dreadful trivial horror into her letters that are small works of art, and only for him. He is even slightly humble, in a generous way, that she can make so much out of such raw material.

In the end, our heroine, she mildly becomes that, begins another letter: *Dear Edwin*. The day is already transforming. It seems they will go back to their relationship of words on the page, even more gratefully than before, and on his part with more percipience. So it is quite a happy ending, or continuance. Different from hers with Oliver, but not undone. She and Oliver can have both, the bodies embracing as well as the letters, the ardent conversations with eyes interlocked, but then they are not a beautifully written story. Which is about the transmuting power of art, with the neat irony that it is the figure of the amateur and not the real writer in which it is vested.)

On the third morning Oliver lies with his head on her stomach. She gazes down at him; he has that long-limbed high-hipped maybe very faintly androgynous slenderness that you see in pre-Hellenic sculptures. Those divine marble figures with their gleaming sharp-eyed smiles, possessing a clarity that could be a little sinister but is on closer looking self-aware; smiles of contemplation. She lays her hand on that fine pelvic girdle of bone and he curls up with his head on her stomach, which is both hollow and pillowy, and they don't say much, just let their bodies be conscious of one another, because in a little while he will get up and make coffee and it won't be long before he has to leave to catch the train home.

She feels him stir, and tells him this story; he lies back again to listen.

There was one day when Geoffrey was first ill, he was in hospital, two years ago it would be, a bit more, and I'd gone to see him, I used to spend a lot of the day with him, just being together. He was sitting up in bed reading, he felt okay then, and I was in a chair, it must have been quite warm weather because I was wearing sandals I think, at least no socks or stockings, and he had his foot poking out of the bedclothes, he hated having hot feet, my sister said it was because he was Piscean, Pisceans always have difficult feet, and it's true, he did, beds and chairs would stick their legs out and wound him, but he was irritated by having it blamed on a star sign, and I had my bare foot up on the bed, just touching his, our feet were just resting gently together on the bed. Both of us reading, and our feet just resting together. It was lovely. Anyway, the pharmacist came bustling in, and his face was a study, he did a double take, a mild one, suppressed, but I saw it, and I watched his face when he was leaving, he was smiling the kind of smile he might have smiled if he had found us in a passionate embrace, it was complicit, and pleased, aware of seeing something special, and I imagined it turning into a big grin by the time he got out of the room, enjoying his own little frisson; it was oddly intimate. He saw. And I suddenly knew how important it was for us to be sitting there, together, not paying any particular attention to one another, but knowing the other so thoroughly there, in that gentle touching of our bare feet.

She walks with Oliver to the tube, her arm hooked through his, walking at that comfortable swift pace that matches so easily for them, waits while he buys a ticket from a machine. He turns and hugs her, puts his hands round her head so her hair slides against it and kisses her mouth, beautifully, and a kind of quotation.

She walks away without looking back, and that's a kind of quotation too, and sets off for Selfridges, quite a long walk but she needs it, she is warmly dressed and softly booted and the rain holds off. She wanders round the glittering Christmas shop and its trappings for what it calls the new millennium: champagne, bare little strappy dresses and sandals (who cares that it's midwinter—the English don't), tiny beaded handbags. She buys some food and catches a taxi back to the apartment. She is sitting in the back, the seat-belt done up like a good Australian, dreamy, when there's a violent bang and she is thrown forward against the belt. The bag of provisions tips over and spills. The people from the car that the taxi has run into—it seems incredible, she didn't think London taxis ever ran into anything, were somehow magically able to twirl and twist in the traffic, always missing disaster by the snicker of a hair—the couple jumps out, full of anger. It's their fault, the taxi driver shouts, pointing to two gaudily dressed women on the pavement. At first she is shocked; how can he blame two women on the pavement for his inattention? Is the old

Adam still pointing the finger? But then she understands. When the women dart out into the traffic, sliding between the cars, one middle-aged, the other very young and more limber, except for carrying a baby, well, not a baby, a large walking-age child, but it is swathed in tightly wrapped blankets so it imitates a baby, she can see its rolling imprisoned eyes, it's real, not a bundle of clothes. Its weight and unwieldiness hamper the slight young woman, and she looks in danger of losing hold of it.

The women are begging. They run out among the cars, holding out their hands, making motorists so afraid for their safety that they give them money. It's a kind of blackmailing begging: look, their bodies say, we are in danger, of being run over, of dropping the child under your wheels, reward us. The women's clothes make them look like gypsies, their bright flounced skirts and shawls and dangling jewellery could come out of a pantomime, and maybe they are gypsies, and maybe they are masquerading, claiming the stereotype. Possibly it isn't even their baby.

The run-into couple come to understand this, watching in horror the ducking and weaving through the stopping and starting cars. The taxi driver is deeply upset, he was afraid of their being run over, he was paying attention to avoid them, not the car ahead. And despite the shattering crump of the noise not much damage seems to be done to the rubber bumper of the rammed car, and they go on their way. Clare has picked up her groceries, they are safe back in their bag, she is unhurt, but the taxi driver needs comforting, he is still trembling and agitated. It should be stopped, he says, it shouldn't be allowed, where are the police when you need them, it's criminal, innocent bystanders, poor motorists, there's bound to be a really terrible accident. You'd blame yourself forever but it wouldn't be your fault. She gives him a good tip.

. . .

And so she sits in a pretty flat in London, the first-floor drawing room of a merchant's house, with tall windows and ceilings and a mirrored marble mantelpiece with long-stemmed lilies, the Annunciation kind, in a row of wine bottles, three of them, the wine drunk and now the bottles making vases for the flowers Oliver bought her. He has always given her flowers, well, now and thirty-something years ago, the extravagant flowers she loves. She has a glass of wine and a fig on a pale blue plate. Nice plates in this apartment, Spode mostly, a pleasure to use. The wine is called le Pigeoulet de Brunier, lucky it didn't break in the taxi. The fig is slightly sharp, full of rich seeds. Oliver doesn't like figs, she found that out when they were shopping, but he isn't here, she said, No I don't want figs when she found out he didn't like them, and neither she did, but now he isn't here and she has bought figs.

There is time, without men around. Time to think, to write words on paper, time to go to Selfridges and find some of her favourite solid graphed paper, to search out some cartridges with black ink for her pen, to sit at a desk in a tall London drawing room with the pale sun extinguished though the sky is still light, and the alabaster lamp lit so she is looped in a pool of light with these words that she is writing down. Maybe she will become a woman who writes with a

273

glass of red wine always there, never getting drunk exactly but never the glass empty.

Opening the bottle of wine seemed a good thing to do, coming back to the empty flat.

She goes out on to the balcony, looks at the rows of brownish brick houses with their ground floors cream painted over rusticated plaster more or less fresh, their entrance ways like little bridges across the areas (only fancifully drawbridges) and the doors painted bright blue or red or black or brilliant cream, with shining knockers and numbers, and these doors proclaim the life inside: we are paying attention, they say, we are spanking and sharp and we are telling you that the house in here is kept very well. And Clare is a woman on her own in London, and in a minute she'll lie down and have a little nap, just to keep her strength up.

And of course the lives in these houses could be just as disorderly and dangerous and damaged as anybody else's, it just doesn't show, it usually doesn't.

In the morning Clare dozes in her bed in the drawing room beneath the tall sash windows. A thin light squints along them; it's too early yet to see whether it's going to be one of those days of pale dazzling sun which make you gloat, make you look at the bare trees and the last leaves bathing in this thin rich liquid wash of light and recognise how precious it is. A bane of being Australian is that the sun is too often hateful, an enemy. Beautiful, but you need to keep your distance.

She dozes, and dreams of inviting old lovers for dinner. Cooking them a fine dish of buttered parsnips. Parsnips the sweet root vegetable that she is fond of, the rich earthy taste, the comforting wintriness; she cooks them in butter so they brown a bit then serves them in a blue and white Spode dish with a lot of extra butter.

She's only half asleep in this dream, so she watches herself dreaming it, though she isn't controlling it, she is enjoying it. And when she wakes up properly she knows what it means: Look, she is saying, I know how to butter parsnips, here is the vegetable in all its rooted earthiness, and here is the butter, great wodges of the French unsalted butter she bought at Selfridges, this is how you butter parsnips. As all your fine words cannot do. Does anybody know this any more? That fine words butter no parsnips? You can bet the old lovers do. When they see the real thing in a blue and white Spode bowl. With some black pepper to sharpen it up.

Of course, this is a dream. The butter on her parsnips isn't real either.

And its meanings disingenuous. Because she doesn't want her parsnips buttered. She has other fish to fry.

If I were not already married I would ask you to marry me. If I were free I would want to be with you always. And they go home to their loving wives and their connubial pleasures, from breakfast to fucking, and are comforted. While she, she is her own mistress.

With time to think, time to compare. A wickedness she has never achieved before. Neither of her lovers matches, in his heyday, her beautiful brilliant Geoffrey. The urgency of the one, the mind-stopping abandoned losing yourself little-death sex, the gentleness and dreaminess finding yourself of the other: Geoffrey was both. But Geoffrey was her youth, and his, her young lover, the father of her children, the companion of her days, the love of her life. He was all those things together and her friend as well. Her best friend. These men love her, sometimes desire her, will be kind to her when they can manage it, are her friends. And they go back to their own lives. All they can offer is a little help in the drawing-up of her erotics of grief.

She did have Geoffrey for thirty-five years and maybe that should be enough. No. Of course it shouldn't. It isn't, not at all, but it's something. Thirty-five years of Geoffrey compared with fifty or sixty of certain others, oh yes, if you want to measure that you can. Measure. She can't get away from her scales and calibrations. Because it is all out of kilter.

Your problem, she says to herself, is you want moments to go on and on. As they did with Geoffrey. So they become a whole way of living. Now you have to be satisfied that sometimes there will be moments, just that, moments, and they will pass and be gone but still exist, just as her life with Geoffrey still exists, there will be moments like small richnesses in a novel, like epiphanies minor or greater, and they will pass and you can hope that other small luminosities will come.

The kiss at the tube station: would three or five or a hundred have been sweeter? It's a memory now, and one kiss in the memory may be more powerful simply because it's the only one.

Less is more, she says to herself. You are a novelist, you know that.

But she also knows that sometimes more is so much more.

She gets the shuttle to Heathrow and checks her baggage for the Paris plane.

I do not suppose I shall see Paris again, said Geoffrey. Oh well, she replied, who knows. I expect I shan't myself.

When she said it, she knew she was lying. She expects to see Paris again. God willing, as the leisurely Moslem woman charging her groceries at Selfridges (the Pigeoulet, the figs) said when asked would the shop be open on Sunday. Yes, she said, till six o'clock. God willing. *Inshallah*, Clare knows is the Arab word. And God willing, she will see Paris. Her luggage is gone, she is waiting to be called. Geoffrey's Paris.

the sons
of heaven

OF COURSE, THAT ISN'T THE END
of it. How fine if it were. Brave Clare, clever Clare, jetting off
to Paris and a new chapter in her life. In fact, she falls into a
pit.

A pit, a trough, an abyss. Is abyss a bit fanciful? A bit
melodramatic? When she's in it she doesn't think so. It feels
like an abyss.

It's a cold that does it. Or maybe Oliver's unwitting words.
I should hate to travel on my own. I don't think I could stand it.

There were a lot of replies she could have made to that.
She looked at him and thought of them but felt too tired. It
was as though those words punctured something and her
strength began to drain away.

You are tough, he said. I don't think I am, she said.

Strong is what she is, not tough. But the strength isn't part
of her substance, like muscle or sinew, as toughness would be.

It's something she contains, and conserves, and it can drain away. She thinks of a china cup, so good at containing: hot liquids, cold, a bunch of flowers, borrowed sugar. Until it cracks, and leaks, and maybe breaks. So strong while it's whole, but all the time so fragile too. And once it's cracked it's done for, it's no good, its next step is to break. Whereas she hopes her cracked state is temporary, that she will be healed and strong again.

This is the trouble with metaphor, it may take you places you don't want to go. But perhaps you ought not to refuse. Perhaps the crack is final in people as in china.

On her first night she goes to dinner with old friends, Parisians, whom she hasn't seen since Geoffrey's death. They are sad about him, they've known him longer than she has, without him they might never have met one another, and they are chastened by illnesses of their own. The sense of mortality is vivid. In fact they are quite okay; one is recovered from his cancer, has been clear for a good while, the other has had an odd turn and is being checked in all the technological detail she knows so well. Nevertheless, they have been forced to pay attention to their own deaths. She talks about Geoffrey, as is her wont. He is still so lively in her mind, how could she not? They all three speak of him with affection and delight and small jokes. But she fears that she there as Geoffrey's widow is a warning of what life can do. She's the emblematic skull, which says, *As you are, so was I. As I am, so shall you be.* Her situation will come to one of them, one day, maybe not too long away. This is the end of the marriage contract: I love you, and I will stay with you, and in the end I will bury you.

The Paris hotel is in a courtyard off the rue Jacob. It's very pretty, with a kind of conservatory where you eat breakfast and beyond that a garden with white iron furniture, no more than a view in this cold weather. The conservatory is extremely flowery, with poinsettias and white hyacinths in pots as well as in patterns on the looped bobbled curtains. Through its roof you can see the tower of St Germain des Prés. Her room has flowery curtains, too, very scarlet and orange, with fabric on the wall in wide stripes of the same colours plus a chalky bright blue; when you sit on the narrow bed you can nearly reach over and touch the opposite wall. When you sit on the lavatory you can't shut the door. Of course it is a single room. The hotel is comfortable and warm and very quiet. Terribly full of couples, on the stairs, handing in keys, crossing the courtyard, and even not walking together or touching and sometimes quite bad-tempered with one another, nevertheless carving out that space in air that contains them both and proclaims their belonging.

She goes out, and walks along the streets, marvelling at the rich caves of the shop windows in these ancient grey buildings, walking down to the river and along past the mostly shut *bouquinistes* to St Michel and then back along the rue St André des Arts, stopping at a big cafe restaurant that's always been there, at least for more than twenty years as she knows it, to drink a glass of their favourite gewurztraminer which is always very good here. The establishment is called l'Alsace à Paris. They do spectacular *choucroutes* and know where to find good Alsatian wine. Once on a long summer evening when the triangle of the place St André was filled with tables they had dinner here. She can't recollect what they ate, but does remember the green iron drinking fountain, called a Wallace, said Geoffrey, after the Englishman who made a present of quite a lot of them to the people of Paris so that even the poorest would have clean drinking water, and this fountain with its cheerful iron cherubs spouting water was beside their table and the children who would have been eleven and eight in that year kept filling their glasses which was great fun and much cheaper than the Badoit they would drink on such occasions. Badoit because it was fluoridated and she was keen to keep this up for their teeth's sake, and indeed even now they have no cavities. They liked it because it tasted good, and was fizzy. Once they went to buy a large plastic bottle of it in a supermarket in the rue de Rennes, round the corner from their apartment, and dropped it on the terrazzo floor, when it exploded with a loud noise, and a shop assistant comforted them.

The gewurztraminer was still good, slightly deliciously oily and full of flavour. It came with pretzels which she didn't eat because they were salty and she'd want another of the small round green-stemmed glasses of wine and it was quite expensive. She sat on the sheltered terrace surrounded by a hedge of winking Christmas trees. The long triangle of the place was empty. No tables. Just bare branches. It was very cold. She went back to the hotel and lay on the bed and folded herself in her red linen wrap the colour of a persimmon in the hand of the Christ Child and then in the quilted bedcover and knew she had a fever. She'd walked down the wrong street to the river, forgetting the way the rue Mazarine curved round which meant she'd had a long walk back along the quais to St Michel. Geoffrey would never have made that mistake, he knew these streets by heart, from when he was a student here in the late fifties. This part of Paris was one of the sets of narratives of their lives. His landlady with her husband and little dog who all sat placidly and getting fatter in their own apartment, on the rents of all her other properties. The Algerian bomb that went off down the street. Police raids, and one night a shoot-out. Going to the dentist and being told to give up drinking until his tooth was mended. (The goodness and nature and cheapness of the food and wine at the student restaurant was another narrative.) Geoffrey said of course, he'd stop drinking wine with dinner. Wine, said the dentist, who's talking about wine, I said to stop drinking. Alcohol. Don't drink alcohol. Wine's okay.

And the classic story, being given giant pills to take away the pain. Muttering that they looked hard to swallow. The dentist guffawing. You don't swallow them. You put them up your bum.

The old French belief in suppositories. Don't muck about with your stomach. That's got to be kept in good nick for eating and drinking. Apply painkillers from the other end.

She got up and put on her coat and gloves and two scarves and went out again. The stairs, the lobby, the courtyard still traversed by couples. She bought aspirin and took a roll of film to be developed, to make sure her new camera was still working properly. She's taken a picture of the tower of the church of St Germain des Prés reflected in the mirror of the breakfast room of the hotel, among the bobbly pink and red curtains, the poinsettias, the painted tin chandeliers; she wants to see how it's worked. She still has a hankering after arty photography.

She went back to bed and slept and woke and was feverish and sweated and felt miserable and said words to herself like *abyss*. The long dark night of the cold. She wondered if Oliver hadn't said how he couldn't bear travelling on his own, she might have borne up better. She recognised that she was dropping her bundle. And she also thought that maybe she needed to.

I shall never see Paris again, said Geoffrey when he was ill, and she replied, Well quite likely I won't either. Knowing she was almost certainly lying. Maybe she should have made it be true, she thinks, sweating and not in her right mind in a narrow bed in a narrow room in Paris. Maybe I shouldn't have come without him.

Paris is Geoffrey's gift to her. Without him she would have surely visited it, would have liked it, as nearly all the world who's been here does. But she wouldn't have lived in it, housekept, sent her children to school, learnt it as she did with Geoffrey. Paris belonged to him, and he gave it to her. Then she wrote articles saying that Paris was a tart, and belonged to nobody, that possessing her was an illusion, and a good thing too. All true.

She dozed, and tossed, her mind wandered. She got up and took aspirin. She had a shower, put her clothes on and went and bought some food and wine which she didn't eat or drink, except for some clementines. Next to the hotel was a shop which sold old linens, sheets and pillowcases, towels, teatowels, soft faded quilted bedcovers, glasses, plates, flowery fragile teacups. Twice she went in and talked to the woman about making curtains from old sheets. Nothing original about this. She saw it in a magazine.

That's a bad cough, said the woman.

Oh, it's going okay, she said.

There were some heavy sheets, coarse, dark cream coloured, rough. Never used, said the woman. They'd soften up a lot if you washed them.

They have a seam down the centre, sewn with small stitches. Narrow fabric, said the woman, needs to be joined.

There's two small red initials as well. *J. B.*

The first time the woman clearly thinks she's just a passer-by. An idle tourist entertaining herself. The second time she takes her a bit more seriously. Maybe she will buy sheets to make into curtains. Clare herself isn't sure. She does need curtains, the dining room is newly painted pale yellow and the old greenish curtains, twenty years old, and quite dispirited, don't look any good; she is serious. But it may be all too much effort.

I'll ring up my daughter, says Clare, and get her to measure the window. She likes ringing her daughter, this loving little thread of connection over the phone is something to hang on to.

They're big, says the woman. Two metres by two and a half.

Could you send them to Australia, asks Clare.

Ouf. The woman shrugs. So expensive. They're very very heavy. Five hundred francs perhaps, more. Why don't you take them with you?

Well, because they're so heavy.

I could make a parcel. Give you a plastic bag. She pulls out one of those big red and blue striped zippered bags.

I'll get the measurements checked, said Clare. She went back to the hotel and climbed under the covers again.

This went on for two days. She went out, came back, got into bed and slid down into the pit again. It was very strange, but not uncomfortable, she liked being there, swirled around in its dark supporting fluid, you could even see it as nourishing; salty, elemental. Amniotic, even. And she disporting in it. She has time and space and solitude to take pleasure in these words: disporting, amniotic. Words will save her.

When she floated up to the surface and climbed out she brought with her immensely important things, that she held on to, placed carefully along the edge, but when she looked at them she couldn't see what it was they had meant, she held them in her mind as her hands would have held stones and examined them, but their beautiful meaningful patterns could no longer be discerned; like stones they needed their native wetness for their patterns to be seen. She peered at them, and tried to remember, but all she could recall was how important their inscriptions had been, not what they said.

On the morning after her third night in Paris she lay in bed and thought she might be all right. Still with a cold, but the fever gone. She was meeting Helen at the church of St Germain at ten o'clock. Helen has been in England visiting the husband she was divorced from more than a decade ago. She remains on good terms with him in a way her friends think is heroic. Not just for the sake of her children, though that matters; for the integrity of that part of her life, the number of years when she was married to him, and believed she loved him. Now she's spending four days in Paris, staying with colleagues at the embassy.

Helen was late and by the time she came Clare was feeling very strange; she couldn't see, the light had gone out of what she looked at, it was dark, blind. Helen sat with her and after a bit Clare said she thought she could make it back to the hotel but then she fell fainting in the porch. There was a christening forming, she'd watched the verger lighting candles before the dark came, and wondered what for, it was too early for mass, she'd checked at the door. It ought to have been shameful, fainting in the porch of the church of St Germain des Prés with a handsome bourgeois christening gathering on the steps, but it wasn't. It was a huge and difficult thing that was happening and she had to concentrate on getting through it.

What did you have for breakfast, asked Helen.

Clementine. Her voice came in a croak.

And for dinner?

Clementine.

It's lack of food that's the problem, said Helen. Probably. Though you should get checked out by a doctor. Strokes, you know. That sort of thing.

Eventually in a cafe she had a *grand crème* and some bread and butter and felt better. They walked about a bit. She showed Helen the sheets in the antique shop. Helen said they were beautiful, but what about the symbolic meanings.

What.

The trousseaus. Never used.

Oh, said Clare. She was too tired to think of that.

They went to a cafe and had lunch. She ate *andouillettes* which she always did at least once each visit so she knew she really was in Paris, and bought them half a litre of Côtes du Rhône, because she was grateful to Helen for being there, for being company, a friend.

Later, people commiserated. Poor you, how terrible, being sick in Paris. Oh no, she said, it was good. It was a kind of marvellous experience. To herself she said, mystical, even. Looking back she saw it as one of the most significant parts of her trip away. It was like her grief. It was important to her, it mattered. Like the grief, not something you'd say, when offered, oh how wonderful, yes please. But when you had to have it, then it belonged to you. It made you what you were. You would keep it, jealously, as a prized possession.

And though all her precious salvaged stones with their now undecipherable messages were themselves meaningless and she'd thrown them away (or back, perhaps) that didn't mean that the whole experience lacked meaning. She didn't entirely understand it, yet, but she felt it. It was about love. It was about loving people. It was about her being good at that. It was about the loss of her loves, that was why it was a pit, but it was also full of nourishing amniotic fluid because love wasn't lost; there was bleakness, and terror, but buoyancy, and safety. Loves are lost, but love isn't. It's a hard idea, and whether it drowns you or saves you is by no means sure. Or which is which.

So it was probably just as well that Helen had come along and pulled her back into the real world of tripe sausage and mustard and rough red wine. That world of sickness and lost love and love found, you couldn't stay in it very long, any more than you could a womb.

There was a Proust exhibition at the new Bibliothèque de France, Mittérand's building this, as Beaubourg is Pompidou's, and she went on the new metro that served it, from Madeleine to Bibliothèque. All the platforms have transparent walls, so nobody can jump or be pushed or fall on the line, with doors that open to match the doors of the train when it comes in. The train is all one long articulated body, silver black and gleaming, you can see it curling round, climbing up, plunging down. At one stage it goes down deep, under the river. Moreover, it doesn't have a driver; Geoffrey always said the metro didn't need drivers, they were only there to keep the passengers happy, and maybe to notice if they were caught in the doors. She so badly wants to tell Geoffrey about this new one—not even needing him to see it in person, just having him somewhere she can tell him, hear the lift of interest in his voice, so he will know that this technical thing that had always fascinated him had come about—that sadness overwhelms her, and she is nearly undone again.

Tricky stuff, the grief-striking possibilities of the metro.

But the Proust exhibition takes her mind off loss. It's showing the things Proust would have read, seen, heard. She is aware she has a tendency to believe that great artists sprang fully formed, and needs to keep reminding herself of what she knows but forgets, that they began in doubt and uncertainty and the fear of hope unrealised, just like everyone else. There are wonderful things, like lifeless muddy copies by Ruskin of Italian paintings, and bicycling posters, Fortuny gowns, photographs of actresses the family knew, and actors, and the theatre phone, a direct line from the theatre, so in bed in his cork-lined room he could listen to plays; when Clare picks it up she can hear Sarah Bernhardt's harsh melodramatic voice, and almost capture the enchantment of her classical French. Best of all are his handwritten manuscripts, displayed in tall flat cabinets, the notebooks with pasted-in extensions hanging down a metre or more. And wonderful typescripts entirely rewritten, with more fold-down pastings. Even the proof sheets put out sheaves of interleavings.

She copies out Proust's own words referring to this:

> . . . car, épinglant ici un feuillet supplémentaire, je bâtirais mon livre, je n'ose pas dire ambitieusement comme une cathédrale, mais tout simplement comme une robe.

Her own interest in cathedrals as metaphors draws her attention to this, and bowerbird that she is, she starts looking for a way of plaiting it into her own nest of words.

> For, pinning on here an extra page, I would build my book, I don't dare be so ambitious as to say like a cathedral, but quite simply like a dress.

She wonders if she could see herself as building her book like a dress, if dress is the word, maybe for Proust it ought to be something like garment, but that's clumsy, why not dress. It's good to think about Proust, to remind yourself that the best thing life can offer a writer is the chance to write. Nothing else matters. However dull or tragic or messy the life, it is still a life to write in.

She rang up her daughter and got her to measure the dining room windows, and when she went back to the shop it turned out that the coarse creamy sheets were too short, they were only two metres and she needed two and a half.

Ah, said the woman. I do have some others. She brought out a pair of much finer linen, handkerchief weight (a good heavy handkerchief), very plain, with one narrow hem and the other finished in wonderfully long and tiny-stitched drawn-thread work. They were three metres long. Also unused.

How do you know they haven't been used, Helen had asked, and Clare had replied, Because she says so, but anyway you can tell, and when she saw them Helen agreed.

These are more bourgeois, less peasanty than the creamy ones. They feel cool to the touch, almost polished. They are like the sheets in Séverac, that she's written a whole novel about, except that these aren't embroidered white on white with flowers, ribbons, ears of wheat, just hem-stitched in that long elegant way. You imagine a woman sitting bent over her work and forming her minutely skilled stitches and thinking . . . of her future, the marriage they are meant for, not necessarily with any one in mind. Wondering. Or a fiancé, perhaps, and sewing her sheets she dreams of what it will be like to lie in them with him. Or perhaps there's a bunch of girls, gossiping, passing the time giggling, being malicious, rude, silly, having enormous fun, free for this small space of time. Before they become wives, or spinsters.

She doesn't ask why they are unused, she knows the possible answers as well as the shop woman, and no more than she will she ever find out which is true.

When her friend Maggie got engaged her mother told her she wouldn't be properly married until she had six pairs of good double-bed sheets. I'll just have to live in sin then, said Maggie, but in fact by the time the wedding happened she'd got her six pairs. Clare and her sisters have sheets of their mother's, never used, not trousseau sheets but bought thriftily and saved and never used. These sheets may be of such a provenance, kept in a linen press for use one day but never needed. Especially as French housewives used to have a lot of sheets, they only washed them about twice a year, perhaps a fine day in late spring, then again late in summer, all the women of the family doing a huge boil up and spreading the linen on the meadows to dry. There's a story by Colette, with all the servants out in the paddock, that's the word used, spreading the sheets to dry on this rare washing day. A chandelier falls on a young man, and there are no servants to help, but it turns out brilliantly well because he and the young lady of the house are able to find out that each is in love with the other. He pretends to be unconscious and lets her kiss him in despair that he is dying.

And the other possibility is that they were sewn by one of that great number of women who were made widows before they ever were wives by the First World War. All those names on all those memorials in all the tiny towns and villages of France, and for so many of them a woman would never marry. Would live out her life in her parents' house. Her brothers killed too, often, and she the dutiful daughter. Like *la Cousine*, who died aged eighty or so in 1970, and left the family home to the grandson of her cousin, who is Clare's old friend whom she dined with on Wednesday, which is how she came to live in the Séverac house and grow so fond of it. To write a novel about the town and its grim and glamorous stories, and *la Cousine*'s embroidered sheets, the millions of tiny stitches, white on white, a novel where a woman of another country and another generation can look and marvel at the skill, and the beauty. Reading these other lives like a primer from which she might learn. And who knows if *la Cousine* knocked back numerous proposals of marriage, or once had a fiancé who died, or lived her life unmarried because whoever he might have been was killed in the carnage of that war. The fact is that she didn't ever marry, and never used her copious trousseau linen. But her heirs do, and value it. They're not selling it to antique shops.

Clare is going to Biarritz tomorrow. She calls in at the linen shop again and tells madame who greets her like an old acquaintance and admires her French and asks her what she thinks of the country, what critical things does she have to say, she is sure that there must be many, she tells madame that indeed she will buy the sheets and when she gets back from Biarritz on Saturday at 5pm she will come and pick them up, in their parcel in a cheap red white and blue plastic zippered bag, ready to fly home to Australia on Sunday. Ready for Clare to choose her own symbolic meanings for them.

Already going into the shop full of the belongings of dead people and trying to decide whether or not it is a good idea to buy the sheets is part of that miraculous feverish time, one of its rituals. That will be one of their meanings.

Did you buy any clothes in Paris, people ask.

No. She bought old never-used linen sheets to make dining room curtains. And in London in a market in the churchyard of St James in Piccadilly, she bought Georgian silver teaspoons.

★

When she comes home after nearly two days of travelling she marvels at the light in her house. Of course it is summer, not deepest winter, though sometimes there the sun did shine with a fierce feeble wintry brilliance. But here: her house is surrounded by trees, a golden elm, a liquidambar, oaks, a mulberry, a catalpa, big solid northern hemisphere trees, and they don't so much filter this bright high mistless antipodean sun as absorb it and give it back with a faintly green tremulous luminosity, so you perceive as you walk through the house that you are walking through palpable light. She gets out her sewing machine unused for years and sews her linen sheets into curtains. The drawn thread hem is along the bottom, the top folded over because it is too long, and when she sits at her sewing machine pinning this fold she sees that the top hem on one of the sheets is done with cream thread that looks a bit grubby and faintly frayed and part has been unpicked where it wasn't straight and done again and you can see the line of holes where the stitches were, and it looks exactly like her own bad primary school sewing, the unpicking, the grubbiness, and this fills her with affection for the long dead Frenchwoman, or perhaps girl, who made them, and who could never have imagined what fate would be theirs. She sits in her dining room admiring the fall of the fine linen; she eats yoghurt from a silver spoon and feels its pitted thinned-out surface on her tongue.

Things are the sons of heaven . . .

The hands that used the 1828 spoon are generations over and over turned into dust. The green light gleams through sheets that have spent the better part of a century in lavender drawers, unused, and whether because of tragedy or plenty no one will ever know. And here they are, the spoons, the sheets, alive and well on the other side of the world, being seen. Being gazed on and delighted in. There's a woman looking at the frail blazing brilliance of the Georgian silver, at the sheeny polished coolness of the old linen, and she is thinking, these are beautiful. Thinking, Geoffrey would have enjoyed them.

And the words that are the daughters of earth, she has them too.

She is happy. For now. She knows about love.

The robust little rose bush called Love Potion has bloomed again. She picks several of its small crimson flowers and breathes in their dark scent, this scent that perfumes the blood. And fills it with desire. Smell the desire. And she does.